Super Max and the Mystery of Thornwood's Revenge

ALSO BY SUSAN VAUGHT

Footer Davis Probably Is Crazy
Things Too Huge to Fix by Saying Sorry

Super Max and the Mystery of Thornwood's Revenge

SUSAN VAUGHT

A Paula Wiseman Book

Simon & Schuster Books for Young Readers

NEW YORK · LONDON · TORONTO · SYDNEY · NEW DELHI

SIMON & SCHUSTER BOOKS FOR YOUNG READERS
An imprint of Simon & Schuster Children's Publishing Division
1230 Avenue of the Americas, New York, New York 10020

SIMON & SCHUSTER BOOKS FOR YOUNG READERS
is a trademark of Simon & Schuster, Inc.
For information about special discounts for bulk purchases,
please contact Simon & Schuster Special Sales at 1-866-506-1949 or
business@simonandschuster.com.
The Simon & Schuster Speakers Bureau can bring authors to your live event.
For more information or to book an event, contact the Simon & Schuster Speakers
Bureau at 1-866-248-3049 or visit our website at www.simonspeakers.com.
Jacket design by Chloë Foglia
Interior design by Hilary Zarycky
The text for this book was set in New Baskerville.
Manufactured in the United States of America
0717 FFG
First Edition
2 4 6 8 10 9 7 5 3 1

Library of Congress Cataloging-in-Publication Data
Names: Vaught, Susan, 1965– author.
Title: Super Max and the mystery of Thornwood's revenge / Susan Vaught.
Other titles: Mystery of Thornwood's revenge
Description: First edition. | New York : Simon & Schuster Books for Young Readers,
[2017] | "A Paula Wiseman Book." | Summary: Twelve-year-old Max is determined to
investigate the connection between a hacker's online attacks of her grandfather and
other town officials and suspicious activity at the supposedly haunted Thornwood
Manor, even though her grandfather, who is Blue Creek's police chief, wants to keep
Max and her souped-up wheelchair out of police business.
Identifiers: LCCN 2016050926 | ISBN 9781481486835 (hardback)
ISBN 9781481486859 (eBook)
Subjects: | CYAC: Wheelchairs—Fiction. | People with disabilities—Fiction.
Hackers—Fiction. | Robbers and outlaws—Fiction. | Haunted houses—Fiction.
Mystery and detective stories.
Classification: LCC PZ7.V4673 Sup 2017 | DDC [Fic]—dc23
LC record available at https://lccn.loc.gov/2016050926

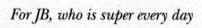

For JB, who is super every day

ACKNOWLEDGMENTS

Special thanks to Chris Nelsen, whose brilliant mind gave my son more independence than he's ever known—and Super Max her knowledge of electronics, wires, and things that go ZAP in the night.

Have you ever seen a little girl run so fast she falls down?
There's an instant, a fraction of a second before the
world catches hold of her again . . .
A moment when she's outrun every doubt and fear she's
ever had about herself and she flies.
In that one moment, every little girl flies.

—CAROL DANVERS (Captain Marvel)
Captain Marvel, volume 7, number 9, by Kelly Sue
DeConnick, Marvel Comics, January 16, 2013

Super Max and the Mystery of Thornwood's Revenge

PREFACE

Super Max the Mighty Invincible can see a haunted house from her bedroom window.

Thornwood Manor is one hundred and twenty-five years old, and it's excellently creepy. It's the most famous pile of creaky boards in Tennessee, if you don't count Graceland, and counting Graceland in any comparison is pointless, since Elvis is still so famous he's like the big giant gyrating dead ambassador to the universe.

Elvis has his songs, and Thornwood has its rhyme, penned by a local poet. It isn't a very good rhyme, but like the haunted house, it's spooky enough to raise a few eyebrows.

In years long past, dark and old,
Thornwood's heart beat small and cold.
A penny earned was a penny pinched.
With relentless greed, his fate he cinched.

In the deep of night came evil served,
A thirsty poison, well-deserved,
And to his grave went Thornwood unrepentant,
Vowing to punish his town and descendants.

When December's chill comes to kill the year
Blue Creek will remember fear,
Of wrongs imagined, he swore to avenge,
Come the day of Thornwood's Revenge.

Historians agree that Hargrove Thornwood began as a brilliant banker and businessman, controlling and a bit cruel, but not unusual for the time he lived. He came to Blue Creek and charmed the locals by employing nearly every soul in residence to build the Town Square.

Then came the great Panic of 1893, which wiped out the savings of so many of Blue Creek's wealthier residents and threatened to ruin the town. The Panic decimated Thornwood's bank and left him with little money, save for the funds to keep his local property and his personal comfort. Economists have written papers on how Thornwood could have sold some of his belongings or his fine mansion—how he could have parlayed his remaining assets into employment for his neighbors and rebuilt his fortune through the success of Blue Creek's recovering businesses.

But he wouldn't turn loose of a single acre, dollar, or piece of silver.

No.

Not one.

Hargrove Thornwood chose a path of avarice, and greed often becomes its own form of madness.

He began to imagine that his family and the citizens of Blue Creek were responsible for his financial losses, instead of his own poor planning and the national financial woes of 1893. He started to believe his relatives and neighbors had to be cheating him and lying to him. He called in loans, demanded brutal hours from his employees, and destroyed what was left of the town's economy—but he still didn't recover enough of his fortune to suit him.

That's when Thornwood took to terrorizing the streets with midnight carriage rides. People wrote about how his ancestral crest, a murderous-looking owl flying with a thorny branch clenched in its talons, seemed to glare down on them as his buggy careened around Town Square, seeking victims for him to accuse of treachery and theft. Nobody wanted to go near his mansion's front entrance, where carved owls fixed their beady gazes on anyone who dared to darken the stoop.

Finally, his son and oldest daughter ran away from him and disavowed their heritage. Most biographers note that their desertion drove Hargrove Thornwood to new depths of malice. He ranted that his belongings were disappearing, and that his staff were somehow poisoning his food and drink. He stopped going into town, and he kept his wife and youngest daughter under lock and key. When the little girl somehow escaped to go live with her brother and sister, Thornwood took to his bed, and his wife's health soon declined as well.

As the old miser lay dying, he swore that his spirit would survive the grave. He raved that he would make sure no one enjoyed the home or comforts that had been his, and that all of his descendants would suffer the same financial ruin he had endured. As Christmas approached, he thrashed in his bed, screaming that one day, in the frozen hours of December, he would return to destroy the town of Blue Creek and whatever was left of his lineage once and for all, finally and forever.

These deathbed rantings turned out to be prophetic. After he died, Thornwood Manor was rumored to be haunted, and the house seemed to torment and eject all occupants. Thornwood's progeny didn't have much success in love or business. But worse, much worse, was Thornwood's promise of revenge on the town that suffered his abuse. Long after Thornwood shuffled off this mortal coil, people in Blue Creek believed his threats to return and make them even more miserable.

Living in terror of the deranged banker's vengeance, townspeople refused to tend the mansion's grounds, fearful that Thornwood had left deadly traps or poisons hidden in the dirt. Every time some minor disaster hit, Blue Creek blamed the unforgiving ghost of Hargrove Thornwood. Yet, as years passed, nothing *really* dire happened. Time moved on. People grew older and spoke less of what used to be.

Eventually, Thornwood's declaration of doom for Blue Creek became superstition and legend. The problem is, legends don't fade or disappear. Just ask poor Elvis, wherever he might be, because he knows the truth.

Legends never, ever die.

Not the good ones, like the King. And definitely not the bad, horrible, awful ones, like Hargrove Thornwood.

They linger, and they wait, and sooner or later, they find their way home.

1

DECEMBER 1

Superheroes should never be grounded.

But if I had to be grounded, being stuck in my grandfather's workshop wasn't all bad. Toppy and I sat close together in the giant metal outbuilding, since I wasn't allowed to be on my own with tools and wires for a while—which was so completely bogus, because that fire was totally an accident.

Holding my breath so I wouldn't holler at Toppy about my punishment and get kicked out of the workshop, I snapped a connector onto the circuit board on my table. Toppy had one of our kitchen chairs clamped upside-down on his workbench as he used wood glue and finishing nails to stabilize one of the legs.

"Come on," he told the chair, his breath fogging in the chilly air. "Work with me." He tested the leg. It wobbled. He glared at it and adjusted his trapper hat. "Max, hand me the Phillips-head."

I grabbed the screwdriver from my table and rolled it over to him.

"Thanks." He gave my circuit board a quick once-over. "You about done with that thing? If we're out here much longer, I'll need to turn on the heat."

"One minute, maybe two," I said. "It's just a kit, and I didn't change much."

He went back to the chair, twisting the screwdriver and mumbling at it like it could understand him. I squeezed the red clown-nose on the top of my joystick. It honked as I motored back to my table. After that, it took me only a few seconds to snap the last circuit into place on the kit board, check the extra panel of LED lights I had added at the top, and then plug the main connector into my iPad.

I cued up a song and pressed play on one of Toppy's favorite Elvis tunes.

"You ain't nothin' but a hound dog," the King declared, and my circuit board lit up and changed colors in time to the music, just like it was supposed to do. Toppy let go of the chair leg and watched.

"Cryin' all the time," Elvis sang.

The little panel of lights I had added fired up and blinked SFC Stinks every four seconds.

Toppy's eyebrows lifted.

SFC Stinks.

SFC Stinks.

"That's—" Toppy started to say, but just then the little panel flashed again, twice as bright as it should have been.

I shielded my eyes. "Uh-oh."

Toppy squinted at the glare. The panel made a popping noise, and the last three letters went dark.

SFC St

Another flash of light made me wince.

FC St

A pop and a fizzy noise.

C

C

C

The last little bulb went supernova and cracked. Sparks shot from the edges of both boards. I leaned back as flames licked out from the added LED panel. The stench of burning plastic made me cough, but before I had to grab sand to smother the fire, it burned itself out.

Toppy came over to my workbench and unplugged my iPad from the smoking circuit board. He handed the iPad to me, then pointed to the extra wires I had used to attach the LED letter panel to the main board and the battery I chose to boost the power. They were smoking, too.

"You, ah, put a resistor in that LED panel you made?" my grandfather asked.

"I did," I said.

"Well, either you didn't wire it correctly, or the resistance was too low." Toppy patted my shoulder. "It drew too much current, so it shorted and blew the resistor. That's why your circuit board burned up."

I stared at the fried boards, miserable. Four weeks of allowance, poof. Up in smoke. Literally. "I'll work on my design."

"How about next time you want to make a blinking sign, you start with a circuit board meant to power blinking signs, not flicker to iPad music. And the right resistors, too."

I dug through my memory, trying to figure out where I'd messed up in my math. Those enhancements *should* have gone off without a hitch, even if the main board came from a kid's kit.

"You can't always make something haul the load you want it to, Max," Toppy said. "Not when it wasn't made to do that work."

I didn't answer, because I didn't agree, and I was sooooo close to working my way off grounding from the fire. The other fire. The big fire. The real—oh, never mind.

"Let's go, Max," Toppy said. "It's getting that time."

Like I said, superheroes should never be grounded— and superheroes definitely shouldn't be forced to watch sappy brain-eating holiday movies on the Sentimental Flicks Channel. SFC. Yeah, as in the big, blinking, flame-spitting **SFC Stinks** sign.

On the giant-screen television that dominated our living room wall, a girl squealed as a guy who just happened to be a secret prince rode up on his horse to return her lost puppy.

I groaned.

Toppy, who had ditched his down coat and trapper hat when we came inside, ignored my sound effects. He kept his bald head bent over the crossword puzzle on his worktable, but when I groaned a second time, he shot me a sideways glare. "Finish that report if you ever want to see your best friend again."

I bumped my joystick and backed up my wheelchair until I could look him in the ear. "This has to be child abuse."

"There are actual people who suffer actual abuse in this world." He scribbled a word into the puzzle. "Show some respect."

The threat of more days without seeing Lavender and more nights of my grandfather's heinous version of being grounded hung in the air between us. Movie credits rolled, and I muted the schmaltzy music, leaving the room quiet except for the pop-hiss of cedar burning in the fireplace and Toppy's slightly too-loud breathing. The air smelled like evergreen and winter, and the secret mug of Earl Grey tea with honey steeping next to Toppy's crossword book gave off a shimmery feather of heat.

With a sigh, I picked up my pen and scribbled a paragraph about the movie's ending, then slid my paper across the table toward Toppy. He took it and held it over his crossword, reading silently. The muscles in my neck tightened as his bushy white eyebrows lifted once, then twice. He tapped his pencil on the paper.

"Good insight about weak characterization. The Central Park Prince movies don't offer much in the way of literary merit."

I leaned hard against the back of my chair. "Literary merit? Who uses phrases like that in actual sentences in this actual century? No wonder you can't get a date."

"Wouldn't date on a bet." He kept reading. "And I'm not the nerd who can name every superhero in both the DC and Marvel universes."

"Hey, it's a useful skill."

"I'll be waiting on proof of that assertion without holding my breath." Toppy held up my report. "If I accept this as your final paper, we're agreed that you won't modify anything else in the house's electrical system without discussing it with me first?"

I squeezed the oversize clown-nose on my joystick tip, making it squeak. "If I had tightened the nuts on those wires, we would have been fine with my added fuses. I just wanted the breakers to stop blowing."

"Well, they're all tight now." Toppy's green eyes drilled into mine. "The three thousand dollars to replace the burned fuse box and repair the scorched wall was bad enough, but all that burned-up mess could have been the whole house. It could have been *you.*"

"I won't touch the house electric again," I conceded. My fingers trailed along my armrests, the leather covers currently painted with silver and gold runes I saw in a movie about faeries and King Arthur. "But my wheel-chair—"

"That chair is no different than your legs. You do what you want with your own body, Max. Don't let me or anyone else tell you any differently." Toppy pushed my paper to the side and almost went back to his puzzle, but he paused long enough to add, "Though I'd rather you not bust the thing trying to make it fly or float on water or whatever you come up with next, seeing as I don't have an extra ten thousand lying around to buy you a new set of wheels this year."

"Yes, sir," I said, my guilt rising like the heat off his tea. I hated how much my chairs cost, even though Toppy usually didn't make a big deal out of it, even when I broke something or fried some wires trying new ideas.

"And no, you can't have a tattoo until you're eigh-teen."

I sighed.

The phone rang.

Toppy and I both jumped and stared at each other. I caught the sudden sadness and concern on his face. The lines on his forehead deepened even as my stomach sank. Nobody would call at eight o'clock on a Friday night except for Mom.

My fists clenched on the arms of my wheelchair. "I don't want to talk to her."

Toppy held up one hand as the phone rang again. Caller ID flashed across the television screen, noting **Blocked Number.**

So, not a California area code. Not Mom.

Toppy answered the old-fashioned desk unit. "Yellow?" Pause. "Wait, who is this?" Pause. "Facebook? Bunch of cat pictures and whining, far as I can see." Pause. Then Toppy's head flushed a bright shade of red. His eyes narrowed, and his jaw set, and when he spoke, his normally mellow voice ground out in a low growl. "Now you wait one minute, Margaret Stetson Chandler."

I shot forward and bumped his chair with mine. When he startled, I leaned forward and grabbed the phone from his hand before he could say anything we'd all regret. Margaret Chandler was his least favorite person in the entire universe. She also happened to be Blue Creek's most revered businesswoman, owner of Chandler Construction, and the mayor. Which made her Toppy's boss.

"Hello, Mayor Chandler," I said, happy because she wasn't my mother. "Is there something I can help you with?"

"Maxine." Her voice switched from cool to warm as she spoke to me, then blazed right on to red hot. "You tell that—that—that *man* to take down what he posted. Right now, or I'll convene the City Council and we'll have his separation papers finished by morning. I will not have somebody speak about my business and my family—and my *hair*—in that manner!"

I pulled the phone away from my ear, looked at it, then realized I couldn't see whatever kind of confusion had infected Mayor Chandler through the mouthpiece. "I'm sorry to interrupt, ma'am, but are you talking about a Facebook post?"

"Yes!" She hollered so loud I heard her without the phone being back against my ear. "It's right there on his page, and every single one of his posts is shameful. You're a beautiful young lady, Maxine Brennan, and you know I adore you, but your grandfather is old enough to know better than to misbehave on social media. It's unbecoming for a city employee, and absolutely inappropriate for the chief of police."

I managed to get the receiver back against my ear without losing an eardrum to her shrieking, but it was a near thing. "Mayor Chandler, Toppy doesn't have a Facebook page. He doesn't have a computer at home, he doesn't have a smartphone, and he won't let me have one, either."

"Phones are for dialing telephone numbers," Toppy grumbled. He had already gone back to his crossword puzzle.

"How can you say he doesn't have a Facebook page?" Mayor Chandler sounded very skeptical, but at least her volume ratcheted down a few digits. "I'm looking at it right this very moment. Every post seems designed to make the town or me look foolish."

Wow. I briefly wondered if Toppy had taken up Facebook over at the police station, but just then, he bit at his pencil eraser, absorbed in trying to find an eighteen-letter word for who-knew-what.

No. Toppy and Facebook, that just wasn't happening.

"Just a minute, ma'am. I'll be right back." I put down the receiver, hit my joystick, and whizzed around to my side of the big drafting table, where my iPad rested on a custom stand Toppy built for me to hold it steady and at the exact angle I needed to be hands-free in my chair. I pressed my thumb to the fingerprint sensor, unlocked my screen, and pulled up Facebook. Then I typed my grandfather's name into the search bar, but got nothing.

I had to stretch to get the receiver, then work not to get tangled in the cord (no, Toppy wouldn't even do cordless). "Mayor Chandler? I'm on Facebook, but I'm not finding any page for Toppy Brennan."

"It's not under Toppy," she snapped. "It's listed under his real name. . . . Oh." She trailed off, the fire in her tone burning out completely. Once upon a time, a million years ago, Mayor Chandler had dated my grandfather. They were both in high school, before he joined the Army. They hadn't been together very long, maybe a few months, but long enough that Mayor Chandler knew Toppy never ever went by his legal name. "Interesting. I mean, that's unusual. I mean, why would—oh, never mind. I'm coming over."

She ended the call.

I hung up the receiver and put my hand on top of Toppy's crossword.

He glanced up at me, pencil poised over my third knuckle. "What was all that going-on about Facebook?"

"Mayor Chandler's coming over. We've got ten minutes, assuming she wasn't already in her car when she phoned."

For the briefest moment, Toppy looked like a mortified SFC heroine just after the hero shows up and catches her in flannel pj's. Because that's exactly what Toppy was wearing. Red-checkered no less. With matching red fluffy bunny slippers I had given him for his birthday.

"The mayor," I said, hoping to jar him out of stun.

"She's coming here. Right now. I'll get rid of the tea."

My grandfather was seventy-four years old with arthritis in both knees. I never would have known that when he exploded up from the worktable and blew out of our living room, dropping a few not-okay-for-school phrases on his way to his closet.

2

When Lavender and I were little, we played super-heroes *all* the time, when we weren't reading about them. She helped me etch my first ever Superman S into the back of the chair I had a few years back. After that, we welded a searchlight onto one of the push-bars, and I wired it to my battery and used it to stun people while I intoned, "I'm Batman" whenever somebody asked my name. Worked great until the bulb exploded.

Back when I still believed I'd be Super Max one day, I pretended my chair could go anywhere I wanted it to go, and turn into boats and cars and airplanes and spaceships. I had Batman cleverness, Spider-Man agility, Superman hearing, and Superman laser vision that caught every detail, every nuance of whatever we decided to investigate. Sadly, laser vision, real or pre-tend, didn't help much with examining Facebook.

"Smells like Earl Grey in here." Mayor Chandler wrinkled her nose as she settled on her knees beside me at the worktable. "My grandmother used to drink that stuff."

I couldn't see Toppy because he was standing behind my chair, but I know he must have turned red in the face. He didn't want anybody to know he'd swapped his coffee for tea. He thought it made him seem old. As fast as I could, I expanded the Facebook page she told us about and pointed at it to get Mayor Chandler's attention. I smiled, hoping my face looked completely innocent.

After reading the Facebook page for a few seconds, my smile gradually shifted to a frown. "Somebody went to a lot of trouble setting this up."

"Mmmhmm," Mayor Chandler agreed.

As we studied the Facebook page of Thomas Lelliett Brennan, Elvis crooned *Welcome to My World* in the background. Toppy's CD player, the one that looked like an old stereo, was on its last legs, and the disc hitched every now and then, skipping to different songs. "Anybody could have snapped that header photo of the Blue Creek Police Department," I said. "It looks pretty recent, like they took it from Town Square. And I'm sorry. I didn't choose this music."

"Yes about the picture, and I understand about the music," Mayor Chandler said. Then, "Lelliett?"

My grandfather stepped up on my right and cut her a side-eye.

"Family name," I told her, hoping the two of them didn't go from zero to brawl in ten seconds flat.

She pointed to the profile picture of Toppy, wearing his uniform complete with its bright blue hat. "This page has been updated since I saw it. That's new, and it looks like his departmental identification shot."

Toppy shifted from foot to foot. He was wearing pressed black slacks, shiny black shoes, and this year's winter sweater I bought him, the one with black shoulders, red stripes, and a snowflake in the center. He smelled like a pine tree. Every few seconds, he gave Mayor Chandler a once-over then looked away—then looked back again. Finally, he stared at the muted television as a secret princess galloped through Central Park on her white stallion.

"Public record, then." I frowned at a symbol in the upper right corner I couldn't quite make out, so I expanded it some more. "That looks like—hmm. It's like a drawing of a bird."

"An owl," Mayor Chandler said. "Carrying something."

I squinted at the dark lines and angles. "Thorns," I said. "It's carrying a thorny vine, or something. Oh! It's like a tattoo of the Thornwood Owl!"

Mayor Chandler's head automatically turned in the

direction of the mansion up the hill from our house. "Okay. That's a little strange."

"So is this," I said, pointing to the next photo on the timeline. It showed a young woman with blond curls so bright they probably made people see spots. She was wearing a really ugly striped dress and holding a baby.

The post read, **Heartless Widow Chandler won't escape Thornwood's Revenge.**

Mayor Chandler winced as I enlarged the picture. "That's from fifty years ago." Her hand lifted to her ash blond ponytail, blue eyes narrowing behind her small gold glasses. "Good lord, old photos should just self-destruct after a few decades." She sighed, then added, "*Blue Creek Gazette* did that article on my husband's construction business after we got that big contract with the state parks. I was already running the front office by then."

I glanced at her faded jeans and white sweater, and the bomber jacket with its worn elbows. She didn't wear cartoon-y makeup and striped dresses now. I was glad. She always looked pretty to me.

"She won't escape Thornwood's Revenge," I said. "Is that a threat?"

"Everybody's always citing that old legend," she said. "It's just another way of saying I ought to get tortured by a demon—or poisoned by a shallow-dug well. Wasn't that how Thornwood and his wife died?"

I had read every book about the Thornwood Manor haunting, most of them more than once. "Yes, ma'am." I popped open another window on the iPad and clicked the bookmark for my stored copy of the old Thornwood website, the one where people could schedule tours before the floor in the mansion's main room caved in and the city had to close down everything.

The Thornwood Owl bloomed into view, winging across a dark night sky with its evil-looking bramble clutched tight to its chest. It faded to a page about how Thornwood lost most of his fortune, turned into the meanest man alive, and then how weird things started happening at his mansion, like noises in the night and his prized possessions disappearing. The last paragraph of the history read:

> The coroner noted odd horizontal stripes on Thornwood's fingernails and his wife's also, hinting at arsenic poisoning. The Thornwood Manor well was found to be contaminated. Despite persistent rumors of homicide, a state surveyor pronounced the well to be shallow-dug and contaminated with natural arsenic. No doubt this was due to Thornwood's penny-pinching and bellicose management of his mansion's maintenance crew, who hurried in their duties to escape his berating.

In the end, Thornwood lived and died by his
own frequent assertion: In this life, a man well and
truly gets what he pays for.

"I don't plan to sip from an arsenic-laced well,"
Mayor Chandler said, "so we can move on."

I closed that page, leaving her old big-hair photo
front and center.

"Library has the *Blue Creek Gazette* going back to June
1, 1897," Toppy said. "Scanned it all into their computers. Whoever did this likely got your picture from those
archives."

Mayor Chandler and I both looked at him, because it
was the first time he had spoken since she got there. He
cleared his throat, and the top of his head turned pink.

"Do you have to go to Blue Creek Central to search
the archives?" Mayor Chandler asked. "Or can you do it
through their website?"

"They don't have anything but branch hours and
community events online." Toppy ran his fingers
through hair he didn't have, seemed to realize what
he was doing, then dropped his hand back to his side.
"When an officer needs something, they have to go on
over to the Third Street branch."

My iPad chimed with a message. It dropped down in
a black banner, tagged with Lavender's purple dragon
profile picture.

Dude. Did Toppy drink too much eggnog? Have you seen Facebook?

It's a fake page, I typed back. Mayor's here. Laterz.

I swiped off Messenger and checked the next picture. Another shot of the mayor, this time when she won her first election the year after her husband passed. Widow Chandler not much for grieving, the post said.

"At least my hair was smaller by then," she groused.

"I can't tell who this jerk wants to embarrass," I said. "He's going after you and Toppy both."

"It's me," Toppy said.

When we looked at him again, he shrugged. "I piss people off every day."

After a few seconds, Mayor Chandler said, "Can't argue that."

The laugh popped out before I could stifle it, and it was my turn to get the side-eye from Toppy.

Mayor Chandler softened her jab with, "We should check your cases and make sure nobody you helped convict just got out of prison or jail."

He nodded, and we went back to scrolling through the page. My watch alarm beeped, and I weight-shifted in my chair, moving more onto my right hip and taking pressure off the bottom of my spine. I had to do that every four hours during the day, so I didn't get pressure sores and die from nonstop sitting. And even if my equipment and appointments cost a lot of money and made things harder for Toppy, I didn't want to die, especially not from a giant hole in my butt cheek.

After I settled myself and refreshed the page, it updated with a new picture, and my stomach clenched at the sight of a way-too-familiar mangled Ford pickup, and the high school graduation photo next to it. My grandfather's hand came to rest on my right shoulder, and Mayor Chandler stood and touched my left shoulder.

"You don't have to enlarge that one, honey," she said.

I did anyway.

My mother's seventeen-year-old face stared back at me, grinning. She had green eyes like Toppy, and reddish-brown hair like his before he went bald. My eyes were dark brown, and my hair, too. Since I didn't know my dad, I had no idea who I looked like, but it wasn't Mom or Toppy.

I had seen this shot about a million times. Maybe a billion. It was the yearbook photo the *Gazette* had used to report on the wreck Mom and I had on the Pacific Coast Highway near Monterey Bay when I was four years old. Mom was twenty-three by then, but the paper chose a picture locals would recognize.

I didn't remember the crash, or anything much about my life before that. Probably not a bad thing. If I could remember walking, I might miss it more.

Difficult Year for Chief Brennan Continues:

Granddaughter Seriously Injured in Early Morning Coast Collision

Two weeks after Toppy's wife, my grandmother Ada, died from cancer, a tanker truck had come around a curve in Mom's lane and clipped our front bumper. When we spun into the bank, the ancient pickup Toppy had given Mom came apart like a toy. I couldn't walk anymore, but at least I could pee for myself and take care of my own business, so all in all, it could have been a lot worse.

It was an accident. Nobody's fault. That's what the article in the *Gazette* said, but whoever made this new fake Facebook page had scanned the article and trimmed off the text, leaving just the headline and picture. Above the photo, the post read,

Eight years since disaster, and four years since my daughter blew through her settlement money and pawned off her disabled kid on me. I've always let my only child shirk her responsibilities. It's a wonder Blue Creek trusts my judgment at all.

"Shirk," I mumbled. "Who uses words like that?" *Pawned off . . . disabled kid . . .*

Toppy's piney aftershave made my eyes water. From a thousand miles away, Elvis told us he was "a steamroller, baby, 'bout to roll all over you."

27

Mayor Chandler X'd out of the enlarged picture and scrolled away from the accident shot. There were a few more photos of her with snotheaded comments in the posts, and then some clips of police department problems from the past. The screen looked a little blurry, but I coughed and wiped my eyes, then shook off both the hands on my shoulders.

"It's all photos somebody could get from the library or online," I said, then got mad because my voice shook, and totally furious when I realized the rest of me was shaking, too.

Mayor Chandler scrolled back to the top of the page. "People are commenting—and the page already has two hundred and fifty-four followers."

Toppy folded his arms. "So? Doesn't take a genius to see the whole thing's a bunch of hooey."

"Not that simple," Mayor Chandler muttered, pulling out her phone. "This is social media. Public pages can go viral. People in China might be reading this tomorrow."

I ignored Toppy's grumbling about the page needing a whiny cat picture to be complete, and how viruses were things people got shots for, and reported the whole mess to Facebook. "They'll probably take it down," I told him, "but it may be a few days, and a lot of folks in town will see it. Some idiots may even believe it's yours."

Mayor Chandler cleared her throat, and I realized she had been one of those idiots for a minute or two. I wanted to fall through my chair cushion, but before I could apologize, she patted my shoulder.

"I'd suggest you put a message on the police department phone, Chief Brennan," Mayor Chandler said. When she saw the look on his face, she tried again with, "Toppy, trust me, some people will fall for it, just like I did. You'll be getting calls."

He scowled at her for a second like he didn't quite believe anybody would be pathetic enough to pay that silly Facebook page any attention. She held his gaze, matching his stubborn with her own. Seconds ticked by. About three deep breaths later, he relented and picked up the desk unit receiver and started dialing.

I went to my personal Facebook page and wrote a quick post about the fake account. Then, as Toppy droned on the police department main greeting about having the good sense to ignore social media nonsense, the mayor held out her phone to show me the message she was posting on Blue Creek's official city page. She used phrases like "ludicrous fraud" and "unconscionable slander" and "catching the perpetrator responsible for this deceitful poison-pen assault." That ought to do the trick. People would be looking up what she meant for hours.

Toppy hung up the phone, and it rang almost

immediately. Caller ID popped up on the muted television, showing a California area code as the *Aloha from Hawaii* CD hitched.

"No," I said before Toppy could answer it. "Just, no."

He answered it anyway.

Heat rushed through every inch of my body.

Before he finished his, "Yel-low?" I snatched up my iPad and booked out of the living room without even saying good-bye to Mayor Chandler.

I rolled so fast I would have overshot my door and punched another accidental hole in the drywall, if I hadn't practiced being Super Max most of my life. I swung wide better than a NASCAR pro and got my door locked before anybody came after me. It took me another few seconds to stack up my comics and graphic novels, find my headphone jack, jam it into place, stuff the pink buds into my ears, crank the music (anything but Elvis), shut off the lights, and get to my bedroom window.

Deep breath.

My jaw hurt, and I realized I had my teeth clamped together.

Deep breath.

I didn't want to keep getting madder, because I didn't like myself when I threw things and said a bunch of ugly stuff to people I loved.

Deep breath. "Hammer," I said out loud, starting

with the Marvel Comics H-named superheroes, even though I couldn't hear myself over the music pounding in my ears. "Herbie. Hairball. Hammerhead . . ."

My teeth unclamped. With each name, I faded more and more into the music, letting myself pick up the song's rhythm.

By the time I got to Hulk, I no longer wanted to turn green, triple in size, grow mutant muscles, roar my name a lot, and shred my bedroom. I finished the Marvel H's for the sake of completionism, and made a mental note to start with the Marvel I heroes next time I needed to recite.

Then I just stared out into the night and rubbed the sides of my head. The pounding in my temples slowly got better. Then the heat I had been feeling gave way to guilt because I had gotten so mad all of a sudden, and rolled so fast I could have busted holes in the walls with my footplates, like I used to do.

Bad.

Bad, bad, bad.

Just when I thought I had gotten control of my temper, boom. It would hit again. Over something stupid. Usually over something stupid named MOM.

Let it go, let it go, let it go. . . .

Toppy hadn't come to get me and make me talk to Mom.

That, at least, was good.

Of course, with the door locked and the lights off and the music loud, I could pretend not to hear him if he knocked.

Yeah, that would work.

And then it would be just me, Toppy, and another week's worth of being grounded and awful puppy-princess movies.

3

Super Max wouldn't let this Facebook stuff get to her, Lavender texted. WWSMD?

She'd investigate, I wrote back on the iPad. And we're doing that. I told Lavender what we'd figured out about the fake page so far. Music still jammed in my ears, blocking out the world except for the messages on my iPad.

Gotta be somebody local, since they had to go to the library? Lavender typed.

Maybe, I typed back. Or visiting. Or got help from a local friend.

What's their beef with Toppy?

No idea, but he's been arresting people for half a century. He's going to check his cases.

How about Mayor Chandler's hair helmet? A gagging stickman emoji popped up, and I smiled.

I've been trying to talk her into purple highlights.

Bug-eyed heart-face emoji. It'd be a good look for her. NN.

Nine o'clock. Offline time for my best friend. NN I sent, along with a sleeping kitty emoji.

Toppy didn't have an offline time for me. I wasn't totally sure he understood the interwebz were open 24/7, but what he didn't know wouldn't hurt him.

I sat in the dark and checked the fake Facebook page as my current playlist cycled through my favorites. No more updates. I made a folder in Photos, then saved all the pictures, and screencaps, too. If Facebook took down the page, I'd still be able to see what had been posted.

My face felt cool from being so close to my bedroom window with the curtains open. I knew if I touched the glass, cold would sting my fingers.

When I looked out into the night, winter moonlight bathed the field between our house and Thornwood Manor, making a few rolled bales of hay look like pre-historic cows on some alien planet. I had a straight-on view of the back of the mansion, with its three floors and the four-story tower-thingy right in the middle. According to architecture fanatics who commented on the Thornwood sites, it was an "Italianate tower" instead of a turret because it was square, not round.

Rows of windows, six on each floor, seemed like dark gateways to other dimensions. When I first moved in with Toppy, the mansion had creeped me right out and given me nightmares. Now I was used to its hulking silhouette.

My watch beeped, and I moved in my chair, shifting to my left hip because the hour was odd. I did right hip on the evens. What had Mom wanted when she called? One of her obligatory check-ins?

Pawned off her disabled kid. . . .

Jerk. I wished I knew who made that Facebook page. I'd pawn my fist off on his or her face, that was a promise.

My own face suddenly felt hot again, and I shut my eyes.

Mom might have seen the fake page already. She was probably upset. Toppy would calm her down. He was better at that than I was. Then he'd have a little time with Mayor Chandler, maybe give her some tea if he didn't get nervous. Even though he kept telling me he was "too old for any of that foolishness," I was pretty sure he liked her—when he wasn't wanting to kill her.

Deep breath. Don't get mad again. Don't do it.

I relaxed my jaws, then my neck muscles and my hands, and then all my muscles, top to bottom. That's one of the things this counselor taught me to do a couple of years ago, when Toppy drove me to Nashville to get help for my anger after I hollered at a teacher in class. If I kept my body chilled, I wouldn't lose my temper so much, and if I did get really mad, I could distract myself and calm down before I exploded. So I used my superhero lists, and relaxing my muscles, and music. And avoiding Mom. Avoiding Mom really cut down on my blowups.

Oops.

My jaws had gotten all tight again, so I started over on my relaxing.

Even though Toppy teased me about being a comics nerd, I had grown out of a lot of my superhero obsession. Sort of. Still liked the comics and movies, maybe a little less than Lavender. But when we were younger, Lavender and I drew stick-figure cartoons where Super Max in her chair rocketed in to save the day. Lavender the Magnifico was never far behind, wearing her lightning bracelets and booming thunder at all who opposed her.

Deep breath, and hold.

Deep breath, and hold.

It made me happy to think about those silly pictures and stories.

Deep breath, and hold.

A few seconds—or maybe minutes—later, I checked my body. My muscles seemed relaxed, and the heat had left my face. Once more, I could feel the cold radiating off my windowpanes. I let out a long, slow sigh, closed my eyes, opened them—and froze.

Blinked.

Shut my eyes and opened them again.

"No way." I ripped out my earbuds. My fingers fumbled with my iPad, tapping the camera icon, then lifting and aiming. My first shot flashed, and I swore, knowing I'd get nothing but glare from my own windows. I turned off the flash and jammed my finger on the button, taking a burst of Thornwood's tower.

A single light flickered on the screen view as I took another burst, and another. My heart seemed to jump against my ribs as the flickering light moved to the next window, then vanished. A few thudding pulse-beats later, it appeared in the third-level windows, and disappeared. Second level. First level. And . . .

Gone.

I waited, barely breathing, squinting through the darkness at the back of the mansion.

What had I just seen?

A ghost? A ghost walking by candlelight. Wasn't that one of the Thornwood ghost stories? Lavender had all the same books I did, maybe a few more since her mom used to run the tours from Something Wicked, her shop on Town Square.

"Don't be silly," I told myself.

But there had been a light. Had somebody broken into the mansion?

I kept watching for a long time, minutes that felt like hours. No light. No movement. Nothing.

I positioned my iPad so I could see it and the mansion, too, and I opened the bursts I had taken. The shots were mostly a lot of gray and black nothingness. I could make out a pinpoint of light, but only because I knew where I was looking. When I enlarged the shots, they got too grainy to see anything at all.

There had been a light, for sure.

I went to my favorite Thornwood Manor website, waited for the owl logo to load and fade, then scanned the history page until I got to the paragraph I wanted to send to Lavender:

Twenty years after Thornwood's death in 1895, his eldest grandchild tried to set up residence in the mansion. The man fled less than a month later, complaining of frightening noises, terrible nightmares, and lights shining in locked rooms. The heir hired various caretakers, but none lasted more than a few weeks. One poor gentleman tumbled down the front stairs and broke his neck, marking the end of human habitation in Thornwood Manor.

I sent that to her, then sent the next paragraph, too.

In the Roaring Twenties, when the real estate company caring for the home allowed evening tours, guests reported cold spots and visions, and many thought they saw flickering lights in the mansion's windows, as if someone walked the floors carrying a candlestick.

I watched Thornwood Manor for another few minutes, but it stayed dark. I pulled the best of my photos into an editing app, circled the little bit of light, and sent them after the paragraphs for Lavender to find in the morning.

Top of Thornwood turret. Oh, crud. I erased "turret" and put "tower," and recorded the time I took the bursts. Then I added, **See you tomorrow. It's been one seriously weird Friday night.**

4

DECEMBER 2

"You're sooooo wrong," Riley Soza said to David "Bot" Botman, owner of Bot's Electronics, one of the bigger stores on Blue Creek's Town Square. It sat directly across from the police department, but the courthouse in the middle blocked the view. That meant Toppy probably wouldn't see me spending my allowance on a bunch of wires and circuits, which was for the best. Panic wasn't good for him this early in the morning, especially when he had to go in on a weekend to search his arrest files with Mayor Chandler, trying to find who might have created a fake Facebook page to make them both look pathetic.

"Superman is much better than Spider-Man," Riley insisted. "*So* much better." He flexed the puny muscles of his way-too-long arms. "Strength, invulnerability, plus he can fly."

Lavender sat at the parts counter gazing at Riley

with unicorn-star eyes. She thought his long, dark hair was adorable. In fact, she'd been kind of silly about him since he came to live with Bot as his foster son three years ago. He was just one grade above us, but, like, half a foot taller than Lavender's five-two. Every three seconds, she played with her red curls, tucking them behind first one ear, then the other. Sometimes, she fidgeted with the coat on the back of her chair. Her purple *Magic Wins* sweatshirt glittered in the shop's winter lighting, and she kept scrubbing her dancer's tights and fuzzy leggings against the counter's glass, making squeegee sounds that gave me chills.

I don't think Riley noticed.

I tried to go back to studying different wire grades, calculating length in my head as Bot boomed, "Boy, you don't know what you're talking about." His voice bounced off routers and switches and circuit boards and soldering irons, dragging my attention back to the never-ending Great Superhero Debate. I tell you what, if I really were a superhero, I would *not* want these geeks arguing about my strengths and weaknesses. In my head, I saw my stick-figure self in my stick-sketched rocket chair jetting by just long enough to drop a load of "dislike" thumbs on the store's flat yellow roof.

Bot shifted his bulk in front of Riley, shaking a fist but grinning at the same time. With his white hair and white beard and big build, he looked a lot like Santa

Claus, but with a ton of tattoos. "Supe is scared of rocks. *Rocks!*" The dark skin around his eyes crinkled as he laughed. "Spidey's scared of nada, and his extra senses trump super-strength any day."

"I like Carol Danvers," Lavender said as she stretched out her leg and pointed the toe of her purple everyday acro shoe at the far wall. "She can fly, too, and she loves *Star Wars,* like me. Ms. Marvel aces Superman and Spider-Man both."

Bot and Riley gaped at her.

Riley grabbed his chest and faked a heart attack. "Oh, no you did *not* just say that."

Lavender stretched her other leg, then bent her arms and gave him a bring-it-chump finger wiggle.

"I thought Lavender always championed Wonder Woman or Squirrel Girl," Ellis Pritchard said as he leaned on the glass display case I was staring at.

Jeez! I almost jumped out of my skin. He always snuck up on me because he was small and quiet compared to Riley and Bot. He had cut his blond hair since I saw him a couple of weeks ago. It stuck up in bristles around his pale freckled face, making him look my age instead of nineteen.

"Arguing for a Marvel against the DC heroes is her latest tactic to destroy their arrogance," I said. "I don't think she'll get very far. She ought to challenge them to a rap battle or a dance-off. She'd win those, no question."

Bot and Riley talked over each other in their hurry to convince Lavender that Superman, Spider-Man, or basically any guy super was better than her girl super. Ellis shook his head. When he grinned at me, I grinned back automatically. I didn't have any brothers or sisters, but if I could pick somebody to be an older brother, I'd definitely choose Ellis.

We both loved electricity and designing circuits and gadgets. We both didn't really have a mom because ours took off. He got raised by his aunt, like I was being raised by Toppy, only his aunt died at Blue Creek Nursing Home last year. He never talked about his dad, and I figured Ellis was in the same boat as me, not even knowing who that was. So, see? Lots alike. Except he kicked my butt with computers. Lavender and I could hold our own with apps and programs, but Ellis—he could make computers tap dance if he wanted to.

He glanced at my chair and took in the rows of yin-yang symbols I had etched down both push-bars since the last time I was in the store. "You trying a Zen phase, or are you planning to take up surfing?"

"They make wheelchair surfboards and water chairs," I said. "But I'd probably get seasick in the ocean."

"Zen it is." He saluted. "We could all use a little healthy meditation. What can I do you for this week, Max?"

I pointed into the display case. "Ten-gauge wire will handle forty amps, right?"

Ellis's blue eyes narrowed with suspicion. "You up to something that'll summon the fire department again?"

My face got hot. "No! And that was two weeks ago. Am I ever going to live that down?"

He grabbed my coil of wire. "Mistakes follow people. Especially three-alarm blunders. Like . . . your grandfather's new Facebook page?"

"That's just junk," I told him. "Somebody did it for a prank."

"Seriously?" He looked skeptical.

"Yeah." I waved a hand in the general direction of the police station. "Some hacker with a grudge. Used the wrong name. Well, a name my grandfather would never choose, I mean."

Ellis hesitated, then frowned. "Huh. Pretty sophisticated for a prank. If it's not really Chief Brennan's page, where'd all those old photos come from?"

"Like Toppy would even know how to take a picture of a print and post it. He's never used the camera on that old flip-top phone he likes." I laughed. "The hacker got them from the *Gazette* archives, best we can figure."

"We?" Ellis raised his blond eyebrows, and I realized the shop had gotten quiet except for the vintage rock Pandora station Bot liked to pipe in through the always-expanding sound system.

"Toppy and Mayor Chandler and Lavender and me, and now the librarian and other officers, too." Lavender came over to me as I added, "Most of the department's in this morning, checking it out, trying to see if there's any real threat involved. Last time I talked to Toppy, he had questioned the librarian. All the pictures had been accounted for in *Gazette* stories, and they were piling up cases released from jail this year to get a fix on who might have tried it."

"There are, like, a hundred-fifty-million fake Facebook accounts trying to steal people's identity and money and stuff," Lavender said.

"And they rake in the dough," Ellis said. "One way wealth gets redistributed from silver-spooners with big bucks to smarter people born with fewer resources."

Bot wagged his finger at Ellis. "Internet Robin Hoods are criminals, not superheroes."

"It's not fair that money controls who a person can become," Ellis said.

"It doesn't," Riley argued. "Well, I guess it does some. Maybe a lot."

"No cynicism allowed in my shop, boys and girls," Bot announced.

Ellis gave Bot a thumbs-down, but he stopped talking like he thought it was cool to steal from the rich.

"I don't think the police will ever figure out who set that fake page up," Lavender said, "but it got taken down this morning."

"Well, that was quick work," Bot said. "But I didn't

think Mayor Chandler and Chief Brennan got along that well, from, well—you know. Back in the day. But now she's helping him?"

"She has a nice side," I told him. "Plus, the hacker posted an awful old photo of her. Hey, you rang that wire up wrong, Ellis."

Ellis studied the old-fashioned cha-ching register's big numbers and grimaced. "Yeah. That'll be $12.93 for fifty feet, not $1.29. Sorry."

"Dork," Riley said.

As Ellis punched him in the shoulder, I fumbled in the pouch hanging from my wheelchair arm and came out with my last grubby clump of five-dollar bills. When I forked them over, Ellis frowned and pinched them between his thumb and pointer like they might be contaminated.

"It's just honey," I assured him. "From making Toppy's tea. Oh, crud. Look, don't tell anybody he drinks tea with honey. He says people will think he's going soft in his old age."

Riley cracked up, and so did Lavender. Bot hustled off before anybody asked him to touch the sticky money. Ellis stuffed the bills in the register and gave me my change, looking like he ate something really sour. Then, as I zipped up my change pouch, Ellis asked, "So, you want me to try to trace the Facebook page? I have some data-mining programs I wrote. I could try them out to see if I can find the server the page-faker used."

"You can do stuff like that?" Lavender asked, sounding impressed.

"He wishes," Riley said, and then laughed at his own joke.

"I can try," Ellis said. "May not get anywhere, though." He held up both hands like he wanted us to know he wasn't promising anything—or, more importantly, setting himself up for endless teasing if he couldn't pull it off.

Lavender fiddled with her hair. "Seeing as we don't have any sophisticated cybercrime investigators in Blue Creek, and Mom said the FBI won't help out unless the fake poster starts outright threatening people or breaking big federal laws, you're probably our only hope."

"That would be awesome, Ellis." I handed my bag with the wire coil to Lavender, and she put it in my wheelchair backpack, then handed me the coat I had draped over the chair's push-bars. "Thank you. You have my e-mail address if you find anything?"

He gave me the thumbs-up. "It's in the store records. Just you be careful, Max. There was a lot of talk on that page about Thornwood's Revenge. Seriously creepy stuff."

Lavender helped me put on my coat, shaking her head. "Mayor Chandler says that's just more junk. People have been telling scary stories about that scary man and his scary house for decades."

"When you read all the old stories about Thornwood Manor, it's not such a joke," Ellis said. "You know his youngest daughter was just about your age when Thornwood's wife snuck her out of the mansion and sent her to her brother and sister in Detroit, but she—"

"Died less than a week later in a carriage accident," I finished for him. "Yeah, I know. And I know people said nobody was driving the carriage."

Riley counted off on his fingers. "And then a caretaker broke his neck, and tour guests saw spooky stuff, and don't forget the one grandson who tried to live there and had to run away. I know Thornwood was a jerk, but you have to respect his supervillain-fear-me game. People are still scared of what his ghost might be cooking up for Blue Creek, and I bet it's nasty as he— um, heck."

"Fire, storms, floods, more hauntings," I said. "What else could Thornwood's Revenge turn out to be, if it's hitting a whole town?"

Lavender did a dance stretch, bending over to her ankle with her leg stuck out to one side. "I don't believe in ghosts."

Ellis laughed. "Better not tell your mom that, given all the ghost-y stuff in Something Wicked."

"Yeah, I know." Lavender groaned. "But just because she's superstitious doesn't mean I buy into unscientific principles. I like comic books and sci-fi, but I know what's possible and what isn't."

Riley and Ellis looked at her like she might be growing horns.

"I'm out," Riley said, jerking his thumb toward parts storage and heading in that direction.

Lavender held open the shop door and I rolled out into the cold winter air. Sunlight blazed into my eyes, making me drive sightless for a few feet until I could stand the fresh outdoor glare. I pulled my hand off the clown-nose joystick and the chair rolled to a stop near a parking meter. When Lavender caught up, dancing different jetés in wide circles around my chair, we headed toward Something Wicked.

Lavender landed nearby and posed, hands above her head. "I wonder how many people Toppy's arrested in his career. Has to be hundreds, or maybe thousands. Those records aren't all on the computer. Searching them will take—"

"Forever," I agreed as she took off again, spinning and hopping. The few people out in the chilly morning gave her plenty of room. "But whoever this is doesn't like Mayor Chandler, either. Maybe that narrows the cases a little."

The air chafed my cheeks as Lavender once more came to rest near my chair and said, "I still think it has to be somebody local, or at least somebody who grew up in Blue Creek, or who lived here for a while."

I rolled forward, careful to miss her toes. "Will they stop with messing around on social media, since Facebook took down that page?"

"I doubt it," she said. "We should keep a watch on Twitter, too. And I keep thinking about that light in Thornwood Manor."

"Yeah." I didn't like the way my chest felt, all tight, with my heart beating kinda funny. "It flickered like a candle, straight from all the scary stories. But I don't know what it means. Seems weird the Facebook page with the Thornwood Owl in the corner and that light would happen on the same night—and the hacker said stuff about Thornwood's Revenge. We should go up to the manor and look around."

Lavender's eyes widened. "That makes about as much sense as tap dancing on an anthill. That place is halfway to condemned, and—and—"

"I thought you didn't believe in ghosts."

"Shut up, Max." A dance shoe flashed in front of my nose like a karate kick.

I rolled more slowly, lining my chair up with the door of Something Wicked. "I saw a flickering light in Thornwood's windows."

"Then tell Toppy!"

"Right." I honked my clown-nose and stopped outside the shop with its display window of books and crystals and dream catchers and incense packs, arranged with peacock feathers and hay and chunks of geodes. "Toppy doesn't believe in ghosts, either."

Lavender pulled open the shop door, setting off fairy-chimes and bells. "No, but he believes in vandals and robbers who might break into old haunted mansions."

"I don't think a robber was carrying that light. We should check it out. All of this might fit together somehow."

"No," Lavender said as I rolled into the smell-cloud of cinnamon and exotic spices and old books that was Something Wicked. "I am not getting arrested or grounded for the next decade."

"You don't have to get grounded," I told her as I pulled off my coat and tossed it on my chair's push-bars. "Doesn't your mom still have keys from back when she did tours? Let's ask her. She could let us in and burn sage or something to—you know, ward off ghosts, just in case they do exist."

Lavender let the door slam behind us, wrecking the melody of the chimes. "Absolutely not, and that's final, Max."

5

S ure!" Joy Springfield said, her brown eyes glittering with excitement. "I'll take you two up to Thornwood Manor Monday, after school. I love that old heap of a house, and I haven't been up there in almost a year."

"Mom!" Lavender looked up from her phone and glared first at her mother, then down at me. I was sitting on the floor using Ms. Springfield's metallic paints to add more dragons to my wheel covers, to go with the rainbow stripes and unicorns Lavender had painted on them last month. I wondered how long it would take people to notice that the dragons were eating the unicorns. I had also painted a couple to look like they were full and farting out rainbow stripes.

We were all sitting around a table in the back, surrounded by statues of dragons and unicorns, occult books, and stacks of science fiction and fantasy paperbacks, eating kale-wrapped tofu bites and arguing about Thornwood's Revenge.

"The floor's falling in," Lavender said. "And you're not even supposed to have that key anymore!"

"Junior Thornwood knows I've got it." Ms. Springfield waved a hand, graceful as ever in her sky blue peasant shirt and jeans, her long red hair tied back with a thin blue ribbon that curled against her shoulders. She smiled at both of us. "I'll text him. He'll probably be glad to have somebody give it a look, other than the cleaning crew that goes in once a month."

"Do you talk to Junior Thornwood often?" I asked, intrigued.

"Every now and then," Ms. Springfield said. "We met back when we were kids, when his family would come to town to check on the house. He used to be scared, you know. Of being in that house, and of Thornwood's Revenge swallowing up Blue Creek while he happened to be visiting. But he's done okay for himself up North."

I couldn't help noticing how Ms. Springfield smiled when she talked about Junior. "He's what, Thornwood's great-great-grandson?"

"No, it's way more than that," she said. "Five greats down the line, I think. But he doesn't like to talk about his family history much. I think it gets old. That's why he wouldn't let the city fix the floor when it collapsed."

"I know," I said. "I read that in *Complete Haunts and Haints of Middle Tennessee*. He called Hargrove an ambitious man who made unfortunate choices, and said it was time for the legend of Thornwood's Revenge to die."

"He should just sell the place," Lavender said. "Let somebody else fix it up for tourism."

"Well, it's still his ancestral home," Ms. Springfield said. "If tours start back up, that'll just keep all the stories going." She pointed to a big green ledger book lying under a bunch of newer brown ones on her bookshelf. "Besides, there are lots of valuables in Thornwood. The inventory we had to keep when we did tours, it was massive—and antique dealers made regular offers."

I hadn't thought of that. "Wow. I bet ghost hunters would pay a fortune for Thornwood stuff, wouldn't they?"

"But if the cleaning crew only goes in once a month," Lavender said, "why did Max see a light?"

"No idea," Ms. Springfield said. "The power's on right now to keep the heat and protect the water pipes, but nobody should be inside the house at night."

Lavender's face filled with worry. "We should tell Toppy."

"I will, I will." Her mom sounded a lot like me when I had to disagree with Lavender about something—insistent but hopeless at the same time, because it would take a Batman-level superhero to win an argument with my best friend. "I'm sure Toppy will be fine with it—he'll probably come with us."

Lavender frowned. "Yep. There's a Twitter account." She leaned down and showed me a page with a Thornwood Owl in the spot where a photo should be. "About thirty tweets. I reported it already. Seems like it got set up a day or two before the fake Facebook page—so, see? The cyberattacks started happening before the light showed up in the Thornwood Manor windows. They probably aren't related. No need to go risking the ridicule of the whole school—never mind the entire town—if we fall through some board and get stuck upside-down in the floor."

"Thornwood's not *that* dangerous," Ms. Springfield said as I put down my brush and took Lavender's phone with my paint-flecked fingers. "The floor in that room just rotted."

Lavender ignored her as I scrolled through tweets on Lavender's phone—tweets people out in the world might think my grandfather actually wrote.

Crime rate in Blue Creek going up. Guess I suck at my job. #badcop

Mayor Chandler shouldn't run for reelection. Sign petition. #dragonlady

I don't know why I took on caring for a handicapped kid. #parentingfail

Somebody needs to purge the corruption in Blue Creek.
#thornwoodsrevenge

They were all bad. I tried not to focus on the "handicapped kid" snark. The hacker managed to find nasty stuff to say about Bot and Bot's Electronics, the post office, Something Wicked, and even the local grocery store—#badlettuce. Poor Danique Mitchell, the woman who owned Danique's Foods. She'd be so upset. She was way proud of her fresh produce and cheeses.

On impulse I went to Pinterest, and a few seconds later I pulled up yet another fake account in my grandfather's name, this time using his initials superimposed on the Thornwood Owl. It had one board full of photos of Toppy and Mayor Chandler, all with weird or ugly facial expressions and postures. Snapchat—just never mind. Those filters were awful, and the captions would get me grounded if I said them out loud.

Lavender pulled at my hand and turned her phone until she could see it. She winced and closed Snapchat, then stared at Pinterest for a while. "Looks like they took screenshots from videos and freeze-framed them halfway through eye blinks and movements." She took the phone and blew up a picture and turned it toward me. My grandfather gazed back at me through half-drooped eyelids, cheeks flushed red, nose even redder. His right hand was out in front of him like he was warding off a bad fall.

"Toppy looks drunk there," Lavender said. "But he's probably just about to sneeze or cough or something. I wonder if the hacker is going to start making memes with these pics."

Ms. Springfield had a look at the photos, and her smile fell away. "Oh, poor Mayor Chandler. That one looks like she's picking a beagle's nose."

My watch beeped, and I shifted my weight. Lavender reported the Pinterest and Snapchat fakes, then handed her phone back to me. I called the police station and let Mayor Chandler know about the additional social media troll accounts—but I left off the picking-a-dog's-nose part.

"We'll need to check each of these for threats, and respond to them on the city and police department websites." She sounded tired and irritated. "I don't even know what all other sites we should visit."

"I think there are too many possibilities," I said. "And the hacker can make new ones any time. Looks like he's using the Thornwood Owl as a signature."

The mayor let out a soft groan. "Life was easier when people who were mad at me rolled my yard or lit bags of dog poop on fire and dropped them on my front steps."

"Ew. That's gross."

"And effective." Her voice seemed happier now, as if burning dog doo and toilet paper messes cheered her up. "Hard to squelch the instinct to stomp out the flames even when you know something disgusting is probably inside."

"Well, at least all this is just online," I said.

"Exactly. This is frustrating, and we don't know where it's headed—but for now, it's just words."

I shifted Lavender's phone in my grip. "So, how are you going to explain Pinterest and Snapchat to Toppy?"

Mayor Chandler laughed. "Not even gonna try. It's all nonsense to him—and honestly, he may have a point about ignoring social media. Talk to you later, Max."

We hung up, and I forked over Lavender's cell.

"You know, Max," Lavender said, "you totally should use all this mess to make Toppy get you a phone. For safety and all."

"Lavender Dusty Springfield," her mom said, horror lacing each word, and Lavender closed her mouth.

Fairy-bells tinkled, and Ms. Springfield got up to go see if it was a customer, still giving Lavender a shame-on-you frown.

I capped the paints and set them and the brush aside. It took me a few seconds to pull myself back into the chair, but once I was seated, I powered up and rolled toward the front of the store, and Lavender came along behind me. "Tell Toppy you need a phone in case this freak kidnaps you or something," she whispered. "It's not manipulating if it's true, right?"

"Right," I said, working to let the thought go. I had

tried everything to get Toppy to understand that everybody in the universe other than me had phones of their own, but he wouldn't bite. *I got you that iPad whatsits. Just use that.*

And I did, and it was great, especially since he let me get wireless on it through his phone account, but I didn't take it out of the house very often. Too afraid it would break and leave me with nothing. *Just because something's new and the latest-greatest doesn't make it good,* Toppy often reminded me, *or even necessary.*

A phone felt necessary to me, but Toppy—

Whoa.

Ms. Springfield had stopped right in front of me. I let go of the clown-nose and my wheels stopped just short of her Birkenstock clogs. Lavender squished into the back of my wheelchair with a little "Oof."

"May I help you?" Ms. Springfield said to a woman decked out in an army-green Tennessee State Trooper uniform, right down to the tan shirt, green tie, and green pants with a darker green stripe down the center.

The woman had to be six feet tall or more, with broad shoulders. She pulled off her great big green trooper's hat with its rank badge and gold cords and acorns to reveal very short hair, all white with just a few hints of black. The lines on her face underscored the white hair. She looked to be about Toppy's age. She had no expression at all, though her dark brown eyes darted around, taking in every detail of the shop like she might be searching for bad guys hiding in the bookshelves. When she finished, her gaze came back to Ms. Springfield, then to Lavender and me. The name badge on the right side of her chest read *Captain Merilee Coker.*

Captain Coker raised a paper in her hand, studied it, then nodded as if she had answered some unasked question. She ignored Ms. Springfield and focused on me with a quiet but stern, "Maxine Brennan?"

I tried to speak but couldn't get out a word.

Lavender said, "Oh cripes, did you set something else on fire, Max?"

The trooper's heavy eyebrows lifted. I backed into Lavender just enough to knock her sideways.

"We will have no fires," said Captain Coker.

"We will have no fires," agreed Ms. Springfield, holding her arms very still at her sides. "How can we help you, officer?"

"Captain," the uniformed woman corrected. "Captain Coker. And I need to speak with Maxine Brennan."

I raised my hand and managed to squeak, "Present."

Captain Coker eyed Lavender and her mom. "Do the two of you have substantial contact with Miss Brennan?"

"Substantial?" Lavender sounded offended. "Uh, yeah. She's my best friend."

"They're together or texting every waking moment,"

Ms. Springfield said, talking fast. "Does that count? And would you like to sit down? I have a table in back."

Captain Coker gave us all hard, long looks. She probably didn't have any trouble arresting people. I bet if she glared at them, they confessed all their crimes and probably even made stuff up for good measure.

After way too many seconds, she said, "Do you want to talk to me in front of these people, Miss Brennan?"

Why did I have to talk to a trooper? What had I done?

Impulsive . . .

Quick to anger . . .

Good leader, but tramples other people's feelings . . .

That's what the school had said about me after I got in all that trouble a year ago—but counseling had helped. I was doing better. I hadn't done anything I wasn't supposed to.

Except almost accidentally burn down your house . . .

I started to sweat like it was the middle of summer. "Yes?" I said, hoping it was the right answer. "And I'm Max."

Captain Coker waited another few moments as she studied all three of us. Then she tucked her hat under her arm. "The table would be fine."

Ms. Springfield, Lavender, and I crammed into one another trying to turn around. Ms. Springfield sort of squirted backward, then shooed Lavender and me ahead of her. Somehow, we made it through the store to the round table without knocking over any bookshelves. Lavender even managed to get the kale-bite trash swept into the can before the trooper settled into her chair.

Lavender and her mom sat next to Captain Coker, seeming tiny. The tall trooper looked like a grown-up in a kid's seat at school.

She placed her hat on the table and gazed at me. I tried not to squirm and mentally went over everything I had done in the last month, year, and my whole life, ever, anywhere, for any reason. Seriously, what would a trooper want with me, now that I was doing better with my temper? Unless screwing up house electrical boxes was illegal. And if that had been illegal, Toppy would have hollered at me about that when he was hollering about everything else, and—

"Miss Brennan," Captain Coker said, "I'm here to do a welfare check. Do you know what that means?"

My thoughts spun in slow circles, like a top winding down before it fell over and quit moving. "No, ma'am."

She leaned forward.

I pressed myself against my wheelchair and wished I could fall through its back.

"I went to your home," she continued, "but when no one was there, your neighbors suggested I check for you here, or at Lavender Springfield's home. I have to talk to you today, because someone called Social Services and reported that you were being abused and neglected. Since it's the weekend, police respond instead of child protection workers, and since the alleged caregiver involved was a local law officer, State was asked to make the check. State as in the nearest State Police headquarters, which is mine."

"Abused and neglected?" Lavender asked. "Max? You have to be kidding."

The trooper looked at Lavender, her expression clearly conveying that humor did not exist in her behavioral repertoire. Lavender cleared her throat and decided to examine her purple and gold fingernails.

"I'm not abused or neglected," I told Captain Coker. "I even get home health check-ups once every month to be sure I'm not getting any pressure sores, and that I don't have any new medical needs, and Toppy takes me to Vanderbilt to the Spinal Center twice a year—and more often if I need it."

She took this in without comment. Then she pulled a pen and a small notebook out of her pocket and started writing. "When you've done something wrong," her eyes moved to Lavender, "like setting something on fire, how does your grandfather discipline you?"

I wanted to explain the whole fire thing *so* badly, but figured I should play it like court on TV—just answer the question. "Toppy makes me watch awful sappy movies and write book reports about the plots. I mean, really sappy. From the Sentimental Flicks Channel, you know? No aliens, no werewolves, no superheroes—just princes and puppies, and everybody's in love, and it's so stupid—"

I made myself breathe.

Shut up, Max. Just answer the question, then SHUT UP.

Captain Coker's rock face cracked at the edges, and her mouth twitched. "I see. Well. That's . . . creative."

"It's terrible," I said, then rushed to add, "but it's not abuse or anything, right?"

"I guess that depends on your cinematic preferences," the trooper said, eyes on her notebook.

Did she just crack a joke? I forced another breath into my lungs.

"What happens when your grandfather gets really angry?" Captain Coker looked up suddenly, eyes locking with mine. "What else does he do?"

"Well, he doesn't take away my iPad because he says it's like my wheelchair, something I need to get things done, so that'd be like taking away a body part, and he'd never do that." I was trying not to babble, trying so hard. "He hollers sometimes, but only if I do something really ignorant that scares him. Usually he just gives me a look that makes me wish he'd ground me for a thousand years instead of making that face, and then he lectures me. I don't think lecturing is abuse. Do you? I mean, no matter what your lecturing preferences are, lecturing just really stinks and makes me feel horrible. But lecturing isn't abuse. I know it's not."

Captain Coker kept her pen poised but stopped writing. "I'm not sure my grandchildren would agree with you, but I understand. Now, if I were to go to your home—which I'm going to have to do—would there be food in your refrigerator?"

"What? I mean, yes, ma'am. Of course we have food." This was getting seriously weird. I couldn't figure out why anybody would report we didn't have food.

"Can you tell me what you have to eat in your house right now?" Captain Coker asked.

I closed my eyes and took a deeper breath, slowly growing more aware of the shop smells again. The spicy air actually helped me calm down enough to tell the trooper, "Butter, milk, eggs, sour cream—we have a lot of that for nachos and baked potatoes and stuff. And Swiss cheese for Toppy and provolone for me, because I think Swiss cheese is ooky."

I opened my eyes.

"Swiss cheese is ooky," Captain Coker said, making a note. "Got it."

"There's salad dressing and a bag of lettuce that might be a little old because we should have had it last night but we had a roast instead because Toppy said he was hungrier than rabbit food. Oh! We have rabbit food, too. I mean, carrots and cucumbers, and there's lunch meat—smoked turkey because we both like that, though I guess that doesn't count as rabbit food because I don't think rabbits eat turkey. There's biscuits in those tubes that go pow when you open them, and some spicy sausage because Toppy and I both like the hot stuff, and apple juice, and leftover tortilla soup, and I'm pretty sure we have bacon bits and pepperoni and pizza dough we haven't used yet. And cherry preserves, and—"

The trooper held up her hand.

"Please don't make her list the contents of the cabinets and pantry," Lavender said before Captain Coker could ask another question. "That would take a week. Toppy believes in having two of everything."

"The house is very well-stocked with food," Ms. Springfield agreed. "Chief Brennan teaches a community college weekend course in disaster preparedness, and he really practices what he preaches. He also has emergency kits and propane in his workshop, and an extra fridge and freezer, and a storage cabinet full of dried and canned goods. He and Max will probably be the sole survivors of Armageddon or the zombie apocalypse."

"I—" Captain Coker began. "Zombie what?"

"Was the caller a man or a woman?" Lavender asked.

The trooper's face went stony again, and I thought about smacking my best friend on the head, then wondered if I could get arrested for that.

"I'm not at liberty to give out that information," she said, voice cold as the air outside.

Lavender looked annoyed. "I'm only asking because Chief Brennan and Mayor Chandler are being cyber-attacked, and I'm wondering if the same person who's hacking them made the call about Max being abused and starved or whatever."

When the trooper looked surprised, Lavender added, "The chief and the mayor, they're over at the police station right now, searching through all of Chief Brennan's files with half the department, trying to figure out which of the people he arrested just got out of jail and might be trying to get even. I thought that knowing whoever made this bogus report was male or female might speed things up for them."

Ms. Springfield gave Lavender a gentle elbow to the side, and Lavender hiccupped and hushed.

"We weren't aware Chief Brennan was being harassed," Captain Coker said. "He hasn't reached out to State yet."

"It just started last night," I said.

"Well, State might be able to help if they want to ask us." Captain Coker made another note. "After I see your home, that is. We need to head over there now, Miss—well, Max."

"I'll drive," Ms. Springfield said.

The trooper looked up, frowning. "That won't be

necessary. I'll take the child with me. That's policy."

"You have a wheelchair-accessible van?" I patted the arms of my electric chair, then honked my clown-nose. "This doesn't fold, and it weighs over one hundred pounds. More with me in it."

Captain Coker's mouth came open. She looked at my chair as if really seeing it for the first time. "I—er—"

Ms. Springfield put her hand on the table, and her voice got almost as cold as the trooper's. "Please don't suggest taking Max without the chair and leaving her helpless. No policy should ever mandate anything like that, and if it does, it's barbaric."

"Well, no," Captain Coker said. "Of course not."

"I take Max home a lot," Ms. Springfield said. "I'll just go swap my car for Chief Brennan's wheelchair van. You can follow us."

The trooper stood, looking chastised. She picked up her hat. "That will be fine. Thank you."

She hustled out of Something Wicked like she was seriously embarrassed. When the door chimes jingled, Ms. Springfield got to her feet. "I'm going to get the van and tell Chief Brennan what's happening. Meet me out front."

"Yes, ma'am," Lavender and I said at the same time.

As she left to go across Town Square, I pulled on my coat.

"Okay," Lavender said, adjusting her dance leggings. "This is a hot mess."

"Yeah," I said, remembering my earlier conversation with Mayor Chandler. "I think we're officially past 'just words' now."

Later that night, after Captain Coker had inspected our house, complimented Toppy's housekeeping, ogled his workshop tools, scrutinized the contents of our military-precise, alphabetized, and overstocked pantry, left one card for Toppy and another for me, and made her departure, Toppy sat on the edge of my bed. He had come to tuck me in like I was little again, just in case I was upset. Which I was. But I didn't really want to tell him that.

He was wearing his flannel pj's and bunny slippers, but he still smelled a little like a pine tree from where he cologned up for Mayor Chandler. I didn't say anything about that, either, as he adjusted the covers on my shoulders.

"I'm sorry about all this, Max." He patted my hand.

"It's not your fault."

His smile looked sad in the low light of my bedside lamp. "Kinda feels like it is."

"Nope," I told him. "You always tell me when bad guys do bad things, it's their fault, not anybody else's."

"I do say that, don't I?" The phone rang, and he glanced at the desk unit next to my lamp. "That's probably your mother. You know, if this sorry scoundrel

69

wants to make more trouble, he's likely going to pull her into it. I need to tell her about all this, and then she'll want to talk to you that much more."

My sigh was automatic. The phone kept ringing and I kept ignoring it. I didn't feel mad, just tired, and sort of trapped, which I hated more than anything. "Fine. Tomorrow. Or the next day."

"She is who she is, Max." Toppy's smile was definitely sad now. "If you could love her for herself instead of who you want her to be, you might be happier, and that temper of yours—"

"Is a lot better." My fingers dug into my covers on both sides.

"It is. I'd just like to see things with your mom get easier for you."

"I am who I am, too," I said, trying to ignore the words flashing through my mind. *Impulsive . . . quick to anger . . . tramples feelings.* I really was better with those things now. Wasn't I?

"I know I have to be respectful to Mom," I said, making sure my voice stayed calm. "But I don't have to like her."

"No, you don't." Toppy leaned over and kissed the top of my head. "But I want you to tell me one thing."

I grimaced, dreading the question.

"Were rainbow-farting dragons necessary?" He gestured toward my painted wheel covers.

My mouth twitched. "Totally. Eating unicorns gave them psychedelic gas."

He thought about this, then nodded. "I guess that's better than the psychedelic eyes that made your school counselor tell me you needed a psychiatrist."

"They were Cyclops glasses," I said. "I can't help it if that woman never read an X-Men comic."

After he left, I lay in the darkness, staring across the field, watching Thornwood Manor and imagining giant owl-supervillains wielding huge thorn spears winging through the dark hallways. When I couldn't sleep after an hour, I pulled my iPad off my bedside table, flicked open my Paper app, and used my finger to draw pages full of stick-me's and sloppy alien owls with big bloodshot eyes, dueling to the bitter end. I was so intent on sketching a green and purple owl with full feather armor and an evil curved thorn dagger that I almost didn't notice the light.

I stopped moving my hand on the iPad. Slowly, I lifted my head, then reached up and turned off the screen.

The light was on the bottom floor of Thornwood Manor, and this time, it wasn't moving. It flickered in the center window, as if somebody stood just out of sight, holding a candle.

My skin prickled.

Had the light from my iPad been bright enough

that whoever was in Thornwood could see me? I laid the iPad on my table and squinted at the window.

The hairs on the back of my neck stood up. I was sure somebody was in there, looking right at me. Only now they couldn't see me, because I had turned off the iPad.

As if hearing my thoughts, the light danced once and went out, as if snuffed by an angry hand.

6

DECEMBER 4

You're lying," Jace Alton insisted, but his blue eyes burned with curiosity. "Thornwood's, like, condemned now, right?"

I grinned at him from across our classroom table as I sketched in Saskatchewan on the map of Canada we had to finish before the bell, and made sure I didn't write "Sasquatch" by mistake. "Nope. Well, not really. It's closed, but Lavender's mom still has a key."

I labeled the province with a 1905, to indicate when it joined Canada. Jace screwed up his face and stared at a blob on his page that was supposed to be Russia.

"Just put 'REVOLUTION' in big letters," Cindy Morath told him. "It doesn't have to be perfect."

We were almost up to 1920, illustrating what was happening in the rest of the world while the Industrial Revolution was happening in the United States. Mr. Rager, our Social Studies teacher, was a project and paper fanatic, even about seriously boring stuff like the Industrial Revolution. Jace, Cindy, and the other kids in my group had been falling asleep until I mentioned going to Thornwood.

Now everybody was wide awake, and they all seemed hugely impressed. From two tables away, Lavender gave me a SHUT-UP glare, no doubt calculating the number of requests her mom would get for illegal tours of the haunted house.

"I've been wanting to see the inside of that place since I moved here," I said. "It'll be fun."

"Sure," Cindy agreed. "If a ghost doesn't eat you. And that's if you don't freeze to death. It's *frigid* outside."

"I know there's a ramp to the front door," Jace said. "But what about the inside? Is there an elevator to the other floors?"

"No," I said. "I'll be stuck on the ground floor, probably—but there's a lot of cool rooms on that level."

Jace grinned. "And a giant hole in the floor. If you fall in, I'm gonna laugh."

"Ha, ha," I told him.

"Post pictures," Cindy instructed.

"Yep," I said, turning almost completely around in my chair seat to avoid Lavender's death stare.

Monday afternoon, it was so cold I thought I could see frost on the top of Toppy's bald head.

The five of us stood outside Thornwood, staring at the front of the house as our breath made clouds in the air above us. Toppy zipped his checkered hunting coat, while Mayor Chandler stuck her hands in the pockets of her bomber jacket. Lavender and her mom had bundled up like matching purple Cookie Monsters in wool scarves, leggings, and sweaters. As for me, I had on my black *No Whining* sweatshirt and a black and gold *Vanderbilt Commodores* blanket over my legs, so I was handling the cold okay.

"Let's get this over with," Toppy said, gesturing to the ramp on the left for me, then leading everyone else up the front steps. The whirring of my chair's motor couldn't block out the fierce creaks and pops as he and Mayor Chandler and Lavender and Ms. Springfield climbed the stairs. By the time I looped around the long ramp and came back across the porch, Toppy was stomping boards in front of me, testing the wood to be sure it would hold me.

"I really think the floor is stable, except for the room where it collapsed," Ms. Springfield said. She was working to get a key into the main lock with her left hand and holding her right hand over a keypad to push in a code. "This key sticks sometimes."

As she fussed with the lock, I stared at the front doors I had seen on the Internet so many times. They were solid wood, and a dark, dark brown that reminded me of dried blood. The bottoms were carved like the branches of trees, while the tops had matching Thornwood Owls gripping their menacing brambles. I couldn't help focusing on the owls' eyes, which seemed to be inlaid with something black and shiny, like onyx.

"If this were a spooky movie," Mayor Chandler said, "those eyes would move whenever we stopped paying attention."

"I'm paying attention," Lavender said right away.

"Me, too," I agreed. I used my iPad to take a photo of the owls, then popped a caption of **THORNWOOD CREEPINESS** on it before I posted it to my Facebook page.

"We're here to look for any evidence of Max's light in the nighttime," Toppy grumbled, "not to make some kind of social media event." Then he griped to himself about the Internet and Saturday morning cartoons and Dracula flicks melting people's brains. Mayor Chandler nudged his arm with her elbow and he hushed.

I squinted at the owls and trees carved in the door, realizing words were woven through the branches like a banner. I had only rolled up to the front of Thornwood a few times, and never this close. None of the websites focused on the panels, so I had never noticed the carved words before.

"Is that Latin on the doors?" I asked Ms. Springfield.

"Pecuniate obediunt omni," she said as she worked the

key in the stubborn lock. "It translates to 'All things obey money.'" The door gave a loud click. "And I got it." She tapped in the code, grabbed the handle on the right, and pushed open Thornwood's front doors.

They moved so slow, I wondered if somebody on the other side might be pushing back, and the loud, high-pitched creak sent chills crawling up my spine. My heart started to beat faster.

Toppy waited a few seconds, then strode in front of all of us, shaking his head. "Warmer inside than out," he said.

"Until we hit the cold spots," Lavender pointed out.

"You watch too many ghost hunter shows," my grandfather snapped back as we piled into the foyer. I rolled over an ornate brass grate in the floor, and it gave a mighty creak. I saw something that looked like wires poking up from one corner, and immediately worried I just tore up something, or set off a security alarm.

No sirens or bells or beeps sounded.

Phew.

I took a picture of the grate and posted it.

Lavender's mom pulled the front door shut, and it settled with a thunk so loud I jumped against the back of my chair. *Trapped!* my chicken-brain screamed. The door probably locked itself. And the lock would stick. And here's where something with fangs and claws would come charging at us, and—

Silence dropped around us instead, pressing like fists into my ears. My fingers curled into the red rubber tip of my joystick. I had wanted to get inside this house for as long as I could remember, but now the sound of my own fast breathing sent chills up the back of my neck. The air smelled like lemon and wood, like somebody had recently used furniture polish.

"Has the cleaning crew been here this week?" I asked Ms. Springfield.

She glanced around. "Not that I know of. Next week, I think. Looks pretty dusty in here."

It did. But, weird. The place really did smell like lemon-scented cleaner. Underneath that, though, there was something else. Something . . . wet. A little dank. It reminded me of the one time I had to go to a funeral with Toppy and hang out at the cemetery while they finished burying the guy who died.

Lemon-scented grave dirt. Wonderful.

My breathing got even faster. My eyes darted left and right, looking at the wooden floors and paneled walls, at the light fixtures added sometime after electricity became common. Cobwebs strung between the hanging lights, jiggling gently in some breeze I didn't feel. I got a shot of the cobwebs and sent it out, but I couldn't help thinking maybe this was a bad idea. Maybe some serial killer was hiding in the closet, waiting to separate us and chop us all to bits. Or maybe there really were ghosts, and one of them would start pitching books at our heads.

"So, Chief Brennan." Mayor Chandler put a hand on my shoulder and squeezed. "If you've never watched a ghost hunter show, how did you know they talk about cold spots?"

Toppy eyed her sideways, narrowing his gaze and frowning as his bald head turned even more red. And just that fast, I could breathe normally again. Lavender giggled, as did her mother.

"Fine," Toppy snarled. "I'll check the top floors and the turret. Lavender, you and Max take the ground floor with Maggie. Joy, if you wouldn't mind, have a look at that cave-in area, but be careful. Nobody break anything, nobody fall into anything. Got it?"

I sighed. "People always separate in scary movies, and that's when the zombies eat them."

"Well, if the Walking Dead get a few of you, it'll cut down on the chatter." Toppy stalked off without waiting for anybody to agree or disagree or yell at him for suggesting it'd be great if we became zombies. He headed out of the foyer and to the left, and a few seconds later I heard the squeegee of his rubber-soled boots on creaking wooden stairs.

He was halfway to the next level when Ms. Springfield said to Mayor Chandler, "Maggie?"

Mayor Chandler sniffed. "It's an old nickname. He

was the only one who—he always—well, never mind."

Ms. Springfield left us, smiling as she walked off to the right. "The kitchen and the door to the basement are this way," she called over her shoulder. "It's more like a cellar, really. Just stay out of the central living room. It's roped off so nobody falls in the hole where the floor rotted through. There's a set of temporary metal steps the city put in. I can use those to get a closer look."

"Okay," Mayor Chandler said, "Let's start in the west wing, girls. This way, past the main stairs. We'll have lights, since the power's on, but obviously, the heat's only set to engage if it gets below freezing inside, to save the pipes."

She started walking, and I pushed my clown-nose forward. My chair whirred, the lights on the control flickered, and it shut itself off.

I came to a hard stop.

"What the . . ." I picked up my hand and frowned at the darkened panel. Dead. Nothing.

Lavender came up beside me. "Did you forget to charge up last night?"

"I never forget to charge my chair," I said. "Not ever."

Mayor Chandler came back to us and tapped the side of my chair controls. My heart thudded as I bit my bottom lip. My chair had never ever broken before, unless I was messing with it to enhance something. Not the propulsion system, anyway. If it wouldn't turn on, we could switch it to manual, but it was hard to roll. And how long would it take to fix? My throat went dry and my eyes blinked really fast. I could try a manual chair again, but my shoulders were so weak I didn't think I could roll it by myself. If it took a long time to get the electric chair repaired, people would have to push me—and if I didn't have somebody to push me, I'd just be stuck wherever I was, and that had happened to me once before, and—

Cringing, I hit the green circle for on.

All the lights flickered. One at a time, the panel areas lit up. "Thank you," I said to nobody in particular, so relieved I almost wanted to lie down and take a nap. Only not in a cold haunted house.

I made sure I was in drive mode instead of recline, and double-checked that I was set on level two of four, to move around inside a building. Then I gave the joystick a little bump to be sure it wouldn't turn off again. The chair bucked forward and auto-stopped, just like it was supposed to.

The mayor raised her eyebrows. "Good to go?"

"Yes, ma'am." I breathed a few times, to make sure I still could, then honked the clown-nose.

"What happened to it?" Lavender asked.

"No idea," I said, even though my mind was shouting *GHOSTS!*

Mayor Chandler pointed to the hallway. "Let's try this again."

My watch beeped, and I nearly jumped straight to the ceiling. But I held it together, shifted my weight, and we headed away from the door, the mayor leading the way, Lavender following her, and me rolling behind them, guarding the rear flank and staring at my controls every three seconds. In between control checks, I tried to take good photos of the house. Dust drifted in dull clouds around us, and cobwebs jammed the cracks and corners.

Mayor Chandler ran her fingers along a table, leaving a trail in the thin gray film. "Guess the cleaning crew doesn't dust much."

Outside the foyer, the narrow main hall hugged the side of the stairwell on the right. The slowly upward-sloping wall of the stairwell was covered in ancient black-and-white framed photographs, the kind that looked burned around the edges. No fixtures hung above, and light from the windows barely reached us, leaving shadows across the whole stretch of boards, the pictures dim under their layers of dust.

Lavender pointed at the pictures. "Daguerreotypes. These are the oldest kind of photos."

The daguerreotypes were framed with fading, flaking bits of gold paint accenting carved bramble designs. The gaunt figure of Hargrove Thornwood stared out at us from all of the shots, his dark eyes hooded, his lips pulled into a perpetual stern frown. Seeing him close up gave me the shivers. Somehow, pictures on websites didn't seem as personal as looking right into a still shot of his blank stare. The black-and-white photos made everything seem twice as chilled and bleak. And seriously, that man's eyes really did seem to follow me whichever way I leaned, especially the eyes in the largest photo, the one right in the middle, with a life-size version of his face. The glass seemed oddly clean compared to the rest, and the way it was positioned, it was like he was staring into every room on this side of the hallway, all at once.

Mine, his expression seemed to say. *It's all mine, and I'm not sharing.* I got a picture of him, but I knew the iPad camera couldn't capture that level of creepy-creepness.

"Who are all those men he's with?" Lavender asked, pointing to a big cluster of photos of bunches of guys wearing suits and tall black hats. "Was his family that big?"

"Those aren't his family members." Mayor Chandler stopped and turned to the dozens of antique photos. "They're businessmen and politicians. These pictures, they're from when he first got here, and they're all about status, not memories. Making business relationships, getting people to take out loans and invest, give him permits to build whatever he wanted to build—my late husband would have approved."

I squinted at the grainy pictures. "All things obey money?"

"Something like that," the mayor agreed. "These are just plain spooky, like shots from an old Dracula movie."

"I've coooome to drink your bloooood," I said in a croaky-crow voice that sounded way too loud.

Lavender cringed. "Ew. No vampire references." She inched away from the full-size version of Thornwood's face and rubbed her fuzzy purple arms with her fuzzy purple mitten-hands. "I had nightmares for weeks after I saw the original *Dracula*. And didn't Mr. Creepy make any pictures of his wife or his kids and grandkids?"

"No," Mayor Chandler said. "There are some oil portraits of his wife, though. One of them is right in there, in the main study."

We moved farther into the mansion, which seemed thoroughly cold, with zero "spots" of one temperature or the other, no matter what those ghost shows tried to get us to believe. As I rolled away from the big picture of Thornwood's face, it was hard not to check back and make sure his eyeballs weren't swiveling to glare at me.

Mayor Chandler steered us through a door on the left, and I rolled into another paneled room, this one lined with bookcases and dominated by a huge fireplace surrounded by the expensive pink marble Tennessee is famous for. The scent of cleanser seemed to get stronger the farther we went. Mayor Chandler switched on the lights.

Immediately, I stared at the fireplace to see if it had been cleaned. The inside seemed oddly polished, but the outside—nah. Just as dusty as the rest of the place, even if it smelled like Lemon Pledge and Windex.

Hanging over the pink fireplace was a huge cobweb-laced painting, its bright colors standing out from the rest of the house. A beautiful woman in a red-striped gown with a wide, round bottom—hoop skirt, I think those were called—looked down on us, smiling ever so slightly. Her brown hair was swept to one side in a tight up-do, but curls spilled under her bright red bonnet and tumbled down one shoulder, almost reaching her waist and brushing the tops of what looked like red velvet gloves.

I had never seen this picture before, not on any of the Thornwood sites. My mouth came open as I studied the vivid reds and blacks and browns. "Is that Thornwood's wife, Mayor Chandler? Is that Vivienne?"

"Indeed. Her parents were French, but they moved her from New Orleans to Tennessee when she was only eight."

"She's beautiful," Lavender said. "And she looks smart. So why would she marry a jerk-sicle like Thornwood, then stay with him until it killed her?"

Mayor Chandler's expression grew distant. "Women

in the past didn't have many choices, and sometimes they didn't have a say in who their parents chose for them to wed. Or maybe she loved him."

"But he was awful." I couldn't quit looking into the eyes of the painted woman, green like my mother's, with the same sort of distant, unfocused expression Mom usually had. At least I thought it was similar. It had been a while since I had seen Mom in person. Did her eyes actually look like that?

"People in love look past lots of faults," Mayor Chandler said. "Sometimes you love people even when you see they have bad problems. And I think that back then, people tried even harder to care about people they were supposed to love, since they couldn't really leave each other."

Frowning, I tucked my iPad between my leg and the chair arm. *People they were supposed to love—and people they weren't supposed to leave.* Like husbands and wives. Or parents and children. My mom certainly didn't have a problem leaving a child behind. *Eight years since the disaster, and four years since my daughter pawned off her disabled kid on me . . .*

The hacker had a few things right. Maybe too right. I so did not want to think about my mother, but her face kept popping into my head. Tears clouded my vision, and I ground my teeth. The beautiful Mrs. Thornwood gazed down her pretty nose at me, her green Mom-eyes so piercing, smiling like she might feel sorry for me.

My chair whirred as I pulled on the joystick and rocketed back across the threshold, retro-pulsing into the hallway. My anti-tip wheels, little plastic spinning things that stuck out behind the real wheels to keep me from flipping backwards on big hills, crashed into the paneling at the bottom step, and a big crack echoed through Thornwood Manor.

Two little spots of light danced on the wall in front of me, like Thornwood's eyes had turned into lasers, threatening to sizzle through the wood paneling. Any second now, they'd swivel to me and roast me alive for hurting the house. For real, I felt like somebody was staring at me, and hard.

My chair switched itself off again. I let go of my controls. "Crud!"

I was stuck now.

7

Max?" Lavender said from the study, still standing underneath the portrait of Vivienne Thornwood.

The dots of light on the wall vanished.

"I heard that crash," Toppy yelled from somewhere above me. "And I know who did it. What part of '*Nobody break anything*' did you miss, hotshot?"

"That sounded like thunder and lightning over my head," Ms. Springfield yelled from underneath the floor where I was sitting.

"Sorry," I said. "I banged into stuff, but I don't think anything broke."

Mayor Chandler came over to where I was sitting, just as I switched the chair back on again. After it powered up, she helped me ease the chair away from the wood paneling. "Little nick on the bottom step. That's all." Her eyes met mine. "No harm, no foul. Let's check the next room."

"Um, okay," I said as Lavender caught up to us. My face felt hot, and I knew I had to be blushing. I honked the clown-nose on my joystick, hoping nobody would notice my bright red cheeks.

Without saying much else, we moved through several other rooms attached to the hallway—a bedroom, a small storage room, and another sitting room, this one with no fireplace or books. We tried the door to the closet under the stairs, but it was locked. A few minutes later, we made it through the kitchen with its closed range and very literal icebox with the door where the giant ice block should go standing open, and its thick chopping block boasting carved brambles on all four legs.

"Nothing looks out of place," the mayor said.

"I'm not sure I'd know if it was," Lavender said, "but I don't see anything weird, and this part faces the field and your house, Max."

I grunted, then realized that sounded way too much like Toppy. Even though I didn't want to, I kept thinking about Mrs. Thornwood, and how maybe she loved her husband even if he was a total barf-head.

Did my mother actually love me? Was there something wrong with me that I didn't automatically love her back?

Maybe I did love her. Maybe I didn't. Mostly, I didn't want to be thinking about her, but it kept happening, and at really bad times.

That jerk hacker. This was all his or her fault.

I hit my joystick and eased my chair out of the kitchen into the huge dining room. It had four floor-to-ceiling windows with green drapes, and hardwood floors with expensive-looking rugs decorated with swirly green and brown designs. The big table in the center, which I managed not to bash into, had a thick green velvet tablecloth, and the table had been set with fragile-looking gilded china, complete with little etchings of the Thornwood Owl in the center.

Mayor Chandler stayed in the kitchen. "I forgot about all this 1840s cooking stuff," she said, sounding fascinated. "This family had the best of everything from that time period."

Lavender wandered into the dining room and got absorbed by the table settings, running her finger along the edge of the china. Her nose wrinkled. "It kind of stinks in here, like wet dirt."

"It smells like fresh graves," I mumbled.

"That's seriously morbid, Max," Lavender said.

"Did you notice we're in a haunted house?" I followed the scent to the far door in the dining room, but when I pulled it open, I found myself looking at a big yellow X made out of caution tape.

Past that, there was about ten feet of solid floor, followed by broken boards and a collapsed hole in the center. A set of metal stairs with handles had been lowered into the hole.

Moving the tape to one side, I inched into the room. The boards under my chair popped and creaked.

"Careful, Max," Ms. Springfield said, her voice rising up through the opening. "I'm right underneath you. The edges of the room are still supported by a beam, but you really don't need to be in here. There's nothing down here, anyway. It's just four walls with no doors."

"Okay." But I had to look, at least once. Craning forward, I gazed down into the cellar, and my eyes widened when I realized it wasn't made out of dirt. Instead, the floor looked like slabs of solid gray rock, all smooth and polished under its coating of dust, like—

Headstones.

Ms. Springfield stood dead center in a maze of her own footprints, gazing up at me. "It's limestone," she said. "From the same quarry used to get the limestone for the state capitol building. If somebody shined it up, it'd be impressive."

"But what is it?" I asked. "It makes no sense that there's no way in or out."

Ms. Springfield shrugged. "No idea. A hiding spot, maybe."

"It's like a priest hole," Lavender yelled from the dining room. "Or maybe a safe room in case of fire or armed robbery."

"Priest hole?" I shook my head. "You're making that up."

"Lots of old British houses have them," Lavender went on, like just everybody should know about priest holes. "Back a long time ago, when Queen Elizabeth I was on the throne in England, you could go to jail or get executed for being Catholic. Priests snuck around to give people communion and stuff, and soldiers tried to catch them. So Catholics built priest holes to hide the priests in case of raids. Pretty cool, except the soldiers caught on and started finding them—and a bunch of priests suffocated waiting for searches to end."

"Nice," I said, and I instantly imagined piles of priest bones right underneath my wheels.

As I studied the limestone, it started to look even more gray and graveyard-y. Slowly, I steered around the hole, taking and posting pictures, until I reached the doorway that led back to Thornwood Manor's entrance. Then I backed away from the pit until my wheels crossed the threshold and I was off the creaking boards. That left me facing the back windows directly level with my bedroom. If I squinted across the field, I could see my own window and the top of my desk.

"This is where I first saw the light, I think," I said, loud enough for everyone in the house to hear me.

A bunch of rattling seemed to come from everywhere at once—below, to my left, and above, as everyone shifted around the areas they were exploring. Stairs creaked as Toppy started back downstairs.

From underneath the floor, Ms. Springfield said, "You sure?"

Her flashlight beam poked up through the hole as I searched around the room, squinting at the intact pieces of the floor. So dusty. But over across the room, the dust had been smeared around in an area where I hadn't rolled. It was right in front of the window aligned with my bedroom.

It looked like smeared footprints, but—yes, there. One that wasn't smeared. I tucked my iPad against my leg again and leaned forward, trying to get a better look in the gray, wintry afternoon light. Yep. Pretty big print, too. Man-size. I couldn't see the details from where I was, but I was betting it was from a sneaker, because I could see some patterns in the tread. And beyond it another, and another, like somebody had looped the hole in the floor. Closer to me, it was less dusty, but there were still a few marks where my wheels hadn't messed them up, maybe partial shoe marks.

"Definitely a footprint," I said. "Well, prints! In front of the window, and heading toward where I'm sitting."

Lavender and Mayor Chandler and Toppy crowded into the dining room doorway, looking in the direction I pointed.

"Careful now," Toppy said. "If there really is a foot-print here, I need you folks not to touch anything else or mess up the scene."

"Coming!" Ms. Springfield called from the cellar.

I pulled off my safety belt and leaned even farther out to stare at the footprint. Lavender started into the room, but Mayor Chandler held her back.

"Toppy said don't disturb anything," she said. "And I don't think that floor's safe."

Toppy glanced at me. Then he startled and his eyes went wide. He was looking behind me.

My heart gave a lurch, and I lost my grip on the chair arms. My hand hit the chair control. It rolled forward, then shut off suddenly and stopped hard. There was nothing I could do as I pitched onto the broken boards, my iPad tumbling out behind me.

Pain blasted up through my hands and wrists as I broke my fall, desperate not to flip into the hole in the floor and explode my entire body on the limestone below. The whole house seemed to shake as everyone rushed into the room, skirting around the hole and charging toward me.

"I'm okay," I tried to say, but wheezed because the fall had knocked my breath straight out of my lungs.

Then, before anyone could reach me, big hands slid under my side and rolled me over.

I found myself looking into square tinted lenses set inside black frames. Big nose. Bald as Toppy, but his head was tan and shiny. Thick brown eyebrows, mustache, a goatee, and pork-chop sideburns that Elvis the King would have envied—and he was big. Like, walking-mountain big, with lots of muscles. He looked younger than Toppy and the mayor, but older than Ms. Springfield. He was dressed in jeans and a T-shirt with a skull on it, and he was wearing a black biker vest with lots of dangly silvery things.

"You okay, kid?" Mountain Man asked.

Ugh. His breath smelled like onions.

Toppy, Mayor Chandler, and Lavender got to my side just as Ms. Springfield clattered through the main doorway. She pulled up short beside the big man, squeaked in surprise, and said, "Junior Thornwood! What on earth are you doing here?"

8

The Blue Creek Police Department was a lot warmer than Thornwood Manor, especially as the sun set. It was also crowded with desks, a few cubicles, and corkboards crammed with pictures, maps, lists, and flyers. Once we got past the small front desk with its single bulletproof window, the whole place smelled a lot like ravioli, burned microwave popcorn, and really strong coffee, with a festive holiday lacing of chocolate brownies and peppermint.

Gag.

"And that's about it, Chief," said the dispatcher, a uniformed woman who looked younger than most of the high school kids I knew.

"That's certainly enough." Toppy patted her shoulder. Then he sighed at the stack of complaints the dispatcher had handed him. I could see a few of them fanned out on top, citizens who called in reports of nasty e-mails with owl pictures on them, nastier reviews of their businesses on Yelp and other commerce-rating sites, mean chat messages, and Blue Creek's town Facebook page being hacked and filled with owls, bad words, and threats about Thornwood's Revenge coming soon. The hacker didn't seem to be pretending to be Toppy anymore, just aggravating people and taunting my grandfather because he couldn't do anything to stop the harassment.

Lavender took the stack from my grandfather and dropped them on a desk next to a computer she had switched on. "Leave those for now," she told him. "Help me instead, please?"

I had my chair reclined so Mayor Chandler could finish fussing over the few scrapes I got on my arms and face from my fall, before Toppy had picked me up and put me back in my chair. She dabbed at them with an alcohol prep she had retrieved from the station's first aid kit.

"I'm fine," I told her. "Are you sure my iPad didn't crack?"

"The iPad is fine." She kept blinking too fast as she dot-dot-dotted me with liquid fire. "You're going to have bruises."

Ouch. It hurt to move. "Don't worry. I get lots of them. Proof that I am not, despite all the rumors, actually a superhero."

"I'm so sorry." Mayor Chandler bit her lip.

Poke, poke, poke . . . that alcohol stuff really burned. "You didn't do it," I told Mayor Chandler. "I'm the one who jumped out of my skin and went splat."

"I'm sorry," she said again, then glanced across the room.

That's where Ms. Springfield was doing her own fussing over Junior Thornwood, handing him coffee and a brownie and asking, "Why didn't you tell me you were coming to town?"

"Wanted to surprise you," Junior said. When he smiled at her, it lit up his whole face and made him look like a nice guy. It was sort of a relief that he didn't resemble his skinflint old ancestor. If I'd had to sit in the police station with the image of Hargrove Thornwood, I'd have been totally creeped out.

"I'd estimate it's a ten," Toppy said. "Same size and pattern I saw in the dust on the stairs to the turret."

I turned my head to the right to see him and Lavender and the computer, despite loud griping from my stiff neck and more fussing from Mayor Chandler. Lavender moved her mouse and enlarged a photo she must have taken of the sneaker print I had seen in front of the window facing my bedroom.

"Maybe a ten and a half, or eleven." Toppy sighed. "Smaller than mine, but the most common shoe size for men in the United States."

"What about the pattern?" Lavender pointed at the rows of square spots in the dust.

"Nike, probably," Toppy said. "Looks like an Air Max."

Lavender gave him a quick, shocked stare until I said, "They have databases of shoeprints. Police, I mean. If he knows what it is without looking it up, it's a popular type."

"Anybody on your suspect list of people getting out of jail wear that size?" I asked.

Mayor Chandler finally stopped alcohol-ing me. "We don't really have a suspect list. Came up empty, and the State Police and the Tennessee Bureau of Investigations are just getting started, but they don't have a lot of leads, either."

Toppy gave her a get-quiet frown. "That shoe size could be half the town—or the state. Gets us nowhere."

"Except that some guy with size ten feet was in Thornwood Manor." I lowered my chair back from its recline and sat up straight. "It proves I wasn't hallucinating."

"I wouldn't say 'proves,'" Toppy muttered, but he gave me a wink.

Lavender leaned back in her chair, staring at the ceiling. "But is it connected to the hacker?"

"Of course it is." Toppy snorted. "No such thing as coincidence in law enforcement."

I tapped both armrests. "Yeah. Creepy person starts doing creepy stuff on the Internet, covering everything with owls and talking about Thornwood's Revenge at the exact same moment that creepy things start happening at Thornwood Manor. No coincidences there. But I can't figure *how* it's all connected."

"Because that's *my* job, not yours," Toppy told me. "I took you into Thornwood because I thought it would put your mind at ease, but I shouldn't have done it. Since somebody really has been messing around in there, it's a police matter now."

Oh, great. I grimaced and caught Lavender's eye, then Mayor Chandler's. *"Police matter"* was grandfather code for *Stay out of this, little girl, and let the grown-ups do their jobs.*

"At least it's not your shoe size," Lavender said. "Max and I can post about it—you know, to reassure everybody you're not the one doing the hacking."

"No," Toppy said. "Let it be, as of now. I mean it."

Across the squad room, Junior Thornwood gave a loud belly laugh. He lifted his cell phone. "Can't understand these things. Thanks for fixing it. I got left behind when MS-DOS switched to Windows."

I looked at his shoes. Well, biker boots. They were leather, black with lots of buckles. And his feet were as big as the rest of him.

"He's too tall." My grandfather came over to me and

put his hand on my head. "I'd estimate six feet, four inches. He'll wear a fifteen, maybe larger. And I just told you, leave it alone."

"Police matter," I said.

He nodded. "I'm not kidding."

"I know."

I sighed, because Toppy was right—about Junior's height being wrong for the shoe, not the "police matter" junk. I wasn't a rocket scientist (not out of the range of possibilities) or a software designer building huge data-bases for the police to use (yet) or a criminal profiler for the FBI (very high on my list), but I knew height sort of dictated how big a foot somebody would have. Junior Thornwood was size huge, in everything. Especially that grin he kept giving Ms. Springfield. It was obvious enough to earn a size-huge glare from Lavender, let me tell you.

"Do you guys have a board started on the hacker?" I asked Toppy, drawing new puzzled expressions from Mayor Chandler and Lavender both.

"You're not looking at it," Toppy told me.

"Meaning, it's somewhere around here?" I gave Toppy a sharp stare, but he didn't answer. To Lavender and Mayor Chandler I said, "Toppy's old-school, and he and his officers put up crime boards for bigger crimes they're investigating. You know, to pin up notes and photos and ideas and suspects. It helps them keep track of things."

"No," Toppy said, looking from me to Lavender and back at me again. "Don't even think about it."

Lavender jumped up and went buzzing around the squad room, hopping and standing on her tiptoes to try to see what was on the crime boards that were closest to us.

"Hey!" Toppy strode toward her. "You stop that, Lavender!"

"Honey, don't." Ms. Springfield went after Lavender, and Junior Thornwood moved his imposing bulk over to me and Mayor Chandler. When he walked up to my chair, I found myself staring straight into the skull on his black T-shirt. It had flames coming out of its eyes.

"You feeling better, kid?" he asked.

"My name's Max." I studied him for a second, then stuck out my hand. "Do you have a thing for my best friend's mother?"

Mayor Chandler coughed. "I'll uh—I'll just . . ." She sidled off out of my line of sight.

Junior swallowed half my arm with his fingers, and very, very gently, shook my hand. "Yes, ma'am," he said, a slight Northern twang to his voice. "I do like Joy Springfield. Always have, since the first time I saw her again after we grew up. It was four years back, after the cave-in at the manor. When she asked if she could take you guys into the old place today—seemed like a good time for a visit."

My eyebrows lifted. Honesty. I hadn't expected that.

He grinned at me, but the grin didn't quite match the glint in his eyes. I stared at him, from his throwback Elvis sideburns to his vest and leather boots. He had a few tattoos on his arms, but I'd seen people with lots more.

"Are you rich?" I asked him.

"Max!" That was Toppy, who now had Lavender under one arm, pulling her away from the crime boards while she tickled him and demanded a brownie and some warm cider in exchange for leaving the squad room alone.

Junior Thornwood's cheeks flushed. "No, ma'am. Comfortable, because of my family's money, but I supplement my living by selling motorcycles. They're my passion."

"So, you're a Thornwood who has been able to make money?" I asked.

For a split second, Junior's eyes narrowed. He didn't speak right away. Toppy always said silence was a powerful weapon when interrogating suspects, so I just watched Junior and waited for more, and he gave it pretty quickly.

"I put my sales lot in Connecticut on the market last month," he admitted. "I've been thinking about coming down here to open a new one."

"Not a lot of people in Blue Creek buy motorcycles,"

I told him. "And are you planning to live in a haunted house?"

"Maybe I could get folks from Nashville to drive up to Blue Creek if my deals are good enough," he said. "And no to the house. I'm not that brave."

He gave me another grin, and this time, the smile reached his eyes. Still, I found myself holding on to my armrests. I wanted to like him, sort of did like him, but something—something felt a little off.

"Max Brennan, stop asking people rude personal questions or it'll be movies and reports for you," Toppy grumped as he stalked past me toting Lavender like a suitcase. He plopped her into the chair nearest me as her mother caught up to them, and he pointed his finger right at Lavender's nose. "As for you, Miss Marple, this isn't a television detective show. You just—"

His ancient flip-phone rang, freezing him midbluster. Ms. Springfield took over on Lavender guard duty as he pulled it out of his pocket, fumbled with the buttons, and finally managed his usual, "Yel-low?"

The top of his head flushed pink.

My heart skipped. "Oh, jeez. Is it the hacker *again*? What now?"

Toppy closed his eyes. Opened them. And stared right at me. My heart skipped harder.

"Yep," he said. "She's right here."

He handed the phone to me.

Cold dread blanketed my shoulders, but not because of what the hacker might be doing. Toppy had just sold me out. I knew it. My eyes stayed locked on his, and I tried to let him know that I wouldn't forgive him, that I'd get even, and that he was an evil piece of skunk cabbage and I hoped he got planted in the back garden and a deer ate his ears off.

"Maxine?" My mother's voice seemed to echo out of the flip-phone and fill the entire police station. "Honey, are you there?"

Oh, I didn't want to answer. I didn't want to answer *soooo bad*. But everybody was staring at me, and I knew she'd just get louder and more worried sounding, so I coughed up a raspy, "Here."

"Oh, good." Her volume dropped enough for me to put the top piece of the phone to my ear.

"I got this e-mail through my gallery site," Mom went on. "It said I needed to come get you right away, that somebody's trying to hurt you and Dad."

Words. I needed to think of some, then use them. They just didn't want to happen. It took me a full five seconds to come up with, "No. You don't need to come get me." Because that would be a hurricane-level disaster. Maybe even earthquake-level. Tornado during hurricane, while an earthquake was happening and a volcano blew up. "It's just some hacker being a jerk online."

Mom let out a loud breath. "I went to look for those

SUSAN VAUGHT

fake pages Dad told me about, and I didn't see anything."

"We got those taken down." My free hand dropped to my armrest, and I squeezed the snot out of the padding. "Listen, Mom. Who sent that e-mail you got?"

"It came through the gallery's contact page," Mom said. "ThornwoodsRevenge@hotmail.com."

I repeated the e-mail address for Lavender to hear, and then added, "Through Mom's gallery contact page," cuing Lavender to start looking stuff up on the station desktop. Thankfully, everyone turned to see what she was doing.

Mom was still talking. "That bothered me a lot. All those old legends about Thornwood's Revenge—what's happening there in Blue Creek?"

"Nothing." *Except cruel, evil Internet stuff. And spooky flickering lights and footprints at Thornwood.* "Toppy says all that legend stuff's just hooey."

A pause. "Sounds like him. But, Maxine, maybe you should come stay with me until the police figure out what's happening. I don't want you in any danger."

"I'm not in danger, and I don't want to come to California." *I'd rather watch Sentimental Flicks movies while eating Brussels sprouts, spinach, and broiled liver every single night for the next million and two years.* "School isn't out yet, and besides, it's almost the holidays. It's supposed to be cold and snow until January. The beach is weird at Christmas—and I don't exactly fit in your apartment, now that I'm electric."

Another pause. This one longer. "The elevator's been working pretty well lately."

"People with kids in electric wheelchairs don't usually live on the third floor, Mom." I squeezed my eyes shut. "When that elevator went out two summers ago, I got trapped there. I hated it. I'm not doing that again."

Very, very long pause. "I can't afford to move right now."

"Yeah. Well, I've had the electric chair for four years." I gripped the phone so hard the casing made click-y sounds.

"I know, honey. I'm sorry."

"Right. You're sorry on the third floor." I realized I was talking through my teeth and tried to make myself relax.

My face felt hot.

"Max," Mom started, and I felt guilty even though I had not said anything really bad. The last time I visited Mom, the fire alarm had gone off in her building, and when we got to the elevator, it wouldn't work, and for a few seconds I thought—well. Never mind.

It didn't matter.

Yes, it did.

I thought I would be stuck inside while the building burned down, and it freaked me out completely. *Stop thinking about it!* More heat in my face. *Impulsive . . . quick to anger . . . tramples feelings*—yeah. That was me, and it was Mom, at least when we dealt with each other.

"Never mind," I said, hoping Mom would let it go, so I could.

Mom gave a sigh, kinda like the ones Toppy and I were famous for. "I don't want to fight with you. How about I just come there and help keep an eye on things?"

My body snapped to rigid. "Don't you have to work?"

"I'm between assignments right now. Just doing a little photo-painting for a show."

My brain pulled up images of the black-and-white daguerreotypes at Thornwood Manor, of that life-size Hargrove Thornwood headshot. I imagined it with fangs and dripping blood, and evil golden beams coming out of its eyes.

"There's nothing to worry about," I told Mom. "Just paint your photos."

"I'm thinking about visiting, Max."

"Why?" I yelled, making everyone at the desktop turn around and gape at me. "There's nothing *you* can do to help anything!"

Silence. Pause. Then Mom, sounding sad, said, "Let me talk to Dad, okay?"

"Fine." I jerked the phone away from my ear and very nearly stuffed it into my grandfather's chest as he came forward to get it. He cleared his throat as he took it from me, shaking his head as he put it to his ear and walked away.

I watched him go and banged my palm on my

armrest. I hit it so hard my fingers tingled. My face probably looked like a rotten cherry, and I felt sweat in my hair.

Calm down. Guilt. Then more heat.

Was Toppy over there talking on the phone and agreeing to something, like Mom coming here or me going there? He better not be. My face flamed. I imagined kicking him right in the ankle and making him drop the phone.

No. That was wrong. I didn't want to hurt Toppy.

I breathed in and out.

I didn't want to hurt anybody.

I needed to calm down, calm down, calm down. Too many people in the room. All staring at me. Lavender looked worried.

Guilt, guilt, guilt. I used to yell at her, too, and she never deserved it.

Iceman. Ikarus. Illuminati. Illyana Rasputin. Imp. Imperfects. Imperial Guard. In-Betweener. Wait. I forgot one. Oh, yeah. *Impossible Man.*

Breathe.

Marvel had way too many characters.

Everybody was still staring at me.

I went through J's and a few K's, and finally, finally stopped feeling so hot. When I thought I could speak without saying a bunch of words that would get me grounded, I asked Lavender if she found anything on Mom's website.

"Yep." Lavender sounded relieved.

She turned to the desktop and clicked on Mom's home button. Photos loaded slowly at first, then faster. A picture of a bird on the beach. A picture of a California brown pelican in flight. She had updated it this week. Not that I checked that often. Well, maybe I did. Mom might suck at mom-ing, but she took wicked good pictures. I tried to shoot stuff with my iPad, and I wasn't half bad—but a real camera and good software and lots of practice, it really made a huge difference. Mom's pictures had been in magazines and on book covers. Sometimes she did shows in California or New York City or other big places.

With another click, Lavender navigated to the contact page. "I found out that her web security stinks. She has a contact page with an e-mail form that doesn't even use Captcha to sort out people from mass-mailing machines. Her spam folder must explode every day. And look. I can type any old e-mail in the address field."

I rolled over, threading between Junior, Ms. Springfield, the mayor, and Lavender's chair. When I got close enough, I pulled the keyboard over, surveyed the web page contact form, and typed **ThornwoodsRevenge@ hotmail.com** into the FROM field. In the COMMENTS field, I put, **Sorry I scared you. Just kidding,** and hit send.

Thanks to her archaic web security, Mom would get

an e-mail from the same spoofed address that scared her, only this one would tell her all was well.

"That was devious," Mayor Chandler muttered. "I'm impressed."

Junior and Ms. Springfield and Lavender didn't say a word. When I looked up at Mayor Chandler, her expression seemed sympathetic.

"After school tomorrow, I'll ask Ellis if there's any way to trace the IP address off Mom's website," I said.

Lavender shook her head. "Hotmail is untraceable."

"Yeah, but that's probably not even a real e-mail address." I felt myself relaxing into my seat cushions. "We might be able to see the IPs for people who used the contact form."

"Okay," Lavender said, sounding a little too agreeable and cheerful. Ms. Springfield and Junior Thornwood kept quiet, and so did the mayor—but I couldn't help noticing they all looked worried.

9

DECEMBER 5

I slid the cup of Earl Grey across the kitchen table and stopped it right next to the bowl of Cream of Wheat I had just served Toppy. Steam rose from the cup and twined with steam from the bowl, making a little cloud in front of my grandfather's face.

He sat in the red flannel Rudolph the Red-Nosed Reindeer print pj's I gave him for Christmas four years ago, and he stared down at the Cream of Wheat. "This stuff looks like vomit, Max."

"It has half the iron you need for the day and no sugar, just honey I added with the butter." I tapped the table next to his spoon. "It's better than a packaged cinnamon bun from the convenience store on the way to the station. Try it."

This earned me my grandfather's best heavy-browed skeptical look. He huffed for a second, then grumbled, "Butter's good for me?"

"Not a lot of it, no, but that little bit won't hurt." I leaned forward, keeping my eyes locked on his. "Healthy. Delicious. *Try it.*"

Toppy screwed up his face like a toddler, but he took a bite of the Cream of Wheat. He worked it around in his mouth, then swallowed. "I like oatmeal better. It's not slick like somebody prechewed it for me."

"Variety is the spice of life, right?" I had found out that instant oatmeal was iron-fortified like Cream of Wheat, so I told him, "I'll fix you oatmeal tomorrow. Fiber is good for the bowels."

Toppy's head flushed as red as Rudolph's nose. "Fine. Maybe we could add blueberries to the vomit-butter next time. Flavor and vitamins, and a little something I can sink my teeth into?"

"Okay." I smiled at him. "If you let me go back in the workshop alone again."

"Why?" He took a sip of his tea. "So you can use my tools to build a rocket ship or maybe a time machine?" He gave my chair the once-over, absorbing *Power* and *Strong* and *Steady*, the words I had carved into the foot-rest bars last night using the engraving tool he got me for my birthday. "Wait. I know. You're going to weld a big unicorn horn dead center on the battery and accidentally blow it up."

"No blowing up batteries, I promise."

"Uh-huh." Toppy didn't sound convinced. "So, all

your friends at school—they impressed with those photos you mailed out about the haunted house?"

"I didn't mail them. I posted them. And yes. They thought the hole in the floor was seriously wicked."

Toppy rolled his eyes.

"I put the best ones up on my wall," I said. "I keep looking at them. Maybe I'll find a clue."

Toppy rolled his eyes again.

Outside the kitchen window, dawn broke across Blue Creek, bright and crystal-yellow, spilling into the dark winter morning. For a second, everything got so bright I had to blink, and Toppy looked like he had an angel's fiery halo right behind his bald head. The smell of his tea tickled my nose, and maybe my eyes, too, because I didn't like thinking about Toppy as an angel, because that would mean he died, and he wasn't allowed to die.

"About the workshop. I want to fill in my engravings with some metal paint and work on my chair controls," I said, my voice a little bit choked. "I bought some wire a few days ago to see if I could increase my speed, but now I think the control box may have a short. The chair turned itself off twice when we were at Thornwood."

Toppy put down his tea, then lifted a spoon of Cream of Wheat toward his mouth. Before he downed it, he stopped long enough to say, "Has it shut off since then?"

"No."

"Maybe it was ghosts."

"Maybe you should let me in the workshop."

A frown. A few seconds of shoveling Cream of Wheat down the hatch. A sip of tea. Then Toppy looked at me, raised his right hand like he was in court, and said, "On my honor, I won't build anything illegal or dangerous, or anything that might start a house fire."

He gazed at me, waiting, hand still in the air.

I groaned, but raised my own hand off the chair controls and repeated the pledge, adding, "And I will do my best not to tear up my chair and cost you a lot of money."

Toppy put down his spoon. He and thirty or so Rudolphs stared at me, red noses glowing. "Okay. You can use the workshop again after school. Don't make me regret it."

"And," I said, sounding ignorant and hopeful even to my own ears, "I need a cell phone."

Toppy answered by laughing and going back to eating his buttered vomit with no further complaints.

Tuesday afternoon Lavender and I had Library Sciences during Language Arts, and we were supposed to be using newly learned research skills to work on our Social Studies paper about Urbanization and Immigration. Instead, we had a corkboard app open on a library Mac, saving to iCloud so we could access it later from home.

So far, we had yellow name cards for suspects tacked at the top for Toppy, Junior Thornwood, Mayor Chandler, and one just labeled ???.

"I think we should add Mom," I said.

Lavender gave me a sideways oh-really look.

"No, I'm not kidding," I said. "She was trying to be all Mom-y on the phone yesterday. She may be up to something."

"Like trying to be a more responsible person?"

"Like trying to get me to come live with her again so she can raid my part of the money we got as a settlement when that truck ran us over and put me in a wheelchair."

"Oh, yeah." Lavender chewed on the tip of her pen. "The hacker said she had spent all her settlement money. How much do you have left? Is it a lot?"

All around us in the library, the rest of the class shuffled between shelves and actually taking notes from books. We probably needed to do something soon to look busy with what we were supposed to be busy doing. "I don't know how much money I have," I said. "Toppy put it in a trust fund nobody can touch until I turn twenty-two. He won't use any, and he won't tell me anything about it."

This made Lavender put down the pen. "So, you might be rich and you don't even know how much you've got? That totally sucks."

"I'm sure Mom knows how much I have." *All things obey money.* The words carved into Thornwood's front doors seemed almost prophetic, and the image of Vivienne Thornwood danced in my head. I thought about how she and Mom had the same look in their eyes. "Maybe we're secretly related to the Thornwoods. Mom got the psychotic greed part, and I got the bad luck bit. What do you think?"

"That's harsh," Lavender said. But she made a yellow card and labeled it *Callinda Brennan*. "And if you were related to the Thornwoods, we'd have read it in some book or other by now. Any resemblance to persons living or dead is purely coincidental—like all the book and movie disclaimers say."

She placed Mom's card on the virtual board right before Toppy's card, because that was alphabetical. She opened a purple card, the color we had chosen for MOTIVE, one of the three elements detectives always looked for when they investigated crimes. She typed *Max's Money* on the card, and tacked it under Mom's name.

I pointed to Toppy's name. "Put *Getting Rid of Max* on a motive card for him."

"No." Lavender smacked her hand down beside the mouse. "That's just pathetic. He would never—"

"It's what the hacker's been saying." I stared at my knees, and my hands on my knees, and my feet, and then my wheelchair footplates. "Well, implying. That

I'm a big weight on Toppy. And he's right. I cost Toppy a lot of money, since he won't use mine. We can't ignore anything at this point, right?"

"Yes we can, Max," Lavender said, her voice forceful. "Toppy lives for you."

I managed to get my eyes to move away from my wheelchair control and upward, in the general direction of Lavender's left shoulder. "He's getting older. It's harder now, probably. Plus, I melted the fuse box and almost destroyed the house and cost him money over that, too."

Lavender let out a groan. She typed *Max Is Pathetic* on a purple card and stuck it under Toppy's name.

Good enough.

We settled on *Getting Even with Old Boyfriend* for Mayor Chandler's purple card.

For Junior, I couldn't decide. "He might just be some twisted freak, you know?"

"A twisted freak who thinks my mom is cute," Lavender said through clenched teeth. "Why would he just show up here in Blue Creek, right when all this is going on?"

"He says he wants to open a motorcycle dealership."

"Maybe he wants to sell Thornwood," Lavender said, "to pay for that?"

"He said he has money. So why would he need to sell Thornwood—and how would the manor being haunted make people pay more money for it?"

Lavender thought about this. "Haunted house publicity. Because that'd get him a lot of business at his new motorcycle lot, right? Even if he didn't want to sell the old home-place."

She typed, *Publicity and Hype and $* on his motive card.

For the ??? card, we put, *Punish Toppy for Arresting,* and *Get Revenge on Toppy,* and *Get Rid of Toppy,* though we didn't really know why anybody would want to do that.

Green cards came next for MEANS. We put more *???* under ??? for that. For Mayor Chandler, we argued for a few seconds, then put *Good Computer Skills.* The same note went under *Callinda Brennan,* since Mom designed and hosted her own website, but Lavender changed it to "decent" instead of "good," because Mom's web security was so bad, and she had fallen for a spoof e-mail address, and probably didn't even know what that meant.

"Junior had to ask your Mom's help with his cell phone at the police station," I said as we tried to decide about his computer savvy.

"That could have been an act." Lavender sounded really irritable. "I think the whole biker-tough-guy thing is just baloney, so maybe can't-use-my-phone is phony, too."

"Okay." I was so not about to argue and get a mouse stuffed up my nose. "And anyway, he does have some money already, so he could hire someone to do the web stuff even if he can't find an on switch for any computer."

Lavender wrote, *Unknown Computer Skills, Money to Hire Help* on his green card. Then she added, *Jerk*.

I kept my mouth firmly closed.

We got to Toppy, sat there for a second, then both of us burst out giggling. Toppy. Computer skills. Riiiiight. Lavender put a big X on his green card.

Then she opened up white cards for OPPORTUNITY, and put an X for Toppy there, too, since he'd been with me or somebody basically every time the hacks had happened. And anyway, after that Facebook page and the first few fake accounts, the hacker had stopped trying to pretend to be my grandfather. We opened Mayor Chandler's white card, and—

"Well, well, ladies." Ms. Zevon, our Language Arts teacher, pushed between us, glaring down at the screen. "Must not be working too hard over here, with all that noise."

She was wearing a black and gold pantsuit, and she smelled like spiced tea. Her face, usually stern but peaceful, had gone all hard.

Lavender tried to click the corkboard closed, but Ms. Zevon patted the top of her hand. "Nope. Just leave that alone." She leaned in closer and squinted at it, her colorful scarf and pearl necklace dangling forward as she stared. "What kind of game is this?"

"It's a mystery app," Lavender mumbled.

"We're trying to figure out who the hacker is," I said.

Ms. Zevon stared at us for a few seconds. "You mean that chump on the Internet posting all that embarrassing stuff about your family?"

"Yes, ma'am," I said.

"Admirable." Our teacher stepped back and folded her arms. "I'd even go so far as to say proactive. However, that was not your assignment, was it?"

"No, ma'am," Lavender and I said at the same time.

She made us repeat our actual assignment, then in a feat of interrogation that would have impressed even Toppy, she got us to confess that we had done exactly nothing on the Social Studies project, which was due next Wednesday, the day before holidays started.

That's how we left school with shiny new detention slips. Two hours. On Friday afternoon. The week before winter break.

It should have been illegal.

"Mom's going to murder me," Lavender said, slumping against the frosted window at the back of the bus, in the seat closest to my wheelchair bay.

I tapped my head on my headrest again and again. "At least she doesn't do Sappy Holiday Movie Torture. I'll be writing reports about *Prince Santa Claus Rescues the Kittens* for a month."

"I thought it was puppies."

"Puppies, kittens, ponies, goldfish. It's all the same after a while."

Lavender stayed quiet for a while, then squirmed in her seat. "Is your mom still thinking about coming for a visit?"

"I hope not."

That earned me the extra-special Lavender-does-not-approve look. "I thought you weren't mad at her anymore."

"It comes and goes. I mean, I get why I live with Toppy." When I flopped against the back of my chair, it groaned in the bus's wheelchair locks. "The work she does, it only pays in spurts, and sometimes she really struggles. Plus, here, I'm a lot closer to Vanderbilt Hospital, and Toppy's insurance covers my wheelchairs and everything I could ever need."

"But . . ."

"But, I don't know. She can't handle me, I guess." I gestured to the wheelchair. "Or she doesn't want to. Or maybe she never wanted to be a mom in the first place. The hacker has that bit about her irresponsibility right, at least."

"I don't know if the hacker has anything right," Lavender said. "But that's part of why I keep thinking it has to be somebody who knows you at least a little bit, to dig at you and Toppy about your mom."

My stomach tensed. Somebody who knew us. Maybe

knew us well enough to know how much that would bother Toppy—or me? "The computer corkboard app is cool, but I feel like we need to do a real corkboard, you know? To see it, to be able to touch it and move things around and stare at it live and in-person. Maybe it'll help us think."

"I'll grab supplies from Mom's store and bring the stuff over—oh, wait. I'll bring it next year, when we're ungrounded over the detentions."

I started to let the dread settle in, but my mind lurched to a new possibility. "Does the school call our parents over detentions?"

"I don't think so. Not unless we don't show up for them. I really don't know, since I don't get in trouble." Lavender leaned her head against the back of the bus seat. "And you don't either, not anymore."

"So . . . if we don't say anything about having to stay after school on Friday until Thursday . . ." I wiggled my eyebrows at Lavender.

Her head came up. She pointed a finger at my face. "You're trying to get us killed. Or grounded until we're both fifty. You're absolutely a bad influence and totally evil." Then she grinned. "I like that in a person."

10

DECEMBER 6

I ron Man," Riley Soza proposed, leaning back against the far counter in Bot's Electronics. He had his hair pulled back today, and he was wearing jeans and a holiday sweater, all green and red with ornaments dangling in bad places, but he was still trying to look cool for Lavender's sake.

Bot was out picking up some packages at the post office. The shop smelled like cookies, and Bot had decorated the place with bowls of brightly colored candy on every flat surface. Classic holiday music piped from the ceiling, Christmas stockings hung from rafters, and Bot had sprayed snowflakes on all the windows. Early evening frost kept me from getting a clear view of the police station when I tried to look back over my shoulder to be sure Toppy hadn't gotten impatient and walked outside to hunt for me.

Lavender stood next to me in the corner, swapping

between dance poses and stretches, and goggling at the rad desktop computer Ellis had just finished building for the store's business operations. With the superfast Internet Bot had hooked up at the store, the thing worked like lightning. Pages loaded faster than blinks and flickers. I was so jealous.

Today, at least, Lavender seemed more impressed with Ellis's mad computing skillz than Riley's gorgeous hair. She lifted her hands high over her head, stood on her toes, and arched her back. "Black Widow could take Iron Man with her energy weapons if she really wanted to," she murmured in Riley's general direction, but I could tell her heart wasn't in the fight right now. We had gone a whole thirty hours with nothing new from the hacker, and even though that was great, it made us both nervous. Plus, she was really hating on Junior Thornwood, who had called her mom *no less than ten times since he got to town, I swear it, Max!*

Was the hacker done messing with us, or just resting up, or getting ready for something way, way worse? Was it all connected to Junior's arrival in town somehow?

"No luck tracking the Facebook page or any of the other fake social media accounts, I'm assuming," I said to Ellis.

"None." He kept his eyes on the screen, which was mostly black, reflecting the twinkly Christmas colors everywhere and the yellow outline of the top of his blond head. He worked with a grim expression, following pathways and pings, trying to run down the IP address of the person who had used my mother's contact page with the spoof Thornwoodsrevenge e-mail address; we had tried actually sending an e-mail to that handle, but it bounced.

Ellis had on a black *That Which Doesn't Kill Me . . . Better Run* sweatshirt, complete with a scary looking, very nonholiday bloody eyeball in the center. It fit my mood a whole lot better than Riley's entry into this year's Worst Christmas Sweaters Ever contest. Instead of trying to keep up the superhero fight, Riley came over to us and stood next to Lavender. She ignored him and did a spin-in-place, then picked at a loose red curl, obviously not caring if Riley thought she was cute or not—at least for today.

The sound of Ellis's keyboard tapping blended with the old, worn-out holiday songs. The program he was using to chase the IP signal wasn't store-bought. I could tell. No fancy prompts, no glossy anything. He powered through command after command. Each time a ping came in telling him that he'd found a computer where the message might have come from, he'd copy-paste a cyberaddress and start again.

Another ping returned. And another.

"Why is this message pinging back to so many different computers?" Lavender asked Ellis. "The hacker can't possibly have that many—and how could all of them have sent the message?"

Ellis clicked a few more times, then leaned back in his chair, letting his arms go slack. "They're zombies," he said.

Lavender looked at me, clueless. "Zombies? As in brrraaaaiiinnnns zombies?"

"The hacker's using other people's modems and networks to route his signal," Riley explained. "Zombie networks are robot or 'bot' networks. Bot got his nickname from his last name, yeah, but also 'cause he used to do stuff like that back in the day, until he got in trouble for it."

"So, is that expensive?" Lavender asked, and I knew immediately she was thinking about Junior Thornwood and his money. "I mean, it would take a lot of cash to do something like that, right?"

"Nah," Riley said. "It's code. Viruses and Trojan horses—stuff people click on, and it launches programs that open doors to their computers. Most people never even know their machines are being used."

"More about skill than finances," I said. "Sorry, Lav. Can't nail Junior Thornwood that easily."

Lavender lifted her leg straight up in front of her face, then looked around her knee and offered me a rude hand gesture.

"Junior Thornwood, yeah," Ellis said. "He came by

here to get some help with his phone battery. Weird that he's in town just when the net's lighting up about Thornwood's Revenge."

"Past weird," Lavender said. "I think he's a creeper. Or up to something. He's in this somehow."

"Who is a creeper?" Bot asked as he elbowed through the shop door carrying two stacks of teetering packages.

I rolled over to help, and Lavender came over, too. We helped him load the stacks onto the shop counters.

"Thanks," he said. "Lot of trouble for nothing. I didn't get the supply contract for the middle school and the high school, so I've just gotta send most of this stuff back. The restocking fees will hurt."

Bot sounded sad. I reached out and patted his hand. "I'm sorry," I said.

"Stinks," Riley commented from over at the computer. "Got outbid by some big box store in Nashville."

"Blue Creek should keep its business at home," Ellis said. "That's how loyalty works."

Bot put on a big grin that deepened the lines in his face and made his white curly beard poof out around his lips. "I still want to know who the creeper is."

Lavender gave one of her better theatrical groans. "Junior Thornwood. I think."

"Well, it's easy enough to check his history," Riley said. "Right, Ellis?"

"Well, yeah, since there's not much else I can do

to help," Ellis admitted. "Sorry about the e-mail dead end, Max. This hacker's probably booting from a public WiFi, maybe even taking over computers at the hotspot. If we want to catch him using his cyberfootprints, you'll have to have help from the Feds."

"Feds are bad news," Bot said, shuffling the packages behind the counter a few at a time and stacking them onto a storage shelf. "I'd leave them out of it. Take it from a high school malcontent, the FBI has zero sense of humor."

I frowned. "The State Police and Tennessee Bureau of Investigation are already helping, but they aren't finding much."

"Probably not a priority, since nobody's really getting hurt." Ellis glanced from me to his computer screen again.

"Sooner or later, he'll make a mistake," I said.

Ellis laughed. "Dunno about that, Max. He's pretty good."

Lavender's frown was almost as big as mine. "Toppy says criminals always screw something up somewhere. We just have to find where Junior or his goons left openings."

"You're pretty positive it's that guy from up North," Riley said.

Lavender assumed something that looked like a yoga pose, feet back, arms out. "He's disgusting."

"He likes her mom," I explained to both confused guys.

"Oh." Riley focused on Ellis and the computer screen for a few seconds. Then Riley said, "So, does Toppy have any suspects *other* than Junior Thornwood?"

"Not that he's told us," I admitted. "Lavender and I, we're keeping notes ourselves, but we'll be grounded as of Thursday night, so it'll be a while before we can do much."

That made Riley narrow his eyes. He studied first me, then Lavender. "You know in advance you'll be grounded? What, are you planning another fuse box meltdown or something?"

"That was an accident." I banged my head on the chair's headrest once. "I keep telling everybody, but nooooobody believes me."

"We got a detention for Friday," Lavender said glumly. "Two whole hours."

"I could come keep you company," Riley offered. "Blue Creek High's not much on detention, so I don't get pegged often, like Ellis used to."

"Shut up, degenerate," Ellis mumbled, still typing. "It's only because I wasn't rich. The kids with money— nothing ever happened to them, no matter what they did."

"Yep, we're in the poverty club," Riley agreed. "And it sucks. But at least we have places to live and jobs we love, right?"

Ellis grumbled something under his breath, and Riley went back to offering to keep us company in detention.

Lavender hit Riley in the shoulder. "You show up at our school acting silly, and we'll be stuck staying after school for a whole month, dork."

"You think Black Widow could take out Iron Man, and *I'm* the dork?" Riley tried to look all mean and sarcastic, but failed.

I sighed and glanced out the window, just in time to see Toppy stalking across Town Square, heading for Something Wicked, where he assumed I'd be.

"We have to go, Ellis."

He gave me a sort-of smile. "Sorry I couldn't find out anything. I'll call you if I dig up anything on Junior."

"E-mail," I reminded him. "No cell phone, remember? But thanks for the other stuff. At least we know it's a real hacker and not some wannabe. Maybe that'll help narrow possibilities. I mean, not everybody has serious computer skills."

Ellis pondered this a second, then gave me a single nod. "Just, you be careful. Don't accidentally get yourself caught up in this. I don't think it's about you. And your new footplate etchings are seriously cool. I like the red glitter paint."

I gave him a thumbs-up before honking my clown-nose joystick and heading for the door that Lavender was already holding open. But I couldn't help thinking about how wrong he was. Attacking my grandfather, the only family member I could count on—that totally *was* about me. All the stuff the hacker said, implying how much of a burden I was to everyone, I'd mark that in the "about me" category, too, never mind getting questioned by Captain Coker about being abused. Plus, that hacker had e-smacked Mayor Chandler, and I really, really liked Mayor Chandler.

When the people you cared about got attacked, it definitely felt personal. It *was* personal. Way down deep inside, I wished I really could turn into Super Max with her flying, sailing, tank of a chair and outstanding superpowers, because I was personally going to stop this mess any way I could.

Toppy had errands to run, so Lavender's mom offered to swap cars and drive us home. We lingered at Something Wicked for a while, helping with holiday decorations, and by the time we got to my house, Toppy was already at the kitchen table arguing with somebody on the phone. I figured it was somebody in Blue Creek, mad about something the hacker had done, but as we eased by trying to get to my room without bothering him, I heard the words, "bill," "repair," and "ridiculous."

I quit rolling, and Lavender stopped beside me, her hands gripping the bag with the corkboard and other supplies she had taken from Something Wicked.

"Yes, I understand that you only buy one battery per wheelchair," Toppy said. "But the batteries stop working every year or so and need to be replaced." Pause. "No, she can't just use a manual chair. Her arms aren't strong enough." Pause. "It makes no sense that you would refuse to purchase parts needed to keep her wheelchair running because they're too expensive. What's she supposed to do? Pray for the miracle of walking when her spine is broken? What kind of chicken-fool logic is that?"

I jammed my joystick forward and my chair shot toward my bedroom. Face burning, I wheeled inside and almost slammed it hard before I even remembered Lavender was with me.

"Sorry," I got out as she stood there, petrified, staring at my death-grip on the door.

I let the door go.

She shut it after she came inside, and started unpacking the bag. I rubbed my face and recited superheroes and tried not to feel guilty for scaring her. When that didn't work, I studied the row of ten Thornwood Creepiness photos I had hung on my wall. There was the shot of the entry hall, and some of the daguerreotypes, and then the fireplace, and Vivienne Thornwood's portrait.

I had looked them over before I hung them up, and I had stared at them afterward, too. I had even expanded them on the iPad a few times, trying an inch-by-inch search, but really, they didn't show much. Just old stuff in an old house. Still, I kept coming back to them, bothered because I felt like I should be seeing something. What, I had no idea. But something.

The clean spots were weird, sure. And those old photos—ugh. And really, I could find better shots of Vivienne Thornwood's portrait online, because my lighting was off, and—

"What's that?" Lavender asked from beside me, making me jump.

I realized my hands were still pressed against my cheeks from when I got mad, and I lowered them. "What?"

"That." Lavender pointed at a shiny spot on the fireplace, right at the edge of the hearth.

"A reflection of the light we turned on," I said.

She walked up to the picture and squinted. "Well, the shadow beside it looks spooky."

"That's Mayor Chandler."

She giggled. "Oh." The giggling stopped. She turned toward me, and I went stiff all over, waiting for her to tell me how mean it was that I almost slammed the door on her, and how she hated it when I got mad.

Instead, she said, "That's pretty stupid, how the insurance company won't buy you a battery if yours dies."

I didn't know what to say, so I just nodded.

Lavender stood still for a few really miserable-feeling seconds, then stretched and did a dance step back to my desk and picked up a piece of corkboard and scissors. "What do you think? Taller than wide, or wider than tall?"

"I want to put it on my door, top to bottom."

"Strips then," she said. "Got it."

It took us a while to get the corkboard hung, but we got most of the door space covered, then made our SUSPECT cards.

"Really," Lavender said, "I think we can take out Mayor Chandler. She has motive, maybe, given that she stayed mad at Toppy after they broke up—like, for decades—but she doesn't really have means, and no opportunity."

"Agreed," I said, and took her card from Lavender.

Next, she held up Toppy's card. Both of us stared at it. Really, he had no means or opportunity, but motive—

I glanced down at my expensive chair and thought about the phone call. When I looked at the corkboard on the back of my door again, Lavender was still standing there with his card in her hand. She seemed like she was about to argue that we should junk it, but then she pinned it up without saying a word.

"Now, about your Mom." Lavender waved the next card at me, but I cut her off.

"Leave Mom."

I could tell she wanted to argue, but she didn't. I rolled over to my desk, where she had stacked the blank cards, and dropped off the eliminated suspect. When I got back, Lavender had finished organizing everything under Toppy's name, Mom's name, and Junior Thornwood, and ???.

"I guess we won't know what to put next until the hacker does something else."

"Don't want to think about that," I said.

She crossed the room and plopped down on my bed. "What would somebody plan if they wanted everybody to think Thornwood's Revenge was happening?"

"No idea. When I've read theories, they're always stuff like a giant town-eating fire, or financial ruin, or something else messy."

Lavender froze on my bed, staring at me.

I stared back at her and lifted my hand to my chest, pressing my fingers into the bone and feeling the fast thud-thud-thud that had started after I talked about fire and ruin and messy things that could hurt a whole town.

"Do you think this hacker is going to hurt people?" Lavender asked in a too-quiet voice. "Like, really, truly hurt people?"

"I"—*thud—thud—thud*—"I hope not."

Hargrove Thornwood was just a story, a legend. Except, he wasn't. Thornwood had been a real man. He ruined actual lives. He . . . hurt people. Really, truly. His own family. Workers on his property. The folks who lived in Blue Creek way back then. Maybe his revenge was just a fable, but if some jerk with a grudge against my grandfather and Mayor Chandler decided to make it real, then it would be real.

"I don't like this," Lavender said. She got up, went to my desk, and fished through the colored cards, coming back with a stack of red ones and a black marker. She wrote *Fire* on one, and *$$$* on another, and tacked them up above our suspect list.

"*Epidemic* was one I read about before," she said. "You know, some big sickness that kills half the town, like cholera or yellow fever or . . ." She swallowed hard, and I could tell she was trying to get past being scared. "Pink-purple-turkey-dinosaur-flu." She smiled at her own joke. "Yeah, something like that."

"Use *Disease* for that one," I suggested, lowering my hand and trying to relax so my heart would quit pounding. "Let's see. There's *Natural Disaster* to cover floods and tornados and stuff, and *Killing Spree* to handle all the mass shooting, poisoning, and multiple murder theories."

"Poisoning?"

"Well, yeah, since that's how Hargrove Thornwood died and stuff. Makes a sick sort of sense, if Thornwood's Revenge turned out to be some kind of toxic gas cloud or contaminated water or something."

"That's just wrong," she said, but she added *Killing Spree* to the board.

We stared at our choices for a while, not talking, trying to live with the idea that all of this might end up with way more than just annoying computer hacks.

"I guess," Lavender said, "we could take off *Natural Disaster*, since even the best computer skills can't make a tornado or a flood, not if we don't live below a dam or something."

"Okay." I motored over and took down that card. "We can probably take down *Disease*, too, since I don't think we're dealing with an international terrorist or somebody who can break into disease labs and steal brain pox and start the zombie apocalypse."

"*Fire* and *Financial* and *Killing Spree* left," she said. "That's just wonderful."

"A hacker could do weird stuff at the banks, or at businesses. Could make a real mess." I stared at the red card with the *$$$* symbols and thought about what Riley and Ellis said about the poverty club. "Maybe the hacker plans to steal a lot of money from everybody's bank accounts. I don't think very many people in Blue Creek would be ready for that."

"Banks have okay security," Lavender said. "But yeah. And really, that would be awful but not as bad as killing spree."

"I bet the electric company doesn't have good

security, or the water company. The hacker could probably bust into their computers and turn stuff off. Or steal account information from those places, because they're probably less secure than banks."

"You're kidding, right?" Lavender's laugh sounded a little nervous. "Ms. Jemison runs Blue Creek's water utility district right out of her basement using paper files and an old clunky computer that's not even hooked up to the Internet. It's like computer security, reverse-engineered."

"No way to hack what hasn't ever been online, unless the hacker's right at the computer." I sat back in my chair. "But other businesses in town are online."

"Yeah. Maybe we should tell Mayor Chandler to put out some sort of alert to people who actually do use online stuff."

I shifted around and leaned on my armrest. "I don't think there's much we can do about fires or killing sprees."

Lavender pursed her lips. "Maybe we're just scaring ourselves. We don't even know if this guy is really going to do anything."

"We don't even know if this guy is a girl," I said.

"Point." She sighed. "But that shoe print is from a guy's shoe, so for now, we'll go with 'he' instead of 'she.' And that means we should take down your mom. If she doesn't have the money to get a new place to live that doesn't have stairs, she doesn't have the money to hire somebody to come here and do all this mess."

"Leave her," I grumbled.

"Max."

"Fiiine. Take her down." I didn't really know how much money Mom made from her art. I didn't know if she couldn't afford a new place, or she just didn't want one. Not having an accessible apartment meant she had extra excuses to leave me here with Toppy. But that didn't make her a poison-pen hacker, or a potential arsonist or crazed murderer or whatever this freak might turn into.

Lavender took Mom down, leaving Toppy and Junior Thornwood and ???.

"That's not much in the way of suspects," she said.

"Wonder if Toppy's board has more," I said.

Lavender kept staring at the ideas on our cards. "How can we get a look at the suspects he's collected?"

"No ideas at the moment." I rubbed my eyes. "So, we know that somebody might do something worse than writing nasty stuff on the Internet, because he keeps threatening Thornwood's Revenge. We know he's probably local or visits here a lot, due to him raiding the Blue Creek Library archives and breaking into Thornwood. We know he wears tennis shoes, size ten or eleven, and he has computer skills, hacker level."

"You think we can eliminate old guys because of the hacker stuff?" Lavender asked.

"Not every old guy is Toppy."

"True."

Somebody knocked on my bedroom door, making the cards on the corkboard jiggle. Three raps, fast and hard. Toppy. And he was annoyed by something.

I rolled backward as Lavender went to the door and opened it.

Toppy and Ms. Springfield were standing outside. Both of them were frowning. Ms. Springfield had her arms folded.

"You know, Max," Toppy said, his voice that deadly quiet I usually associated with the moment before a big storm hits with screaming winds and exploding thunder and giant claws of white lightning, "I don't have a personal e-mail address, so I can't read messages from your school."

I swallowed hard but my throat was dry, so I started to cough as a sense of absolute doom dropped over me.

Lavender backed into my chair so hard she stumbled and sat right down in my lap.

Her mother said, "But *I* have e-mail. I might not read them every day, but I do read them. Detention? *And you didn't tell us?*"

Lavender and I both just sat there, looking hugely

guilty, probably because we were totally, completely, hugely guilty.

Ms. Springfield jerked her thumb toward the door. "Let's go, young lady. Right now."

"You stay, Max," Toppy told me, and I heard the sound of a month full of puppy movies in his angry voice.

11

DECEMBER 8

If I really could morph into a superhero, I'd want to be grounding-proof. For that, I'd just need some tiny but cool ability, like being able to erase bits of memory, so when I really screwed up, I could delete the little stretch marked "Bad Decision."

But knowing my luck, Toppy would then grow a superpower that would allow him to retrieve the erased time, along with vital stats on every ridiculous thing I'd ever done ever in ridiculous history. For now, he wouldn't even discuss how long my grounding would last, he was so mad about me not telling him about the detention.

I'm not mad, Max, his somber voice intoned in my mind. *I'm disappointed.*

I sat in the library at Blue Creek Middle School serving the first fifteen minutes of detention and using a gold glitter marker to write *BREATHE* on my armrests in different fonts.

I was already miserable, but not half as miserable as I was going to be, grounded all through Christmas, if that's what Toppy decided.

I was just trying to help, my pathetic whine-voice argued back.

Toppy wasn't much for talking back, even imaginary-in-my-head Toppy.

BREATHE. BREATHE. BREATHE. BREATHE.

Real-life Toppy was *disappointed.* And a little ticked off when he saw the corkboard Lavender and I made. And a little more ticked off when he found Mom's and Mayor Chandler's names in the discarded stack of cards on my desk, and his own name still tacked to the corkboard.

I'm going to tell you again, Max. This is police business. I'm not joking.

I knew he wasn't kidding, but how could I stay out of something that was happening right in my own life, to my own grandfather? Plus, no matter how much I tried to ignore them, the hacker's words kept playing like a text loop through my head, the part where he said I was a pawned-off disabled kid. *I don't know why I took on caring for a handicapped kid. #parentingfail.*

I was pretty sure my grandfather hadn't written any of that. I mean, I hoped he hadn't written it. But I couldn't shake the worry that he might feel that way, even if it was only every now and then, or when I did ridiculous stuff. Which seemed to be often, lately.

Breathe!!! my armrests reminded me. For good measure, I sketched a few on my left arm, then a wobbly *Breathe* on my right, too. My watch alarm beeped, and I weight-shifted in my chair, moving more onto my right hip. Frost etched the library window as I capped the glitter pen and stared out across the field bordering the school on one side, hating that it would be dark when I got to leave. Blue Creek Middle School was actually an ancient elementary school repurposed to hold just sixth, seventh, and eighth grade until the new building, which was a lot closer to my house, got finished.

I'd probably be all the way in high school before that ever happened.

The old cinderblock school sat on the edge of town, out past the closed tobacco factory. It was surrounded by playgrounds, the field I was looking at, and a small section of Blue Creek that liked to swell up to nearly a river during the rainy season. This time of year, it wasn't much more than a few icy puddles trapped between a lot of rocks.

I got bored counting the puddles after a few minutes.

Because it was so close to the holidays, everybody was in a good mood and trying to behave, so there were only six students in the library. The four eighth-grade boys only had half-hour sentences. They sat quietly, pretending they were working but messing with their phones while the detention monitor, Ms. Kendrick, scored her English papers. She didn't separate Lavender and me, so we sat close enough to slide notes to each other, even though we both had books about the Industrial Revolution opened to sections that looked like we were working on the super-boring Social Studies paper. Lavender had note cards poked into various sections of her book, but she pulled one out, wrote on it, and slid it across the table to me.

"This is sooooo tedious."

I wrote, "Totally tedious. And it's cold in here," and slid the card back.

When it returned to me, my comment was lined out, and the new one said, "Totally, truly tedious. And I smell peppermint."

"Totally, truly, tremendously tedious. Ms. Kendrick's got a whole bag of green and red peppermints in her desk drawer."

"Totally, truly, tremendously, terribly tedious. Can't you get detention for eating in the library?"

I almost laughed out loud, then thought better of it. I lined through Lavender's last comment and scribbled, "Totally, truly, tremendously, terribly, terrifically tedious. I've been thinking. One of the hacker's tweets said the corruption in Blue Creek had to be 'purged.' So, maybe FIRE is the thing we should worry about most?"

I slid the card to Lavender, and after she read it, she tapped her pencil against her cheek. I watched as she started scribbling, and when I got the card back, she had dropped the T-word game and said, "Maybe. Good thinking. But it could also mean getting rid of people, like Toppy getting Mayor Chandler recalled—even though I still don't think he should be a suspect. Or maybe the hacker getting Toppy fired or getting other people to do a recall vote on Mayor Chandler. Somebody's already written a letter to the paper about convening a special election for that."

"But who hates them that much? Maybe we should break into the police station Saturday and read Toppy's board."

I stopped writing because the smell of peppermint blasted into my nose.

Lavender closed her eyes, then bent over her book and scribbled like she was taking serious notes. I quickly sat forward in my chair and moved my hand on the page of my book, just enough to cover the last message Lavender had written. My heart thumped, and I imagined getting another detention, maybe one that would make me come to school on the holiday or some awful thing.

"I know you girls are working on your Social Studies project," Ms. Kendrick said from right behind me.

"Yes, ma'am," I said in a shaky, lying voice.

• • •

The boys were long gone, and Ms. Kendrick was finished with her test grading. She alternated between reading *Pride and Prejudice with Zombies* and giving us the work-on-your-project stare, and I didn't want to look at the bloody skeleton face on her book cover, so I actually did make a few notes on my Urbanization and Immigration paper. Unfortunately, what I was reviewing talked about Upton Sinclair's *The Jungle*, and how mean and nasty meat-packing plants were in the early 1900s, and that just made me think about zombies even more. Zombies eating rotten meat and chasing evil plant owners who exploited workers.

"Mom's here," Lavender said.

I popped out of my disgusting zombie fantasy and looked at the clock. Two hours, done! Yes!

But Ms. Springfield hadn't come in the van, and Toppy wasn't right behind her, and he hadn't asked her to give me a message.

"Sorry, Max," Ms. Springfield said as she took Lavender's hand at the library door. "I'm sure he's on the way."

I didn't even bother to sigh. Toppy being late to pick me up somewhere—that was normal. It just stunk worse than usual today.

Ms. Kendrick did my sighing for me, and she grumbled, "I'll call him."

I thought about crying as Lavender and Ms.

Springfield left, then got irritated when Toppy didn't answer Ms. Kendrick's call.

"Texting him," she informed me, and then I wanted to scream, because I didn't think Toppy knew how to read a text.

My fists doubled, but I took a deep breath, listed the DC D-named superheroes, stopping with Doomsday, and got myself together before saying, "I'm going to go to the bathroom, okay?"

"That's fine." Ms. Kendrick worked her thumbs, no doubt unaware she was sending my grandfather a message he'd never find.

I motored out of the library before she could change her mind, but the restroom I could use was, like, halfway to another state. Really, it was all the way on the other side of the building from the eighth-grade wing, just off the sixth-grade wing and near the main office. I was used to having to travel to pee, so I plunged into the deserted hallways. Amazing that the whole place could still smell like sweat and stinky sneakers when absolutely nobody was around.

Golden light spilled through windows onto the cream-colored floor tile, with little streaks of red from the sinking sun. My chair's whirring motor seemed to echo off the empty walls and closed lockers. I rolled down the main hall of the eighth-grade wing, and yeah. Absolutely. No one. Around.

Disturbing.

I never realized how much sounds echoed in the school building, because I hadn't really been in them when nobody else was there. My eyes darted left and right, checking out each side hall I passed, until I turned in to the seventh-grade wing. My chair revved along, but I couldn't go very fast, since I still hadn't gotten to work on my speed options. My chair had a really slow maximum propulsion for safety, but I wanted to tinker with that, if Toppy didn't reground me from the workshop over not telling him about my detention. I didn't know if I could remove the governor that controlled the chair's acceleration without destroying my entire control box, but if I could get more speed for times like this, that would be awesome, and maybe a little like having superpowers, only for real. I wouldn't use the increased velocity and force to flatten thick-heads who refused to move out of my chair's way. No. I totally would *never* do anything like that.

By the time I got to the bathroom and did my business and washed my hands, the sun had finished its slow dive. When I rolled back into the hallway, the world outside had turned gray with dark edges, and the halls had gone dark. I felt really grateful for the lights at the corners of the corridors. My hand pressed against the joystick, I took a deep breath, and—

Whoa.

I took my hand off the joystick and the chair hummed to a stop.

For a second I looked around, then sniffed the air.

Wow. That did not smell like sweat and stinky sneakers. Strong. Acrid. I coughed. Why did the main hall of my school stink like spray paint and Toppy's lawnmower gas?

My fingers curled against my armrests as my mind supplied the image of an evil-looking owl flying slowly through dark school hallways, gripping a bramble.

Thornwood's Revenge.

No way.

But I did smell gas. Was somebody in the school trying to make trouble? Or maybe a huge fire, like Lavender and I had passed notes about earlier?

"Somebody needs to purge the corruption in Blue Creek," I whispered to myself as sweat formed on my forehead.

The dark silence around me seemed to come to life, like it could move on its own, like it was flowing around my chair and opening a giant mouth to swallow me whole. Then a light bounced across the corridor I was facing, way at the end where it T-boned into the sixth-grade wing.

I held my breath so I wouldn't make a single noise.

Something rustled in the hall.

My heart punched against my chest, and the rush of

fear almost made me shout out loud. My hand moved toward my controls, but if I hit the joystick, the click and whirr of the chair's motor would be *so* loud.

The light reappeared, slashing through the darkness at the end of the corridor. A flashlight, for sure. I kept holding my breath even though I was getting dizzy, waiting to see if the light moved toward the center of the hall, where maybe whoever was carrying it would turn and look straight at me.

Janitor, my brain tried to say, but the janitor would just turn on the lights, right?

Thornwood's Revenge. Thornwood's Revenge!

I squinted through the darkness at the school's front doors. They'd be locked, just like most of the side doors. Since Toppy had been seriously late picking me up more than once, I knew the school's door locks electronically engaged at five every afternoon, except for the doors by the library where detention happened. Those locks had to be keyed by hand, when the last teacher left the building.

My heart raced. The only way out was near the library, back in the eighth-grade wing—right past whoever was moving around in the darkness.

That rustling noise came again, very close to the place the hallways joined. I breathed in gasoline. Was the stench stronger?

If the hacker was soaking the hall with gas to light

it, if he was planning to make FIRE like Lavender and I thought he might, I'd never get out. If I tried to roll through burning gas, my wheels would melt and pop. Or I could stay put and die from breathing smoke.

No. Way.

I jammed my hand against the controls, opened my mouth, and let go of a wild animal roar as my chair lurched forward, straight toward where I had seen the lights and heard the noises. My wheels skidded briefly on the waxed tile, making me slide side-to-side. I almost hit the wall, and the gas stunk so bad, and I kept yelling.

The light beam I had seen jerked like somebody dropped it, and I hollered even louder. I wished my chair had turbo engines, and I took the corner as fast as it could possibly roll. My wheels spun, lurched, spun some more, slid, then seemed to hit dry tile and dig in. From behind me, I heard a guy start swearing. The words sounded muffled. I couldn't make out whose voice it was. I wasn't sure I cared.

Smoke slid across my shoulders.

Roll! I wished I could feed my chair rocket fuel straight from my brain. If I could use my legs to run, I could go faster and faster, just by wanting to, but my chair maxed at three miles per hour. Walking speed. And by the sounds behind me, whoever had been carrying that light and splashing gas, they were running.

"Toppy!" I refused to look back, pelting toward the

seventh-grade wing in the dark. I tried to focus on the corner lights, on the triangles of brightness laid out like a trail back to safety.

"Ms. Kendrick! Toppy!" The battery indicator on my chair dropped one slash mark, but the hacker still hadn't caught me and grabbed me.

"Somebody help me!" My voice splattered through the school's dark emptiness. I wheeled into the seventh-grade wing. I couldn't tell where the hacker was, but I imagined him charging along right behind me, closing distance fast. Way, way too fast.

I bit my lip. Tears streamed out of my eyes and I pushed my controller so hard the rubber clown-nose popped off and the real rubber tip started tearing loose. Words left me, and I bellowed a whole bunch of nothing and wondered if I could smell more smoke. Maybe the hacker had gone back to drop matches in the gas. Maybe fire chased me now, and it would sweep into the chair's lithium battery, and the chair would explode and blow me into a thousand bits of gross all over the school walls.

My yells turned into screams.

12

Was I still in a main hall? Had I taken a wrong turn? *Breathe,* my arms and armrests reminded me as I jerked my body left and right, moving like I could force the chair into speeds and angles it wasn't built to do. I tried anyway. More smoke. I coughed. The fire alarm started with a loud squall, followed by three bells, and stop. Three bells, and stop. Lights turned on. I heard locks clicking open and fire doors automatically pulling shut.

"Max?" Toppy's voice boomed over the bells. "Max!"

I pelted toward that sound, leaning forward like my body weight could pull the chair faster.

The turn came up on me fast, but I swung around the corner and almost ran flat over my grandfather and Ms. Kendrick. Toppy had his hand on his service weapon and his eyes on the corner and the hall beyond. Ms. Kendrick clutched her phone and her zombie book. Her mouth hung open, and her eyes seemed huge behind her square glasses.

Three bells. Stop. Three bells. Stop. Three bells. Stop. Toppy seemed to flicker as lights blinked all around him.

"Get Max outside!" he barked at the teacher, even as he punched the button on the radio attached to his shoulder. "Fire at Blue Creek Middle School. Send cars, too."

Ms. Kendrick turned midstep, running for an unchained door. Strobing lights made her look like an old movie.

"This way," she called, yanking the door open and gesturing for me to roll outside.

I didn't take my hand off my control until I was halfway down the sidewalk to the street. That's when I realized Toppy was in a burning building alone, probably facing off with a horrible person who might want him dead.

"No way." I jerked my control to the side, spun the chair toward the school, and rolled full-out back toward the detention entrance.

"Max," Ms. Kendrick said as I motored past her. "Hey!"

Before I got to the door, the chair started to drag, probably because it had a teacher and a zombie book and a phone dragging along behind it.

"Look to your right," Ms. Kendrick said. "Max! Eyes right. Please!"

I was grabbing hold of the door handle. Sirens blared in the distance, and I turned my head to see Toppy marching out of a set of automatically opened doors in the seventh-grade wing. He had his police jacket wrapped around a smoking trash can, carrying it as far from his face as he could get it.

As I watched, he dropped the smoldering can onto playground dirt, watched it for a second, then kicked it another ten feet away from the school for good measure. After that, he stomped on stuff that was still burning and talked into his shoulder radio again. Probably not proper police procedure—but one hundred percent Toppy.

"He's fine, see?" Ms. Kendrick said.

I barely heard her over the blood hammering in my ears, but I let go of the door.

Then I put my face in my hands and cried without even feeling like a giant baby.

"Really, I'm good," I said as Mayor Chandler washed my face for the third time.

She put down the washcloth and offered me her fries from the fast food she brought to the police station. Lavender and Ms. Springfield were finishing up their foot-longs with chili, but I still wasn't hungry, so I declined with a quiet, "No, thank you."

While Toppy, several officers and firemen from

Blue Creek, Ms. Kendrick, and two big guys from the State Police talked in the main area, the four of us were holed up in Toppy's office, which was just a little bigger than my bedroom. A big oak desk stacked with books and papers took up a lot of the space, but he had an old couch with metal legs and orange plastic cushions, a rickety metal chair, and a bunch of signed pictures of University of Tennessee football players decorating the walls between the crime boards. Lavender reached up and took some pictures of the boards, but her mom and Mayor Chandler got up and dutifully turned them around so we couldn't see them.

I should have been thrilled that Lavender got a few pictures, but mostly, I was still freaked out.

"Just a trash can," I said, reminding myself that the world hadn't ended.

"But a trash can with a fire in it," Lavender reminded me around a mouthful of tater tots. "Coulda blown the whole place up. Plus, somebody painted an owl on the hall wall."

I swallowed hard. "Thanks so much."

"It was a small fire," Mayor Chandler said. She was sitting closest to the office door, which was cracked. Every now and then she leaned her head toward the opening, obviously eavesdropping. "Looks like somebody set it on purpose, then tried to stamp it out. Chief Brennan said they found a sooty footprint on the ground outside an open window into the seventh-grade wing."

"Let me guess," I said. "It'll be size ten or eleven when they measure it. Probably some normal sneaker."

"Probably," the mayor agreed.

Ms. Springfield put down her humungous-size cup of Sprite. "Starting a fire on purpose, then putting it out—that makes no sense."

"It could have been a prank," Lavender said. "You know, to get people out early for the holidays. Lots of people have seen that owl on the Internet fake accounts."

"On a Friday?" I shook my head. "What would be the point? Especially if nothing got damaged. Whoever it was, they came to set that fire while I was in the building. Maybe *because* I was in the building."

Mayor Chandler let the door close a bit, keeping her fingers in the opening. "The officers and the firemen aren't sure about that. They think it might have been a coincidence."

I groaned. "You've got to be kidding."

"Detention was supposed to be over, right?" Lavender pushed her last few tater tots around on the napkin in her lap. "Toppy was late. You and Ms. Kendrick should have been out of the building when it started."

"Besides," Ms. Springfield said, "who even knew you two had detention?"

"Did you tell Junior?" Lavender asked, suspicion lacing each of her words.

"Nooo," her mom said, but the way her eyes darted back and forth, I wondered if she was trying to remember what she had or hadn't said to her new best friend.

"Ms. Zevon and Ms. Kendrick knew," I said. "The principals, I guess, or whoever keeps the detention list. Toppy knew, and all of you guys. Lavender and I didn't tell anybody else."

The mayor's eyebrows lifted. "Seriously?"

"We were sort of embarrassed," Lavender admitted. "We didn't want anybody to know."

Mayor Chandler looked even more surprised. "Well. That tickles me. I stayed in trouble half the time I was in middle school and high school. You two must be a lot better than me."

"I doubt any of your teachers or principals are caught up in all this," Ms. Springfield said. "But I guess we could ask Toppy to check out their backgrounds."

"The hacker set the fire," I persisted. "And drew the owl. He was probably trying to scare Toppy. You know, make a point, like, *See what I can do.*"

The mayor leaned back against the office wall. "Maybe. But it's just as likely it isn't related." She hesitated, then continued with, "And I really think you should step back and let your grandfather handle this. Toppy's a good officer and a good investigator."

"Good officer and investigator?" My watch beeped, and I quickly shifted my weight in my chair. "Did you record that, Lavender? We need to put it on Facebook. Everybody thinks Mayor Chandler hates my grandfather."

Mayor Chandler's entire face turned a rosy pink. "I've never hated him. It's just . . . a long time ago, he broke my heart, and I guess I broke his."

"How did that happen, exactly?" I asked.

Mayor Chandler got even pinker. "He told me that we should see other people while he was away in the military. I thought he was through with me, so I moved on and got married." She rubbed both hands against her cheeks. "When he came home, he was furious I hadn't waited for him even though he told me not to. It was—we—we were both so young, Max. But he's still just as stubborn, and half the time he won't listen to anything I say, and when I see that same old obstinate look on his face—oooh. I just want to shake him."

"He makes me mad, too, sometimes," I said, and for no reason at all, a big lump filled my throat and tried to cut off my air. Tears climbed into my eyes, and I couldn't figure out what I wanted to say, but what came out of my mouth next was, "He thinks Cream of Wheat looks like vomit."

The tears escaped my eyes and ran down my face. I wiped them away quick, but not before everybody saw, and the next thing I knew, three people were hugging me and my nose was crammed into the mayor's neck. I had time to think she was strong, and that she smelled like clean clothes just out of the dryer, all fresh and comforting, and then I realized she was crying, too, just a little bit.

"I thought he was going to get hurt at the school," I blubbered.

"I know." The mayor sniffed. "And I'm so sorry."

"Today really sucked," Lavender said under my left ear. She smelled like tater tots, not clean clothes.

"It did," her mother agreed from behind me, her hands squeezing my shoulders. "I think a lot of this week has sucked."

"Maybe it'll start getting better tomorrow," Mayor Chandler said.

"Can you decree that?" I asked. "You're the mayor. Mayors are allowed to decree stuff."

The office door opened, and the mass of huggers moved back to reveal my grandfather. He seemed to fill the doorway, and when he saw that I was crying, he strode straight to me, nudged everyone out of his way, unfastened my safety belt, and lifted me out of the chair to hug me.

I clung to his neck and smelled pine and Earl Grey and everything safe and happy in my entire life, and I relaxed. Over his shoulder I saw Captain Coker in her trooper's uniform. She had her arms folded, and her sharp eyes looked misty and distant, like she might be thinking about something sad or scary.

"We're going to get a little help for a while, okay, Max?" Toppy said. "The State Police and TBI, they'll be giving us support."

"That sounds good to me," I said.

I didn't want Toppy to put me down, and he didn't, not for a long time after that.

13

DECEMBER 9

Early Saturday morning, just about every website associated with Blue Creek businesses crashed. Thornwood Owls popped up in their place, each with a message nastier than the one before it.

Chief Brennan fails to protect local schools. Discipline lax in Blue Creek. #kidsatrisk

Deliberate fire-setting at Blue Creek Middle School, no action from police chief. Mayor Chandler weak against ineffective police chief. #favoritism

Watch your wallets. #moreiscoming

I swear the hacker got no sleep at all—just stayed awake and tried to screw up everything he could for the town. The Chamber of Commerce site was still up, and it seemed like everybody had something to say.

You can do it, Chief Brennan . . .

Whoever this is needs to get a life . . .

Chief, you really need to find this person . . .

Mayor Chandler, you're failing the town by not putting a stop to this nonsense . . .

Maybe it really is Chief Brennan. Maybe he needs medical help . . .

The ones that weren't supportive made me mad, and the people who implied Mayor Chandler or my grandfather might not be doing enough to stop everything—seriously? How could they buy into that mess? Saying a lie over and over again didn't make it true, but apparently it created doubt and confused people way more than it should have.

When Mayor Chandler called at nine in the morning on Saturday, I answered the kitchen phone by the microwave, the one Toppy hung halfway down the wall so I could reach it.

"You're not calling to tell me you've decreed that things will be better, are you?" I asked after she said hello.

The mayor didn't laugh like I'd hoped she would. "I wish I were, honey. Let me speak to Chief—uh, let me talk to Toppy, please."

I frowned, but then I stretched the old-fashioned curly phone cord across the kitchen to the table, where my grandfather sat in the Grinch pj's I bought him for Christmas last year, reading his Saturday newspaper with its "Fire Set at Blue Creek Middle School" headline. His cup of Earl Grey and a bowl of oatmeal with cinnamon and apples steamed in front of him, barely touched.

He gave me a long-suffering look, but he took the receiver, tucked it between his ear and his shoulder, and said, "Yel-low?"

I went back to my iPad and read a couple of short messages from Lavender.

Not grounded yet, are you? And, I'll come over after dance class this morning if you aren't.

Come over, I typed back.

"Well, why do they want to do that?" Toppy asked the mayor. He sounded annoyed, and maybe a little surprised. His head and face slowly flushed red, and he stopped looking at the newspaper.

That wasn't good.

"Well, I know it's bad for business," Toppy grumped. "But it's not like we're swimming in tourists in the middle of winter, what with Thornwood shut down and country music thriving in Nashville."

I fidgeted in my chair, looked back at my iPad, and realized I had an e-mail. When I clicked on it, it was from epritchard@botselectric.net.

Ellis.

Hey, Max.

JThornwood has money issues. Motorcycle lot in Connecticut not up for sale. It's being auctioned by his creditors to pay bank loans he owes. Lavender may be right about him being a creeper, may want $$. Tell her mom to

watch her wallet and passwords. Heard you were around the school when the fire happened last night. You okay?

"How is that going to solve anything?" Toppy got louder with each word. "It's giving that punk exactly what he wants."

I'm okay, I typed back to Ellis. The fire scared me but I didn't get hurt. Thanks for finding out info on Junior. Tell Riley Lavender thinks he's cute. I put a smile at the end of my sentence, but I didn't feel smiley.

As I hit send, Toppy said, "Fine, I'll be there."

He got up, walked over to the wall, and hung up the telephone. Then he just stood in place for a few seconds, and his shoulders curved forward. It made him seem shorter and older, maybe even a little sad.

My pulse jumped. "What's wrong?"

"Nothing," he said too fast. Then his shoulders slumped a little more, and he kept staring at the wall. "The—ah, City Council wants to meet with the mayor and me on Monday."

"With you—or about you?" I started choking my armrests. "About the hacker and stuff?"

"A few of them think maybe it would be better if I took some time off, until all this settles down." He rubbed the back of his neck like he had a cramp. "Maggie wants to get together on Sunday to talk about our options."

My thoughts hopped around until they landed on

truth, but I didn't want to believe what I was thinking. *Take time off.* They couldn't mean—

"So, options?" I asked. "What are they? And do they mean time off like a vacation?"

"A mandatory variety, yes."

I rolled right up to Toppy and looked at the side of his face, at the edge of his frown. "They can't suspend you because some butt-face is running his mouth online. That's not right."

"Don't call people butt-faces." He finally faced me, him and dozens of green Grinch faces. "Anyway, it may not be right, but it is expedient. You know what that word means?"

"Practical. Convenient? Oh." I tapped my head against my headrest. "They want the headlines and social media stuff that's hurting their businesses to stop."

"As fast as possible, especially now that he's actually done something—and at the school, no less. If I'm out of the picture, our hacker friend doesn't have me for a target anymore."

"He'll just go full-out on the mayor then," I said. "Wait. If they decide to suspend you, can't she veto that?"

"Maybe," Toppy said, but he stopped talking when somebody knocked on the kitchen door.

Toppy's head came up, and his hand moved to his hip, where his weapon would have been if he'd been wearing his uniform. Since Grinch pj's don't come with a holster, his service pistol was locked in a safe upstairs in his room.

"Max," Toppy said as he straightened up and managed to look fierce despite his festive pajamas. "Want to roll on out of the kitchen please?"

"Chief?" came a familiar voice from outside. "It's Captain Coker. I've got duty this morning, and I think you've got company."

I stayed in the kitchen, and Toppy walked over to the door and opened it.

Captain Coker stood outside in full State uniform, complete with a green lined coat with brown fake fur around the edges and black sunglasses propped on top of one of those winter hats with ear flaps, dark green and labeled *TSP* like all the rest of her clothes. She blinked at Toppy for a moment, taking in his holiday pj's and me sitting in the background. She rubbed her black-gloved hands together, and then waved at me.

"Hi, Max. I took morning shift in the car we're keeping with you and the chief at all times. And about cars, Chief, there's a car that pulled up outside your house about ten minutes ago, but the woman inside, she's just sitting there."

My entire mind shorted out in a single sound, a *zzaapp* right between my ears, because I knew. I didn't *want* to know, but who else could it possibly be?

For a second I only heard snips and snaps of conversation.

"It's an old red Tercel . . ."

"Yes, it's . . ."

"California tag, 6ZQ . . ."

"My daughter . . ."

Heat blazed through my entire body.

"I'm outta here," I mumbled.

"You stay right where you are," Toppy ordered. "Don't you dare hole up in that room and refuse to speak to your mother."

Captain Coker kept her mouth firmly shut and managed to look anywhere but at me or my grandfather.

Toppy left the kitchen.

Mom.

Mom was here.

I got so hot I had to be sweating everywhere. My hands shook. My jaw clenched. I wanted to scream and break stuff, but I didn't want to scream and break stuff.

Toppy said—

But—

"Whatever," I hollered.

Then I fired up my chair, whizzed to the back door, opened it, and blasted down the house's back ramp.

14

Despite the bright noon sun, it was so cold on the front porch of Thornwood Manor that I thought my lips would turn to ice and break straight off my face.

"I am *not* stubborn," I told Captain Coker and Lavender, who were busy freezing to death with me, one on either side of my chair, our backs to the scary door owls holding the scary door thorns. "The school and my therapist said I was impulsive, that I get mad too easy, and I stomp on people's feelings. BUT I AM NOT STUBBORN."

Also, I wasn't hot anymore. Not even a little bit. One of the benefits of sitting outside at a haunted house, where my mother wasn't.

"You don't stomp on people's feelings," Lavender said. "Not anymore, except for your mom's."

I rubbed my eyes, noting that she didn't argue

with me about the impulsive-get-mad part. "Yeah, well, excuse me if being mean to Mom is a path to the Dark Side. That still doesn't mean I'm stubborn."

"I have evidence to the contrary," Captain Coker said a little slowly, like her own lips had gone numb. "You absolutely would not wait in the kitchen for your mother like you were told, you drove that chair like an off-road vehicle across a field full of sticks and rocks and hay and up a big hill to sulk in front of a spooky house in freezing weather, you refused to speak to me until Lavender here arrived, and let's not forget the part where you ran over your grandfather's toes when he came up here and asked you to come home." She paused, blew her breath into her palms, and rubbed her hands together. "I'd file all that under capital-S stubborn."

"Thornwood may stink," I admitted, "and the cold, too, but at least I'm not having to talk to her. And I won't. Not until I choose to."

Lavender shivered in her dance clothes covered by purple warm-ups covered by her purple coat, mittens, and scarf. "Max's relationship with her mother is complicated."

"I get that," Captain Coker said, studying something way off in the distance. "My mother didn't want a thing to do with me becoming a police officer. Thought it was too dangerous. She didn't talk to me for two solid years when I went to the Law Enforcement Academy."

"That's harsh," Lavender said. "How did you get past it?"

Captain Coker tilted her head like she was thinking. "Time, I guess. She got more proud than scared as years went by."

"She should be proud," I said. "You're good at your job, I think. Right?"

"People make mistakes," Captain Coker said. "Mistakes don't have to be the end of the world—or even the end of relationships."

Lavender laughed. "Nobody gets to end a relationship with their mother. She's . . . Mom, and stuff."

"Oh, you can end a relationship with anybody if you try hard enough," Captain Coker said. "Even parents. You can close your mouth, your heart, your mind—you can blow up relationships, or starve them to death. Right, Max?"

I didn't answer. My mind was too filled up with how Toppy kept patiently urging me to love Mom for Mom instead of expecting her to be someone else, and how when I blew up the circuit board, he said, *You can't always make something haul the load you want it to.*

Lavender started rocking to make herself warmer. "But Max's mother dropped her off here a few years after she got hurt, and she barely visited—still barely visits. And Max got freaked out two summers ago when they had a fire alarm, and Max couldn't get down the elevator at her Mom's place. Seems like Max's mom is the one starving stuff to death."

"Parents can make some of the biggest mistakes of all," Captain Coker said. "Hard to stop loving them, though. And you couldn't get out of her house in a fire?"

"A fire alarm, not a real fire," I grumbled, hating it that I sounded like Toppy when he was huffing and puffing and snorting around about something. "But I was scared it was real. When that elevator wouldn't work, I was stuck."

"I take it you don't do stuck well," Captain Coker said.

The laugh burst out of me, unexpected. "I can't stand feeling like I don't have options. That I'm just . . . controlled, or something. And she won't move to a ground floor place. And Mom's car—it doesn't fit my chair, so she has to rent a van when I go to California. It's like—it's like—"

"Like she pretends you don't live in a wheelchair?" Captain Coker glanced at me.

"Yeah!" I covered my frigid lips with my fingers, surprised they were still warm enough to make a difference. "I mean, yes, ma'am. Like my busted spine will just heal itself and I'll jog up her stairs or jump in her car, or whatever. She won't make room for me in her life—the me I am, I mean. Not the me she wants me to be."

As if on cue, my watch timer beeped, and I pulled

the weight off my left butt cheek and put it on the right one instead. Had I really just hollered that Mom wouldn't love me for me, just like Toppy always hollered that I wouldn't love Mom for Mom?

"Sounds like your mother feels pretty bad about you getting hurt," Captain Coker said, back to staring off into the distance. "She was driving when it happened, right?"

I turned my attention to the side of her face, to the smooth perfect lines of her cheek, and her "stern face" that I was beginning to realize was just how she looked, not necessarily how she was. If she had kids, she was probably really good to them.

"Yes, she was driving," I said. "But that was a long time ago."

Captain Coker raised one hand, palm up. "Probably not to her."

I wondered what it would be like to have somebody strong and steady as Captain Coker for my mother. Sometimes I wished Ms. Springfield had been my mom, or Mayor Chandler. Anybody, really. Anybody but the mom I had, who was currently at my house, probably sitting with Toppy and Ms. Springfield, whining about how I never gave her a chance.

"I'm not sure she feels bad about anything except not having things exactly her way," I said to Captain Coker. "Besides, she's not the one who ended up in a wheelchair. Why can't she get over the wreck? I did."

"I'm glad you did," Captain Coker said. "As for what your mom really feels bad about, I couldn't say. I'm just a Statie and today, a bodyguard, not a therapist." She pointed over her shoulder at the creepy carved doors. "So, you were in this place recently, right?"

"We checked it out a few days ago," Lavender said. "Did Chief Brennan tell you about the lights and the footprint?"

Captain Coker nodded. "He also said there's a big pit in the floor, and the place isn't safe. He told me Junior Thornwood showed up right as all this mess started, but Mr. Thornwood isn't interested in fixing up the foundation or the floor."

"*Mister* Thornwood," Lavender said with so much sarcasm I could almost see its sharp edges in the frosty air.

"Oh!" I clapped a frozen hand against my armrest. "Lavender! Ellis sent me an e-mail—you were right about Junior. He didn't tell the truth about having money. His motorcycle dealership up North is up for auction."

Lavender jumped up, groaned because her feet were so cold, and stomped them, shaking the whole porch. "I knew it! Mr. I've-got-plenty-of-bucks. What does he want from Mom? Money? Or maybe it's just the publicity for the lot he wants to make, or revving up interest in Thornwood so he can sell the place. He just became Suspect Primo, seriously."

She stomped her feet again, and the porch shimmied and gave a mighty POP!

That brought Captain Coker to attention. She put her hand on my chair's push-bars like she could actually move it without the manual toggles engaged.

"Did you get any clear shots of Toppy's crime boards?" I asked Lavender, not worried about the porch since Toppy had checked it out so thoroughly a few days ago.

"The pictures were blurry," Lavender said. "But I'm feeding them through this blur-fixer app and I can almost make out a few names, and—"

The porch popped again, and Captain Coker hit her tolerance for old-spooky-collapsing-house. "Off this bunch of boards," she instructed. "Come on. Let's go."

When we didn't get in motion immediately, she got closer, dwarfing us both and treating us to her sternest police face. "*Move.*"

We moved.

Lavender went down the front steps as Captain Coker followed me down the ramp. Once we were clear of the house, she shot it a mean look, then turned her glare on Lavender and me. "So, crime boards. E-mails. What are we talking about here?"

Lavender glanced at me, and I looked at her. I felt

guilty without really understanding why. "We, uh—" I started.

"We made our own corkboard for the hacker attacks," Lavender admitted. Then she described it to Captain Coker, including admitting that she snatched a few quick shots of the crime boards in Toppy's office, hoping to get a picture of some of the case information.

Captain Coker listened in silence, then stayed quiet a few seconds after Lavender stopped talking. "So what I'm hearing is, you two have been nosing into a police case, you have some theories, and a young friend of yours found dirt on Junior Hargrove faster than the Tennessee State Police." Captain Coker shook her head. "We've got some serious restructuring to do in the Information Technology department, I think. That's probably public record and everything."

"I don't know," I said. "It may not be available for everyone to know yet. Ellis is good at finding out things. Computers are his life, and Riley's, and Bot's. But you can't tell anybody they have hacker skills. Especially not the TBI and stuff. Don't get them in trouble for helping us."

All I got for that plea was a lifted eyebrow.

"They also fix broken computers and televisions," Lavender added. "And they sell lots of cool stuff, and they really know superheroes."

"Well, then," Captain Coker said, "they have to be

straight-up guys—unless they're big fans of Deadpool. He's not my favorite."

"You were corrupted by the movie, weren't you," Lavender said, her serious tone undercut by her chattering teeth. "Max, can we go back to your house now?"

"Haven't you stolen a key to Thornwood from your Mom yet?" I turned to look at the porch again, studying the door and its keypad. "We got most of the code when she kept punching stuff in."

Lavender cleared her throat. "Ix-nay on the e-kay in front of the op-cay, kk?"

"We will not be going into any haunted ouse-hays today, ot-me, gay?" Captain Coker said.

"No haunted houses," Lavender repeated. I almost did the same, because when Captain Coker made pronouncements, it was hard not to just salute or something.

"And why don't we take the oad-ray." Captain Coker pointed at the parking lot, to the street that wound away from the old mansion, down toward my house. "I'm not sure that chair's up for another literal field trip. You and your grandfather are gonna be scraping mud out of your spoilers for a month or two as it is."

"Fiiiine." I powered up, started away from Thornwood Manor—and my chair suddenly shut off. It stopped so abruptly I rocked forward against my safety belt, and Lavender bumped into my push-bars.

I fiddled with the on-off switch and said, "Come on. Not this again."

"Is it busted?" Lavender came around the side of my armrest and stared down at the dark light panel around my joystick.

"What's wrong?" Captain Coker turned and faced us. "Is your chair not working?"

"I don't know." Panic poked at my insides, which made no sense, because we could flip the toggles in front of my big back wheels and convert propulsion to manual, and Captain Coker and Lavender could push me home—or they could call Toppy to come get me in the van. Still, when my chair refused to move, it was one of the only times I really, really noticed my paralyzed legs.

Holding my breath, I flicked the switch one more time.

The chair came on, lights flickering, like it had never been off. I turned it quickly and rolled it toward the road. With everything in me, I wanted away from Thornwood Manor, even if I didn't really want to go anywhere else.

"Wait up!" Lavender hollered, jogging toward me. "Max. Hey, Max!"

But I couldn't make myself slow down until I reached the far edge of the parking lot. Lavender and Captain Coker caught up with me in a few seconds, and together, the three of us headed toward the twisty road that would take us to my neighborhood, my house . . . and my mother.

"So," Captain Coker said as we walked, "I suppose you two thought you'd escape the stay-out-of-police-business lecture, right?"

"Ugh," I said.

"Yes?" Lavender's voice sounded absurdly hopeful.

"Hate to disappoint you," Captain Coker told us, and the lecture—firmer than any we'd received to date—commenced.

"Hey." Mom looked at me with my grandfather's eyes, green with gold flecks, wide and loving. Those eyes had kept me from hating her for years. How sad was that? To keep loving somebody just because they look like somebody else.

And *Hey*. Sigh. Not exactly the way to begin a deep conversation, but that was Mom. She was all about whatever was easiest.

It was just her and me in the kitchen, with everyone else in the living room. I had agreed to come in here with her, to "take our business private." Because, why not make the day as awful as possible.

"Hey," I said back, trying not to stare at her hair, which was long again, but she had gone full ginger. Like, flashing neon RED. That, plus her black jeans and black leather jacket, made me feel like I was talking to a member of a punk rock band. As much as I hated to admit it, it seemed sort of . . . right on her, somehow. But she looked young again, like that photo in the papers from right after the accident, and I didn't like thinking about that.

"Did you hurt yourself driving through that field?" Mom asked.

"No." I sighed. "Mom, I'm not made out of glass. I don't get hurt all the time."

She blinked. Managed to keep the sort-of-smile frozen on her face. Stayed really still in the chair at the kitchen table where Toppy usually drank his tea and ate whatever breakfast I made for him. "Your chair okay after that run across so much grass?"

"Yes."

"I know you didn't really want me to visit." Mom bent toward me and put both of her hands on her knees. She didn't seem to notice when I leaned back to keep from getting too close to her. "I felt like I needed to be here while Dad's dealing with all this. And you, too. You know, to help."

"Okay." *Love her for who she is, Max.* Toppy's voice in my head. Awesome. I hated the day a little harder. "Yeah, so, the stuff at the school was pretty scary. Help might be good."

"I'm sorry you had to go through that," Mom said, and she sounded like she meant it.

My eyes betrayed me by trying to cry. I didn't dare talk right that second, so I just sat still. *It's not your fault.* Those words didn't come out. It really wasn't her fault. I mean, I was in Blue Creek because she didn't want me, so that part was her fault, but the hacker attacking Toppy, and then me getting scared at school, not so much.

"Dad says you and Lavender have been investigating, too—that you poked around in Thornwood, even." Mom's smile came back, less fake this time. "I used to hang out up there when I was your age. Creepy, cool old place. Sad how it's starting to fall apart."

"There's a big hole in the floor and the porch popped today like it might implode." I could make words again. Nice, safe words. "And the old pictures in the main hall are spooky, the black-and-white ones."

"I know! Those pictures are why I took up art and photography." Mom put a hand on my knee, and I didn't knock it off. "I kept wondering what it would be like to paint on shots like that. Add color, try to bring a little of that history into the present. Maybe Junior Thornwood and Joy Springfield would let me get some close-ups and try it on some prints."

Thornwood Manor turned my mom into an artist? Who knew? And why did that feel like more than I ever really knew about her before? I still hadn't knocked her hand off my knee. Toppy would be proud.

Mom seemed to notice me looking at her fingers. "Is this okay, Max? I really don't want to make you mad."

I swallowed past a growing lump in my throat, then managed to nod.

"I hear Dad and Margaret Stetson are talking again." Mom waggled her eyebrows like Toppy always did when he was making a silly joke.

"Who—? Oh. Mayor Chandler."

"Stetson's her family name. Lots of history in Blue Creek, the Stetsons." Mom's expression shifted to something wistful and far away. "Once she married into the Chandler family, people just saw her as part of that clan. Change a name, change your life, I guess. I always wondered if they might take up again after Mom died."

"I don't know if I'd call it 'taking up.' It's more like a truce. They're not threatening to kill each other every day."

"Well, that's progress. Dad's due a little companionship in his life."

"Okay, wait." I didn't shove Mom's hand off me, but I did move it. "What am I for companionship? Nothing? It's not like I have no brain. I can have conversations and be good company and stuff."

"Of course you can. That's not what I meant." Mom

eased back in Toppy's chair, folded her arms, and turned her face toward the ceiling. I thought I saw tears rimming the bottom of her eyes. "I always say the wrong things, don't I?"

"Yes." I chewed on my bottom lip to keep my mouth shut, and felt seriously guilty.

Mom looked at me again, not crying but red-eyed. "Maybe if we talked more, I'd learn what you like to chat about."

My anger punched my nervousness right in the nose. "Chat about this, then. Do you still live on the third floor of a building I couldn't escape in a fire if the elevator didn't work?"

"I—you know I do." Mom's sad face switched over to something else. Maybe mad. Maybe defensive. Maybe confused. "My studio's there, and I get the morning light. I know you don't like that elevator, but it—"

"Can I get my wheelchair into whatever car you're driving now?"

Mom's mouth came open. "Well, no. But that's because—"

"Stop." Heat. So much of it. So fast. I couldn't think of a single superhero name to start a list. I didn't even want to. "It's because I don't fit in your life. Have you ever thought that maybe you don't fit in my life, either?"

And before she could say anything to that, I rolled off to my room, right past all the company, even Lavender.

BANG.

I slammed the door.

But it didn't make me feel any better.

15

DECEMBER 10

T his is a bad idea," Lavender said, fooling with her
phone apps, still trying to unblur the pictures of
Toppy's crime board.

I squinted at the soldering iron, leaning hard
against the metal worktable as I tried not to lose the
tiny wire. My grandfather's protective goggles slid sideways because the strap was too big, but I did my best to
ignore the lump of nosepiece blocking half my vision.

From the corner of my eye, I could see Lavender's
disgusted expression. After a few seconds, she put the
phone on the worktable, then went running across the
concrete floor of the giant aluminum building that
doubled as Toppy's workshop and garage. She had on
two layers of warm-up pants, bright blue today, and two
loose blue sweaters. The sweaters flapped as she executed an impressive tour jeté.

After she landed halfway across the room, she raised

her voice to be heard over the low rumble of the salamander heater I had fired up so we wouldn't get frostbite while I worked. "Messing with your driving controls again is maybe the worst idea in your history of bad ideas—and that's saying something."

"Hey, I built a control box just like my real one, a model, and I tried the idea on the model first."

"Uh-huh." Lavender didn't sound impressed or convinced.

"Just. A. Little. More. There." I switched off the little red tool and carefully put it in its stand on the metal worktable. The workshop seemed to go still as I examined my altered wheelchair drive box. "That *should* work. Went perfectly when I tested it on the model control. And with the bigger wheels I put on this morning, I can get more speed with less acceleration, and now the field and armature have independent controls, and by reducing the field current—"

"Aaaaaaaah!" Lavender smacked her hands against her ears. "I hate electricity!"

I rolled my eyes so high my head almost hurt. "Look, electricity isn't always bad. Most people don't try to chew through plugged-in lamp cords. I can't help it if you got shocked because you were being stupid."

"I was three. Speak English, please, not electricity-ese."

"Fine." I reached to my right and pulled the top to my modified drive box out of an array of jars, boxes of switches, cans full of wires, toolboxes, and discarded chunks of plastic. When I got the top fitted over the joystick, I snapped it into place and made sure the chair would still power up.

The lights on my control panel flickered immediately. I grinned and pointed to the new toggle to the right of the joystick. "All of my fuses have been replaced, and I now have a turbo switch. No more fritzing out when I'm trying to drive, and the next time somebody chases me when they're trying to burn down a school, I can run. We just have to test it."

"Forget *that*." Lavender started prejump stretches. "Toppy and Mom still aren't over the manure thing in your backyard last year. I got grounded for a week, and I didn't even do anything, and if we make them think about grounding, they'll remember we're supposed to be on lockdown because of that detention. Which they may do anyway, when they get back from the meeting at Mayor Chandler's."

"It wasn't manure, it was compost, and I didn't break any bones. You gotta admit, the lift on my chair's tilt function got a lot more efficient after I tweaked the hydraulics."

Lavender twirled a few times, enjoying the space the workshop gave her. "If you like being fired into a pile of cow dung by a ballista. Problem is, Blue Creek's all out of castles to storm."

"That depends on your definition of castle." I wiggled my eyebrows at her.

She quit spinning and folded her arms. "You're evil, and you just want to get away from your mother."

I gave her my best pitiful look. "My chair only shut off at Thornwood. I want to know if it's fixed. Besides, if something freaky happens, you can climb on and I can speed us away. Pllleeeeaaase. Maybe we could find some dirt on Junior if we really look."

"E-V-I-L. And why didn't you get another clown-nose for your joystick? I liked that thing, plus it made people move in the hallways when you were trying to get by."

I eyed the larger black rubber tip I had glued on to replace the tip that used to hold the clown-nose. "I don't know. Not feeling clown-y right now, I guess."

"You'll feel clown-y when you run over somebody's poor cat in that souped-up monstrosity. I don't know why you have to try to change every chair you get."

"I—um." Well. I didn't have a good comeback to that. Because I could always think of ways my chair could be better? Because I wanted to be stronger and faster?

You can't always make something haul the load you want it to, Max. I ran my fingers over the arms of my chair.

"Maybe I'm tired of reading about superheroes," I said. "Maybe I want to be super, all on my own. Otherwise, I'm just another boring person in a boring wheelchair."

The look Lavender gave me was as evil as she accused me of being. "What, you don't want to be all gentle and noble and long-suffering like the wheelchair kids we read about?"

I headed toward her. "I'm running over your foot for that."

She bounced out of my way, laughing. "You aren't boring, Max. And definitely not noble."

"Both feet. Be still."

She darted away again, settling back in front of the heater.

"Seriously, Lavender." I drove forward and turned, putting my back to the door. The salamander roared away behind her, making an orange haze around her blue clothes. "I need to be super for Toppy right now. He's meeting with Mayor Chandler and some friends to try to save his job, all because some freak won't lay off him on the Internet—and I keep feeling like we're missing something at Thornwood, or something *about* it."

"Okay," she said. "But what?"

"The hacker's whole theme is Thornwood's Revenge. He's been in that mansion. I know it. If we just go look better, more carefully, maybe we can find out who he is, or how to stop him before things go any further."

I quit talking because Lavender's eyes had gone wide, and her arms went slack. She focused on something directly behind me.

Or *someone.*

I turned.

Mom was standing just inside the doorway, wearing jeans and one of Toppy's red flannel shirts. It went to her knees. A really fancy camera hung from her shoulder by a black strap. She had her hands in her pockets and her hair loose.

"So, do you two have a way to get into Thornwood?" Mom's voice seemed to echo in the workshop despite the dull roar of the salamander. She wasn't smiling. Her eyes seemed bright and intense, and I didn't get any sense that she was trying to be all cool and win me over, even if she probably was.

Lavender walked over to the heater and switched it off. It went out in fits and burbles, flames jetting, then poofing until nothing was left but the soft popping of its metal torpedo tube. The faint smell of gas drifted around us as Lavender reached beneath the neckline of her bottom blue sweater and lifted up her necklace.

A silver key dangled from the chain, glittering in the bright workshop lights.

The woman in the red-striped gown hadn't changed since I saw her last time. Vivienne Thornwood favored me with her mysterious smile.

Out in the hallway behind me, Mom said, "These

old photos are just as amazing as I remember."

"Have you ever done any research on Vivienne Thornwood?" I called to Lavender, who had headed off through the kitchen.

"No," she yelled back. "Never thought about it. The stories usually focus on Thornwood himself, and that one kid who died even though Vivienne helped her escape."

I gazed at the portrait—and then I sat up straighter. "How?"

"What?" Lavender called.

"How did Vivienne get her youngest daughter out of Thornwood?"

Silence.

And then, "I don't know."

"What about that basement room—wait. No stairs. No doors." I banged my hand on the chair arm. Something tickled the edges of my brain. Something I should be seeing. Something I should be understanding. But what?

I closed my eyes, seeing Vivienne Thornwood's curls and red gloves like burned images on my eyelids. She snuck a child out of the house right under Thornwood's nose, risking his wrath to save something from her husband's madness. He was really awful to her, and to everybody she loved. Vivienne Thornwood was the one who had a right to revenge—on Thornwood. If I were her, I'd have been mad to the power of infinity at Thornwood, and at the people of Blue Creek, too, who never really helped her.

Mom mumbled something about needing a sharper angle. I opened my eyes, held back a drama-queen sigh, and told myself not to roll out to see what she was doing.

And then I rolled out to see what she was doing.

As I sat in the hall doorway and watched, Mom contorted herself to take a picture of a picture, then checked her display and frowned.

"How do you keep from getting a glare when there's glass on the daguerreotypes?" I asked as she let the camera dangle at her shoulder and went and tugged two lamps out of a side room.

"It's lighting and camera settings," she said as she set the lamps into place, plugged them in, and twisted the switches, lighting up Thornwood's picture. "With the right perspective, the right angle, you can get past what's in the way."

I fiddled with my chair controls, backing away from Thornwood, because I still didn't like him and couldn't forget how that picture seemed to have eye beams when I got scared in the house last time I was here. Mom went on for another few minutes about how to take shots of totally glass items with backlighting, and how to get good pictures of metal and shiny stuff like watches and glasses and grandfather clocks with big glass faces. I hadn't meant to be talking photography with her, and I didn't want to find it interesting, but it sort of was.

"You okay, Lavender?" I called out, wrecking the chilled silence and forcing myself away from Mom.

"Uh-huh," Lavender said from the general direction of the gigantic hole in the floor.

From outside on the front porch, the trooper guarding us coughed, then stomped his boots against the wood, probably warming up his feet. Trooper Nelsen hadn't complained or even laughed at us when we marched up here. He just followed us in his patrol car, then stood stone-faced and alert as Lavender and I made a few mistakes, but finally got the code right and made the key turn in the clunky, rusted lock.

When I rolled into the kitchen to check on Lavender, I found her lying at the edge of the busted spot, shining a flashlight around the dank black cavern below. The stairs that had been there before were gone. I figured Junior moved them.

I motored carefully through the door, but couldn't get close enough to see what Lavender was looking at without putting the weight of the chair on questionable boards. As it was, when I pulled my hand off my joystick, the floor gave a big creak, then a loud pop.

"Uh, we okay here?" I asked Lavender.

"Maybe," she muttered.

Behind me, in the hallway, I heard lamps being

shuffled, then the whirr-snap of Mom's shutter. The grave-dirt smell from the hole washed across my senses, and I shivered even though I was determined not to get spooked. I mean, it was broad daylight, and we had Trooper Nelsen right outside. Thornwood might be old and weird, but it was just a big old house, and I refused to be a colossal wimp in front of my mother.

"This room definitely looks like a priest hole," Lavender said. "Yet, not. It's too big. Maybe a deluxe priest hole?"

"That still sounds just . . . wrong," I said. "But if it's not a priest hole, what is it?"

"I don't know." She flicked her light left, then right. "I just can't figure it, at least not without more information."

"Maybe it's a root cellar, or an old wine cellar, or something like a vault. Maybe Thornwood kept valuables down here?" I leaned as far forward as I could, squinting at the dark stone below. "I mean, he thought everybody was stealing from him—but how did he use the room if there weren't any stairs?"

"Maybe it wasn't enough that the room was hidden. If he used a ladder that he took in and out, it would be even harder for people to get into his hidden room," Lavendar said.

I pondered this for a few seconds. "So it had a grate or a trapdoor leading to it, you know, hidden in the part of the floor that's not here anymore."

"It would be dust now," Lavender said.

"And the websites and your mom said nothing was found in the priest hole after the cave-in," I reminded her. "Just dirt and rocks. If Thornwood kept anything in there, it was gone."

"He was so paranoid, he might have just made it for himself to hide if the villagers came for him with pitchforks, or something."

That made me laugh. "You watch too many vampire and Frankenstein movies." My watch alarm beeped, so I stopped leaning and shifted my weight. "You know, when I saw that light over here—maybe the hacker was doing like my mom's doing right now," I said. "Getting the lay of the place. Getting the right perspective."

Lavender switched off her flashlight. "Maybe he was scoping out important things."

"What important things?"

"Valuable stuff he wants to steal and sell?" Lavender sat up. "The best spots to spy on your house?"

I leaned my head against my headrest and stared at the dusty ceiling. Mom moved lamps again, and then she clicked away, taking her photos. Outside, Trooper Nelsen cleared his throat. "What if there's something here he needs?" I asked Lavender. "Or that he needed— for Thornwood's Revenge? For whatever he's planning to do to Toppy or the town?"

Lavender wrapped her arms around her knees and

looked thoughtful. "Money? Valuables? A cache of smallpox?"

"Very funny." I lifted my head and glared at her. "Not."

"Excuse me, sir," Trooper Nelsen called. "I'll need you to stop right there."

My heart gave a quick thump, and Lavender scrambled to her feet. I wheeled around in a hurry, heading back for the hall as outside, a man said something sharp to our guard.

The trooper answered with, "That may be, but again, stop where you are, and we'll sort this out."

"Max?" Mom said quietly as I rolled up next to her.

Lavender moved Mom's lamps against the far wall and stood on her other side. The three of us faced the entryway.

"But it's my house," came a familiar deep voice.

"Oh, great," Lavender muttered. "That's Junior."

I didn't know whether to feel relieved or terrified.

"Should we go out the back?" Mom asked, gripping my shoulder.

I just stared at her.

Reality dawned slowly, and then she looked miserable. "Oh, right. The chair. Only one ramp."

"I respect that, sir," said Trooper Nelsen. "But I'm responsible for the safety of the ladies inside."

"Ladies?" Junior sounded surprised. Maybe a little bit happy. "Is one of them Joy Springfield?"

"No, sir," Trooper Nelsen said. "Her daughter, Lavender, is here with Max and Max's mother."

Lavender gave Mom and me an oh-great look, then marched to the front door and opened it.

"Hi!" Junior said to her, still sounding sort of happy.

The trooper gazed at Lavender, waiting for her to indicate Junior was okay. Lavender didn't. She just gazed steadily at Junior and asked, "Do you want us to leave?"

"Well, I don't—no, I guess not." He stepped into view at the doorway, next to the trooper, looking huge in his jeans and black biker sweatshirt. "But what are you doing here?"

I rolled closer and tried to take the measure of him like Toppy would, studying everything from his jeans and *Harley Hog* T-shirt to his posture to the narrowing of his brown eyes and the sort-of-friendly look on his hairy face. Lavender leaned toward my chair, using her coat fuzz to hide the fact that she was messing with the zipper pouch under my chair arm.

Mom's eyebrows lifted, and I could tell she saw what Lavender was doing. Since I had no idea what that was, I kept my focus on Junior.

"We're searching for clues and trying to figure out

who the hacker is," I told him, watching for any reaction. "Did you move the stairs that led down into the hole?"

"I see." Junior looked surprised, then interested. "And yes, I put them out back. And, did you find anything new?"

"We didn't," I said. "But when you came here as a kid—ever see any ghosts?"

Junior offered me a quick grin. "Used to think I did. Sparkles in the hall. Cold places. Sometimes movement that I couldn't chase down. But honestly, Max, I think it was just kid stuff. My mind playing tricks."

"Do you have any idea how Vivienne Thornwood smuggled out her youngest daughter? The one that got killed by a carriage a few weeks later."

"Not really," Junior said. "Pleaded with some workers, my mother said, but I've never found that part of the story in any books. Maybe she handed her out a window."

"What do you know about the room underneath the floor?" Lavender asked him.

Junior's head swiveled to her. "Nothing."

I took my turn. "Any idea what your great-however-many-greats-grandfather might have kept in there?"

Back to me. He was probably getting a crick. "Knowing that crackpot old miser, it was probably money or gold or guns to shoot at anybody he thought was coming after his money or gold."

Lavender lobbed a big one with, "Do you think you'll get a lot at auction for your motorcycle lot?"

Big reaction: check!

Junior's face turned red so fast, I was worried the heat might burst through the top of his head. The trooper straightened and actually moved toward Junior, like he might step between us, but the porch chose that moment to shake and crack like it was trying to shoot us all.

"Whoa!" Junior stepped backward on the stairs, stumbled, then plopped on his rear end.

Mom ran past Trooper Nelsen, her camera bouncing as she hurried to the fallen man. "Are you all right, Mr. Thornwood? Here, give me your hand."

"Ladies," the trooper said, gesturing to the ramp. Lavender moved to the side, and I hit my joystick.

The chair shut off.

"Cripes!" I banged on the box. "What is wrong with you? I gave you all new fuses!"

I switched it off, then on again. Nothing. Off, on. My breath caught funny.

"Can I push you?" Trooper Nelsen asked.

I felt the back of my chair rattle as he took hold of it, heard Lavender explaining about the toggles in front of my big back wheels, and then Mom and Junior came up the stairs, and the porch really popped and cracked.

"Everybody off!" Trooper Nelsen ordered.

Mom and Junior hurried back down the steps, and the trooper was just bending down to flip the right manual push toggle when I tried my power button again, and this time it worked.

"Got it," I told him.

And since that was as good a time as any, I flipped my special superhero switch for extra speed and gave the joystick a push.

My chair didn't just roll. It *shot* down the ramp so fast I nearly peed myself in sheer terror. The end of the ramp flew toward me, and I knew I'd go airborne if I hit it going that fast. I hauled back on the joystick, engaging the stabilizers and brakes, but I forgot the turbo switch was still on and the chair lurched so hard it nearly tipped and splattered me face-first in the parking lot. My big wheels ground and spun, and I smelled all sorts of burning, melting nasty stuff, and the chair fishtailed before flinging itself backward and almost taking out Trooper Nelsen and Lavender, too.

They both bailed into the yard.

I smacked headrest-first into the ramp rails and my teeth rattled. My wheels were still spinning, burning rubber, trying to bash the chair straight through the railing. I imagined myself in freefall, tumbling and bouncing all the way down the hill to my house like some cartoon.

Hand shaking, I fumbled with the speed switch until I turned it off, took my hand away from the control, and sat trying to breathe while my wheels gradually stopped buzzing and turning.

Lavender pulled herself underneath the railing and back onto the ramp, looking frayed at the edges and really, really pissed. The trooper walked around and came up to me, mouth open.

"What," he asked, "was that?"

"Improvements," Lavender snarled before I could say anything.

"I—um." Breathe out. Breathe in. My face burned, half embarrassment, half frustration. "Uh, I might have overclocked."

"If that means you turned yourself into a cruise missile, then yeah." Lavender glared at me. "Max, that was almost worse than the manure pile."

"Manure?" This from Junior Thornwood, who had walked over to the ramp. He was standing wide-eyed at the bottom, blocking my way down.

"Never mind." Lavender pointed at me. "You're fixing THAT immediately, or I'm telling Toppy."

I glared right back at her. "Back off. If I'd run too fast and busted my head, nobody would freak out."

Lavender looked like I had slapped her.

Instant guilt.

It was enough to throw cold water all over any anger I had.

"Sorry," I said to her. "Really sorry."

She nodded.

Right about that very second, I remembered that my mother was here. She was standing next to Junior, tight-lipped, arms folded, and she wasn't saying a thing. Her expression was a mix of fear and something else. Something a lot like . . . admiration?

"Running too fast doesn't usually knock people over and nearly tear down wooden ramps," Trooper Nelsen pointed out.

The heat came roaring back, all of it, and it seemed to coalesce in my mouth and fire straight at him. "Aren't you just supposed to keep us safe? I don't think that includes opinions about wheelchair modifications."

He raised both hands and backed away, and immediately I felt like a jerk all over again After a few more breaths and closing my eyes for a count of three, I said, "Sorry," for the second time, and when I opened my eyes, he inclined his head, accepting my apology.

"Kid's got a temper," Junior said to my mother.

"Thank you, Captain Obvious," Lavender shot back. Then to me she said, "And I'm sorry, too, Max. Are you okay?"

"I think so." When I looked down at my control box,

I was shocked to see how little power I had left. "But that burst drained my juice to nearly nothing." I smacked my forehead. "I didn't think about the fact that the battery can't handle that much speed. Good thing I wasn't running from a bad guy for real, or I'd have run out of gas in about a minute."

"Can you fix that?" Lavender asked, sounding like she hoped I couldn't.

"Probably only with a better battery," I said.

"Or a second one," Trooper Nelsen said. "Not that I have opinions about wheelchair modifications."

I had to smile at him, all the while wondering where I could put a second battery without increasing mass and drag on the chair too much, because yeah, that probably *would* work.

My attention shifted to my mother, who still wasn't saying anything. Now she seemed distant, and maybe a little sad. Whatever. My wheelchair revisions weren't any of her business, either.

After another minute of deep breathing all around, we moved to the parking lot. It was Junior who broke the silence, saying to Mom, "I guess I need to tell the city to shut the place up for real, parking lot and all. Sounds like the porch is going."

Mom didn't talk to him, either.

"It's too bad, I know," he said like she might be listening anyway. His eyes darted to me, then shifted to

Lavender. "But, as the girls have already dug up from somewhere, I don't really have the money to fix it. I'd have to sell cheap, or turn it over to the city." He rubbed the back of his neck with one meaty paw. "Honestly, I came down here to scope it out myself, to see what I could do to repair it, maybe with some friends."

"It's way past do-it-yourself," the trooper noted. "Unless you guys work in construction."

"We don't." Junior sounded defeated.

Lavender looked confused. I could tell she wanted Junior to act suspicious or mysterious, but other than the little blast of anger we got when she embarrassed him, he seemed mostly like a sad, worried guy, not a bad guy.

"Well," he said, gesturing toward the house, "I'll let myself in a side door and poke around—see what's sound, and what's gone beyond hope of saving."

"I wouldn't advise that, sir," Trooper Nelsen said. "I don't think the old wood's appreciating this cold."

"Thanks," Junior said. "I've got my cell, so I can call if I get in real trouble." Then, to us he said, "I'm sorry, ladies, but I probably need to get all my keys back. If something happened to you up here, it'd be on me."

He held out his hand.

My heart sank.

"I don't have a key," Mom said. "And neither does Max." She glanced at Lavender, who made an irritated noise, put her hand to her collar to pull out her neck-lace, and then felt around, looking bewildered.

"My chain," she said. "The one I had the key on, it's gone." Her gaze jumped from me to Mom, then at the trooper, and finally back to the ramp. "Maybe it broke when I jumped."

This resulted in all of us poking around in the grass around the ramp, and the trooper doing a fairly thorough search with his flashlight, to see if anything glittered. Finally, he gave up and switched off the bulb.

"Don't see it, sir," he said. "It might just stay lost."

"I *liked* that chain," Lavender complained.

"Okay," Junior said. "I'll talk to your mom and get the rest of the keys—and if you find your chain, you can have her get the key back to me."

Lavender smiled at him, but I noticed she didn't agree to anything. As he walked away, Mom gave Lavender a look. Lavender's face filled with fake innocence. I thought about the pouch under my chair arm, and about how Lavender had messed with it. Carefully, without letting the trooper see, I felt the bag.

Something very chain-and-key-like seemed to be inside.

"Back to the house, ladies?" Trooper Nelsen asked us.

I reached over and touched Mom's hand. "Mom, Toppy left us the van. Would you drive Lavender and me to Bot's?"

She focused on me as she fiddled with her camera. "The electronics shop? Honey, it's Sunday afternoon. They'll be—"

"Open," Lavender and Trooper Nelsen and I chorused.

"This near to the holidays," I said, "trust me. Bot won't close until every light in Blue Creek shuts off."

16

It was nearing dark when we parked outside of Bot's, but the shop's lights blazed brightly out over Town Square.

Bot had fake-snow-sprayed *HAVE A JOYOUS EVERYTHING!!!* in all his windows, and other colored spray-snow statements bid everyone *Merry Christmas, Happy Chanukah, Happy Kwanzaa, Gracious Wishes for Tet, Excellent Festivus, Blessings on the Solstice,* and *Ramadan Mubarak.*

Lavender paused as the wheelchair ramp was lowering. "I thought Ramadan was in the middle of summer."

"It is," I said, barely missing her toes as I rolled off and peeled to the right, toward the shop door.

"I believe the Prophet Muhammad's birthday is around now," Mom mentioned as she folded the ramp up, then shut the van door.

"Don't tell Bot that," I said. "He'll accidentally do

something offensive trying to sell more computers."

"He only researches stuff so far," Lavender agreed.

When we got into the shop, I smelled pine and popcorn. Bot had on his Santa suit, and he was helping a young couple examining a toddler-proof iPad case. Ellis, obviously rebelling against the shop theme in his jeans and black T-shirt, showed off three different types of cell phones to another set of customers. Riley met us at the door, dressed in a green elf suit complete with bells, and handing out chocolate Kisses from a green felt bag.

"My favorite super-ladies," he crowed, and then eyeing Mom and the trooper taking up a position by the front door, he added, "And . . . escorts?"

Lavender's eyes rolled so high I wondered if she could see her own brain.

"If they freeze like that," I whispered to her, "Riley's going to accuse you of putting on the Irisless Eyemask of Mystery."

"I'm Batman," she mumbled, unrolling them and crossing them instead.

"You're Riley, right?" Mom stuck out her hand. "I think you had just come to live with Bot when I moved to California."

Riley took Mom's hand, planted a smack on her knuckles, then turned her hand over and pressed red and green candy Kisses into her palm. "My foster dad loves a challenge, m'lady. Says helping me out is penance for his past grievous sins."

"You're talking like an English court servant, not an elf," Lavender said.

He shrugged. "Other than *Lord of the Rings*, I got nothing."

I poked him in the shoulder. "Can we have Ellis for a few, when he's through with those people?"

"Sure, if we don't get a run." Riley's smile made him so cute I had to give Lavender a few taste points. "I can help for a while if you'll play greeter."

He turned his megawatt smile on Lavender and gave her a sweeping bow. She examined her frontal lobe again. But as soon as he wasn't looking, she grinned at him, then at me, and gave me a he's-completely-adorable wink.

"I'll greet," Mom said, and took his bag of Kisses.

She was off to man the door before I could thank her.

A few minutes later, Riley took over a few customer newcomers, and Ellis fired up his desktop with Lavender and me standing by on either side.

"What can I do you for this evening, Ms. Sherlock Max?" He flexed his fingers and let them hover over his keyboard.

"We need architectural plans for Thornwood Manor," I said. "I looked, but nothing's readily accessible except for state library archives that charge a fee."

Ellis pulled his hands back from the keyboard and studied me, his blue eyes lacking any expression I could identify. "Please tell me you're not driving your chair around that tumbledown junk-heap of a mansion."

"We're being careful," I assured him.

He still didn't move to type anything. "Why do you want the architectural plans? Did you find something?"

"Not really, no. We're just trying to look deeper. Cover every base—you know, since the hacker's so focused on Thornwood's Revenge."

Ellis glanced from me to Lavender, then came back to me. "Okay. But you might have more luck at the local library."

"Maybe we can go Tuesday," I said. "Because I want to know more about Vivienne Thornwood, too."

"Girls!" Bot boomed as his customers left the store, packages tucked beneath their arms. He came over to us and hugged Lavender, then me. He smelled like the chocolate Mom was giving out.

"Hey," I said as Bot let me go.

Ellis brought up one of his programs and typed in search phrases related to Thornwood. Then he stopped entering things and asked me, "How do you think Monday night will go?"

"I think it'll be fine," Lavender said.

"Oh, the Council mess?" Bot shook his head. "I can't

believe they're taking it so far. Chief Brennan has a lot
of people on his side."

"They can't blame my grandfather for some evil-
brained hacker," I said. "They just can't."

"You'd be surprised." Ellis frowned. "Has he thought
about taking time off?"

"Toppy never takes time off," I said. "And he's not
about to let some online bully run him out of his police
station."

"But if Chief Brennan took a leave of absence, at
least *acted* like he might resign," Ellis said, "the hacker
might stop. Maybe the guy just wants a win. Give him
one and see what happens."

Bot gave this some thought. "Ellis has a point. No
matter what hackers say or how flashy they get with
their crimes, their real motives can be pretty straightforward—like, to get a bunch of cash, or prove they're
better and smarter, or win some battle or other, even if
the fight's only in their own mind." He coughed. "Not
that I'd know much about what hackers want."

His eyes twinkled.

"I don't think this hacker will quit if the chief blinks in
this stare-off," Lavender said. "I think this guy would just
move on to the next target—probably Mayor Chandler."

"Maybe," Bot agreed. "Or maybe she's just a way
to get at the chief. He might do better protecting the
people he wants to protect if he gives this guy a little

bit of respect, you know? Let him tell the world about whatever made him mad, and the justice he seems to want so badly."

"Or that might make everything way worse," I said. "Make him think he has real power."

The twinkle left Bot's eyes, and even in his Santa suit, he seemed very serious all of a sudden. "Well, if the Council's meeting about the chief's job, seems like he does have power, right?"

I didn't know what to say to that, and neither did Lavender. Thankfully, a small flood of shoppers saved us, drawing Bot away from the desktop station and back toward Mom, who handed him as much chocolate as she gave the shoppers.

"So," Ellis said a little too lightly, like he wanted to keep Lavender and me from getting in bad moods. "Why are you suddenly interested in Vivienne Thornwood?"

"An untried angle," I said, having trouble putting my instincts into words. "Different perspective."

Honestly, I had no idea why I wanted to research her, save for a deep feeling that I should, that I was missing something major, and that it somehow related to her. Out loud, I added, "I think Mayor Chandler will veto anything unfair that the Council does. We'll be okay."

Ellis stared at something over my right shoulder— oh. Bot, doing a little dance and ringing a bunch of jingle bells.

"I think he goes further overboard every year," Lavender said.

"You think?" Ellis's laugh sounded strange. "He starts posting about Christmas in May, counting days. But I won't say anything against him. He gave me a job when my aunt died and I lost my home, and nobody else would let me work. Without Bot, who knows where I'd be."

He went silent for a minute or so, typing and clicking, moving around whatever paths he had found to hunt down Thornwood's floorplans. Then he clicked on a site I had seen before, but barely remembered, and popped up a picture with what looked like an app-generated architectural drawing, kind of like the ones people use to sell houses online. He clicked a set of arrows, and the picture expanded to fill his screen.

"That's it." Lavender leaned in. "There's the main floor. Scroll?"

Ellis complied, showing us all the floors, tower included, and then the underground room we thought might be a big priest hole or vault. On this diagram, it was marked "basement."

Lavender frowned. "This isn't the original plan. Just a copy, put up after the hidden room got discovered."

"So?" Ellis sounded confused. "It's just a basement, right?"

"I think it's something Thornwood built because he

was such a paranoid jerk," Lavender said. "I wonder if it used to go somewhere, you know, like a bolt-hole, or a safe room with a passage out of the house—but without doors, probably not."

"That would make so much sense," I said. "Especially since people really were trying to kill him."

"Except there's no other passages." Ellis gave a quick laugh. "Unless Thornwood's ghost sealed them all up or something."

He clicked off the picture. "So, did you guys figure out anything about Junior Thornwood?"

"Not much," I admitted. "When we nailed him about his motorcycle business being auctioned, he didn't deny it."

I gestured to Lavender. She gave me a sullen frown, but said, "He hasn't asked for money or made any moves to rip Mom off, not that I can tell."

"He just seemed all torn down because Thornwood's in such crappy shape," I added.

"He needs to go back where he came from," Lavender said.

"Yeah," Ellis agreed. "I don't like the coincidence of him showing up when Chief Brennan's trouble started."

My eyes strayed to the shop door, where Mom waved at a guy coming in and offered him candy. "Some people are good at showing up when there's trouble."

Ellis followed my gaze, then reached over and patted my hand. "Your mom probably came to Blue Creek to check on you, with all this mess going on. She just wants to take care of you."

"Something like that," I said, moving my hand away from his. I felt irritable and tired all of a sudden. My watch beeped, and I moved in the chair without thinking about it.

As if to make me stop being unhappy, Ellis said, "Listen, I'll try to get into the state architectural archives and see what I can find out about the original floorplans for Thornwood. I'll e-mail you if I get anything."

"Thanks," Lavender said. "I don't know if that will clear stuff up, or just confuse us more, but we'll try anything at this point."

At that, Ellis gave her a little salute, then got up to go help with the next wave of holiday buyers.

17

Lavender sat with me in the thankfully Mom-less kitchen as I got everything ready for Toppy's nighttime tea. It was getting later, and still no sign of him or Mayor Chandler. The fact that the big summit to prepare for the City Council meeting tomorrow night was running so long—that really worried me.

"What if they actually fire him?" I murmured to Lavender, who was trying again to discover the secrets of Toppy's crime board using yet another unblurring app.

"They won't," she said automatically. And then, "Pictures and writing, but I still can't make out any details." She put down the phone with a frustrated sigh. "We have to get back in that office—when we aren't upset this time, so I can focus."

I left Toppy's cup with honey and tea bags sitting by the electric kettle, rolled back to the table, and fished a silver paint pen out of my arm pouch. "If they fire him, he won't have the money to keep me," I said, writing *Fight* on top of some of the *Breathe*'s I hadn't already worn away, because I would fight not to leave my grandfather.

"Oh, again with the Toppy-wants-rid-of-me stuff?" Lavender made a gag-face. "You need to get off that."

"Maybe." I tried to act like she hadn't hurt my feelings.

Fight. Fight. One day I might get a tattoo with that word. I had to be eighteen for that, though. *Fight.* Definitely. Maybe right on my shoulder. Because I wasn't losing Toppy and my home and my friends without a major throw-down. I couldn't imagine trying to go to some new school in California, and trying to find new friends, and having to prove to everybody all over again that I had a brain and could really do stuff for myself.

Lavender went right on trying to unblur our crime board photos from Toppy's office at the station. I went right on *Fight*-ing and thinking about Toppy getting canned, and telling me that really, it was time, that he couldn't afford for me to stay and I needed to go back to California with Mom. Maybe all things really did obey money, after all.

"So," I said, my voice shakier than I wanted, "about the key you hid in my arm pouch."

"You should keep it," Lavender said. "Mom would only make me give it back."

"Your acting skills are getting pretty scary."

"Too bad my photo editing skills still stink." She grinned at me, and my hurt feelings eased a fraction.

I put up my silver paint pen as voices outside the kitchen got our attention, and a few seconds later, Ms. Springfield came to collect Lavender. I managed to keep a smile on my face, and while Mom was seeing Lavender and Ms. Springfield to the door, I got to my room and closed my door.

For a long bunch of minutes, I studied my photos from the trip to Thornwood. The entry hall with the too-clean grate, the too-clean fireplace, too. Really, that was the only thing unusual at all, that the hacker or intruder or whoever had polished up those spots, and nowhere else we could see.

I reached up and traced the swirly design of the entry hall grate and the bits of wire poking through it. No matter how many times I looked at the pictures, I didn't see anything new, but I just kept feeling like I should.

When I closed my eyes and rolled away from that dead end, I came face to face with our pitiful little corkboard, and its red cards seem to stare back at me, reminding me of all the different ways Thornwood's Revenge might descend upon us all.

Fire. $$$. Killing Spree.

I felt sick as I remembered *Fire* had already sort of

happened, at my school. And *$$$*—well, the website hacks had covered that category, A lot of businesses in Blue Creek had lost money over that, especially since it was the holidays, when people usually sold the most. That left *Killing Spree.*

My shivers came back. The only three yellow SUSPECT cards we had left, *Toppy, Junior Thornwood,* and *???,* didn't feel impressive. And underneath those, the purple MOTIVE cards—*Max Is Pathetic* for Toppy, *Publicity and Hype and $* for Junior, and *Punish Toppy for Arresting* and *Get Revenge on Toppy* and *Get Rid of Toppy* for *???*—also didn't help me figure anything out. We didn't have much for the MEANS and OPPORTUNITY cards.

"Police business," I muttered to myself. Mostly because Lavender and I didn't have enough information to even consider other suspects or motives, or who might have means and opportunity to be carrying out the attacks against my grandfather, the mayor, and really, the whole city.

Don't forget the fire, my mind whispered. *That one might have been an attack against* you.

An attack Toppy had saved me from, of course.

Deep in my heart, I knew my grandfather didn't want to get rid of me. Lavender was right. That whole line of thinking, it was just pathetic. I pulled down his cards, turned my chair away from the corkboard, and

rolled over to the table near my window. I couldn't
help gazing out at Thornwood Manor and noticing that
Junior had left some lights on. For all I knew, he was
still up there. Or maybe it wasn't him at all. Maybe the
hacker had broken in again.

"The bad guy isn't Junior." I felt the let-down inside
as I said it, but I knew it was true. So, iPad in hand, I
rolled back to the corkboard and pulled off his card.

For a time, I stared at the red cards and the single
suspect, the card that read only *???*. My eyes moved
down to the purple MOTIVE card beneath it, and I
felt completely frustrated that I couldn't do anything
to help my grandfather or myself. I couldn't stand that
feeling, not even a little bit.

I opened the iPad. For a while I just stared at the
empty search bar. On impulse, I plugged **Thornwood**
into the search engine. Dozens of headlines popped up
immediately, but I had seen most of them. They were
just variations on stories run by the local news stations.

Except—

Hmm . . .

Thornwood hits on eBay were new. Was that a picture of a table?

It was!

I clicked to the offering, which was posted today.

The table . . .

I rolled back over to my pictures, held up the iPad for comparison—and sure enough, the photo on eBay looked just like one of the hall tables in the picture I took, right down to its cobwebbed legs.

"Who would pay thousands for a dusty old table?" I shook my head and clicked around. Thornwood chairs, for thousands. A clock, for more thousands. There was the dining room table! All in all, I counted a hundred listings, all posted this morning, and I found a bunch of the offered stuff in the pictures I had taken. If people bought the items, the seller would make hundreds of thousands of dollars.

Did Junior put this stuff up for sale? I clicked to look at the seller's name. John Smith, and it listed a PO Box address in Arizona. Probably not Junior then, unless he wanted to hide making money from the people he owed up North.

Mom.

Mom could have taken lots of shots, and—no. Wait. She didn't have time to clean off the tops of the furniture pieces and stage them for good shots before Junior interrupted us, and she didn't have a key to go back and do it on her own.

This felt shady. I pulled open my Notes and copy-pasted several of the entries. Something else to show Ellis, and to give to Toppy. Maybe this big-time try at stealing the stuff right out of the mansion would get my grandfather some federal help.

For my next search, I typed in **Vivienne Thornwood.** Her image came up immediately, the one in the painting at Thornwood Manor—lots of different angles, a few other paintings and some articles.

I rolled to my bed, lifted myself onto the mattress, stretched out facing my wall, and scrolled through the articles. Mostly, they were just different retellings of the Thornwood legend with a mention of the daughter she managed to sneak out of the house—but no specifics. A few pieces talked about how old she was, or where she grew up, and how smart and kind she had seemed. Overall, though, there wasn't much about her.

I frowned.

Vivienne Thornwood had lived and died at Thornwood Manor—but she seemed like a footnote. She wasn't allowed to be her own story. Was it because she was a woman? I scrolled past another shot of her oil-painted curls and came to rest on that seriously spooky picture of Thornwood himself.

"She couldn't have her own story because he wouldn't let her," I decided, staring into Thornwood's empty eyes. "I bet nobody in his life got their own story. He acted so greedy and awful, everyone else turned invisible."

I knew what invisible felt like, because sometimes my wheelchair turned me invisible. People stepped on me or got totally in my way in the school hallway, or didn't seem to see me when I was crossing the street.

Of course, I wasn't really invisible, and being treated like that made me more determined to be seen, to be heard. That made me think of something Bot said about my grandfather earlier, at the computer store.

No matter what hackers say or how flashy they get with their crimes, their real motives can be pretty straightforward. . . .

I sat up trying to figure out why that bothered me so much, and just then, my door creaked.

Mom walked into my room, closed the door behind her, and started to speak to me, but her attention got pulled to the corkboard and the few colored cards left hanging for all to see. A bunch of emotions played bumper cars in my chest, and I couldn't name any of them.

"We had a lot of suspects to start with," I said, irritation winning out—but not irritation with Mom, for once. "Just . . . no good ones, I guess."

Mom studied the board. "Well, the stuff on the red cards is a little scary."

"Lavender and I tried to guess what the hacker would try to do, based on all the legends about Thornwood's Revenge." I waved a hand at the potential disasters we hadn't discarded. "Those are the ideas we didn't toss."

When Mom turned to look at me, she said, "You've been working this case pretty hard."

"Yeah. But we haven't gotten anywhere."

She came closer to me, her expression serious. "You work on everything pretty hard."

"I try." I also tried not to move away from her. That was my instinct, but it seemed mean.

Mom watched me, and then she sat down on the edge of my bed. "I think I realized how hard you work on a whole new level today. What you did with your chair's speed—that was amazing."

"And reckless."

"Lots of brilliant things have a little bit of reckless in them. Innovation is risky and it doesn't always go smoothly."

I couldn't help the laugh, honest. Or the, "What, did you take a philosophy class since I saw you the last time?"

"Maybe I took a Max class." She grinned, and didn't seem offended at all. "I realized I don't work as hard as you do. I give up too easily."

The bumper car emotion explosion started back, this time in my belly. Dread bashed into Worry, and both of those plowed into Pissed Off, but Nervous squirted out ahead. "Wait. Is this about me? About us?"

"Yes." Mom fiddled with the bed covers, but she

held my gaze like she did when she was telling the truth. "When I drove here, I had one thought: that I needed to get you, to take you back to California where you'd be safe."

Nervous blasted away from all the other feelings, and my jaw locked in place. Mom must have seen the NO WAY in my eyes, because she nodded. "I know. And today, I think I got a piece of *why* I don't need to take you home with me."

She stopped talking for a second, and her throat worked like she might be swallowing a lump. I waited, dealing with my own throat-lump. Her eyes wandered to my chair, to my armrests and the new silvery *Fight* marks.

"Even if I had a workshop like Toppy's," Mom said, "I never would have let you try to modify your chair. I probably wouldn't even have let you get used to painting and etching and welding stuff all over it. I'd have been too afraid you'd get hurt, or that people might get the wrong idea about who you are as a person."

Fight. I ran my finger over the word. "Toppy says the chair is part of my body, so what I do with it is my decision."

"He's smart like that. That's why you need him, and he needs you, too, even more than I do."

"You don't need me." My words burst out, almost like a laugh or a swear. "You gave up on me."

"I gave up on me, not you." Mom's expression turned

flat and distant. "I sent you to live with Dad because I had no idea how to be a good mother to you, not after the wreck."

That didn't make any sense to me. "Why would it be any different, being a good mom when I could walk and being a good mom when I couldn't?"

"I don't know. But it felt different." Her expression just kept getting more distant. "Maybe because you getting hurt was my fault. And maybe because I could tell I was being too scared, saying 'no' to you all the time when you needed 'yes' instead."

Since I barely remembered being little and living with her, I didn't remember her saying "no" all the time. But I believed her.

"I didn't want you to get hurt again," she said. "And I really didn't want to let you down a second time."

"You did," I said.

"I know."

"I don't want to live with you."

"I know that, too."

I changed positions in my chair out of nerves, not because it was time to shift.

"Did you—" I almost choked, but I made myself ask a really important question, at least for my heart. "Did you ever really want me? Before the accident, I mean?"

Mom's mouth came open. "Of course I wanted you.

You weren't planned, not at that age, but when I found out I was going to have you, I was *so* happy." Emotions flickered across her face too fast for me to keep up with them. "And the accident didn't change how much I wanted you in my life."

I fidgeted in my chair. "What did it change, then?"

It was a long time, and a lot of face-changing, before Mom came up with, "My confidence, I guess." And then, "I don't honestly know."

You can't always make something haul the load you want it to, Max, Toppy's voice said in my head. *Not when it wasn't made to do that work.*

For a strange second or two, I saw my mother as one of my circuit boards, blinking and flaring and burning out into dark nothingness. Then I saw her as that picture from her yearbook, just five years older than I was right now, not knowing what she wanted to be, or where she wanted to live—not knowing what would happen to her, not at all.

"I . . . wouldn't mind if you visited more, Mom." There. That wasn't so awful. Except it kinda felt scarier than Thornwood's creepy picture, and even the fire at my school. "It hasn't been awful this time. Not the you part, anyway. The only awful thing right now is the hacker."

"Guess we're uniting against a common enemy?"

Mom met my gaze again, and she looked so sad I wanted to get out my silver paint pen and draw a glittering teardrop below one of her eyes. "Like the superheroes you used to talk about all the time when you were younger."

"Maybe."

"I heard what you said in the workshop." She gestured to my chair. "About working on your chair to turn yourself into a superhero in real life. If you really could be a superhero, any of them, which would you pick?"

"It changes," I admitted. "But right now I'd pick Mr. Terrific. He's from DC, not Marvel."

"Why him?"

"He's got fourteen doctoral degrees, and he's brilliant in, like, everything." I jerked a thumb toward my pathetic corkboard. "It would be nice to be smart enough to track down this hacker and get him off Toppy's back. But honestly, Mom, I'm kinda past wanting to be a superhero. I just want to be . . . super."

She looked confused.

That was okay, because I felt confused.

"Super," I tried again. "More like heroes are supposed to be. Like, not getting mad all the time, and not saying mean stuff, and not doing things without thinking and making trouble I don't even intend to make."

"That's hard," Mom said. "I'm not sure I've got those things mastered, even at my age—but can I help you with any of it?"

"No, thanks, but—wait. You maybe could help with tracking the hacker and saving Toppy's job, but only if you're willing to break rules and really make him really, really mad."

Mom folded her arms. "Try me."

"I'm going to send you a photo." I held up the iPad. "It's too blurry for Lavender and me to read. We've been trying unblurring apps, but we're not getting anywhere. Maybe you could."

"What's this a picture of?" Mom's suspicious tone told me she realized I hadn't been kidding about rule-breaking and Toppy-infuriating.

"A better crime board than ours."

Pause. Eyebrow-scrunching. And then Mom said, "Okay."

I pulled up the photo and sent it to her phone, and heard the ding when it hit. A few seconds later, Mom got some more dings, and so did I, but my brain was turning too many circles to care.

"For now, will you take down the rest of the cards on my corkboard?" I turned to my desk, to the stack of cards Lavender brought over, and chose a blue one. I thought about what I had read about Vivienne Thornwood before Mom came in, and how she was the one who had a right to revenge, way more than Hargrove ever did.

So, what if the hacker wasn't a flashy, showy

take-up-all-the-air-space person like Hargrove? What if the hacker was a quiet person who had actually been wronged, like Vivienne, who got tired of nobody knowing, nobody seeing?

I wrote in black marker, *Tired of Being Invisible.*

Mom handed me the old cards and I dropped them in the trash. When she put up the new card, I felt better, even though I didn't really know why.

I thought more about Vivienne Thornwood and how she never got her own story because her husband controlled absolutely everything, even their legend, and I wrote, *Might Have Been Overshadowed by a Bad Person.*

Mom hung that one up under the first one.

Next, I thought about what Mayor Chandler said about Vivienne Thornwood, about how she might have loved her husband even with all his flaws, and I wrote, *Might Love a Bad Person Even Though They Know the Person Is Bad.*

After she hung up the third card, I said, "Do you think maybe Toppy and the police are searching for the wrong kind of suspect?"

Mom gave me an over-the-shoulder questioning look. "What do you mean?"

"Well, they're hunting for criminals who want to get even with Toppy for arresting them." I pointed at the board. "They're assuming the person doing this is a bad guy, like Hargrove Thornwood. Maybe they should be looking for people like Vivienne Thornwood instead—people who got hurt in the situation, like family members of bad guys who Toppy arrested. Husbands or wives, boyfriends or girlfriends, brothers or sisters, maybe even kids. I mean, if somebody really hurt Toppy, I'd try to get even. Wouldn't you?"

"Maybe," she said, and not in that ignore-a-kid way. "It's a good theory."

"Wait! There's a couple more." I scribbled, *Probably Knew About Detention*, and handed that one to Mom, too, followed by *Probably Local* and *Probably Knows Us Pretty Well*. I finished with *Has Good Computer Skills or Money to Hire Hacker*.

She hung the card on the board, off to the side. I snapped a picture of the board.

Tired of Being Invisible.

Might Have Been Overshadowed By a Bad Person.

Might Love a Bad Person Even Though They Know the Person Is Bad.

Probably Knew About Detention.

Probably Local.

Probably Knows Us Pretty Well.

Has Good Computer Skills or Money to Hire Hacker.

There. Those cards felt right. I opened my iPad to send the picture to Lavender, along with the notes about by eBay discoveries.

That's when I found the **WHERE ARE YOU??** message.

And, **Have you seen the news?**

And, **OMG, Max, it's happening! THORNWOOD'S REVENGE!!**

I closed the iPad, crammed it next to my leg, and rolled straight at Mom and the bedroom door. She jumped out of the way. "Max?"

"Check your messages," I said as I threw open the door. "And come on. We need to turn on the television."

18

I got the television on in the living room just as Mom caught up with me. She had her phone in her hand. "Mayor Chandler messaged. She said to stay inside. And Ms. Springfield wants to know if we're okay." She typed fast with her thumbs. "I'm telling them both that we're fine."

" . . . night of chaos in tiny Blue Creek, Tennessee, to our north," the newscaster was saying in the special report. "Multiple residents are reporting that their bank accounts have been cleaned out, and it's possible the town's general fund has been plundered. On top of that, several small fires are blazing in what looks like coordinated vandalism."

"Not good," Mom whispered as she put her phone in her pocket. I felt her hand grip my shoulder, and I didn't push her away.

Fires? My eyes squeezed shut from the memory of

what happened at school. For a second, I could smell that smoke again. My chest got so tight I couldn't even take a whole breath. Then I forced my lids open and stared at the television.

The newscaster kept talking; burning trash cans had been left outside of one of Blue Creek High's buildings, Blue Creek Nursing Home, an abandoned storage center on the outskirts of town, and the office of Blue Creek's only commercial car lot. The fires were small, but they made a lot of smoke and set off alarms everywhere. Police, firefighters, and first responders were running in every direction due to nonstop calls reporting bomb threats, fraud, theft, and just about anything else that creaked in the night.

"Honey, be careful," Mom said. "You're about to dig holes in your armrests."

I glanced down at my fingers. They were curled, my nails poking hard against the leather. My whole body felt rigid. I still couldn't breathe right.

How far would this go? What if the fires came to my house—or to the police station? Toppy had to stop this. I had to help him. I *had* to.

"The voice calling in the threats sounds like a drone," a frustrated nine-one-one operator said on the television screen, talking into the wide-eyed reporter's microphone. "And different numbers show up on the ID each time."

"They're spoofed," I said, my words coming out in a cracked whisper.

"What?" Mom's voice sounded shaky.

"You can do it with a computer," I told her. "There are apps for making phone calls through the Internet. You can put in whatever number you want as the origin—like the e-mail hoaxer did to you through your website."

"Is that supposed to make me feel better?"

" . . . and the total haul from the cyberthefts is estimated to be nearly a million dollars," the announcer continued. "That total could climb tomorrow as more Blue Creek residents wake to this nightmare and check their accounts and assets."

Our front door, which was hardly ever locked, burst open. My heart almost burst open, too. I sat up straight and opened my mouth to scream. Mom jumped in front of me, and then—"Max?" Captain Coker sounded worried.

"Here!" I called back, relief flooding me with heat. "It's okay, Mom. Captain Coker's good." Mom edged to the side of me, her fists raised like she had been planning to punch a monster right in the nose.

I heard the door shut, locks being engaged—and then Captain Coker was striding into the room, closing blinds as she moved. The look on her face made my heart race.

"Ladies," she said in a steady, firm tone, "I need you

to shut off that television and step away from these windows. Ms. Brennan, take yourself a chair into the hallway and sit between the kitchen and the bedrooms, out of line of sight of any doors or windows. Max, follow her."

I followed.

"What's happening?" Mom asked as she arranged her chair as instructed.

"I'm not sure," Captain Coker admitted, and somehow that was even more terrifying than what we had seen on television. "Emergency lines are jammed, websites and automated town functions crashed, bank accounts and public funds have been wiped out, traffic lights have lost their minds, and we've got a bunch of threats coming in. Little fires, broken glass, charred walls and doors, but nothing's burning out of control. Least of our problems. I think the vandal just meant to scare people."

"Where's Toppy?" I asked, surprised I could say anything at all.

"He's at the station with the mayor, working on this mess," Captain Coker said. "He's mad as all get-out, but he's fine. He called me himself to make sure we had you two covered, and I happened to be coming on shift to relieve the trooper you dragged all over the earth today."

Mom let out a nervous laugh. It sounded like a squeak.

She sank into the chair she had carried into the hall and started messing with her phone. I opened my iPad and told Lavender that we were safe at home with Captain Coker. I also resent her the photo of our reorganized corkboard, but I didn't figure she'd look at it right away.

"We'll just stay here away from the windows and doors for a while," Captain Coker said, "until things settle down out there."

Mom bent down and kissed me on the cheek.

It didn't feel bad, having her next to me, so I sort of felt mean, but not really, for the next thing I said.

"I want Toppy," I whispered.

"Okay," Mom whispered back.

Captain Coker said, "I'll see what I can do."

At 2:17 am, when headlights finally swept into our driveway and I heard the *ping-ping* of a familiar old engine, I lowered my head to the workshop floor and lay still, wanting to sob with relief.

Toppy. Home at last. Home with me and safe, where he belonged.

It didn't take him long to check inside the house, then come out to find me in the workshop, my State Police guard manning the door and the propane heater roaring away in the background. I had books about electricity spread everywhere, and my iPad lying on the worktable. The floor looked like ten toolboxes got sick and vomited wires and wrenches and screwdrivers in every direction.

Normally, he would have hollered for an hour about that level of mess and disorganization in his sacred fixing-stuff space. This time, though, all he said was, "You should be in bed."

I put my finger on my place in the electronics trouble-shooting guide I had found and looked up from my spot on the workshop floor. "I slept for a while."

He was standing there in his wrinkly uniform, his shoulders stooped and his eyes heavy with fatigue, holding what looked like a plastic shopping bag.

"Do I want to know what you're doing?" he asked.

"My chair keeps shutting off. I'm trying to figure out why." I marked my place with a long screw, then closed the book I was using. "It's bugging me."

Toppy rubbed the back of his neck with his hand, and the gesture made him look twice as old and three times more tired. "You know, we could actually call the company for a repair."

"I've modified so much stuff, they'd have a heart attack and pronounce it unsafe and illegal and probably a risk to society." I tried to smile, but had a hard time.

He grunted. "Well, any luck?"

"The problem is, some aspects are wireless and some are wired." Butterflies cascaded through my stomach. Something about my grandfather's manner scared me almost as much as anything that had happened tonight, but I kept babbling, hoping it would all get better. "My wired stuff is all good with consistent current, but the wireless is hard to test. Plus, stuff outside the chair can affect it."

"Wireless, but not hooked up to any networks, right?"

"Right. I disabled the reporting-to-manufacturer stuff right away. So whatever's happening, it must be something random—except, it's always happening at the same place."

"Thornwood," Toppy said. "Seems like the solution might be to stay away from Thornwood, Max."

"Somebody's trying to sell all the antiques out of Thornwood on eBay," I said. "The seller account looks like a fake. It's probably the hacker."

"Well, isn't that just par for the course tonight," Toppy said. "He's getting greedier and greedier, like old Thornwood himself. Maybe he'll make his big mistake soon and tip his hand. I sure hope so."

When I didn't answer, Toppy walked over to me, crouched, then sat down beside me on the workshop floor. Almost immediately, he shifted his butt and groused that the concrete was cold.

"Yeah, it's chilly," I said, "but I'm used to it."

"I need a better heat source out here. Maybe a wood-burning stove, or one of those new pellet-jobbies."

"Did you catch anybody?" My question popped out so loud it startled me. "I mean, in town. All the stuff." My fingers pulled into fists, because I needed him to say yes, even though I knew he was going to say—

"No." Toppy brought the bag he'd been carrying across his lap, then set it in front of me. "Here. This is for you."

I pulled myself into a sitting position and peeked into the plastic. Inside was a box holding a decent-model smartphone.

A month ago, this would have made me the happiest Max on the planet, but after the night we'd had, it made me nervous instead. I glanced up at Toppy's unreadable expression. "Why did you get me this?"

He opened his mouth. Closed it. His face stayed all flat and professional-like, but his eyes—something was really wrong.

I steadied myself on my butt and put down the bag. "Toppy, what's the matter?"

"I—uh." He gestured to the bag beside my leg. "You need one. To, you know, call me whenever you want." Pause. Frown. Rubbing the sides of his face.

Oh, this was bad. Worse than bad. I felt like I was freezing solid to the floor, turning to ice.

"Max," Toppy finally managed. "Tonight, in town, things were bad." He rubbed his face again, and I noticed the smudges. Soot, it looked like. And his jacket, it was torn. "Fires and threats—we couldn't be everywhere at once. People were terrified."

Had I ever seen my grandfather look so tired? So unhappy? I shivered as I tried to think of something to say to ease his mind.

"This hacker," Toppy went on, "he's moving things to a whole new level. It's too dangerous in Blue Creek right now."

"Too dangerous." I felt like I was turning to ice. Frozen. A winter statue. "You mean for me?"

Toppy nodded.

"That's stupid." I had never in my life been so angry that I couldn't just jump up and hit somebody, or run. Really run, and never stop until I found the perfect place to hide. "I'm fine here. I've got a guard, and Mom, and you. I'm safe!"

"I worried about you every minute, all night," he whispered. "I should have done this after the school fire, but I guess I was being selfish, wanting you with me."

"Stop talking!" I jerked my hands off the cold floor and covered my ears. "Don't say it!"

Toppy frowned. I didn't move my hands. So he talked loud enough for me to hear him anyway. "Max, you have to go stay with your Mom until we get this mess settled."

I kept my chilled fingers crammed against my ears and started yelling. I didn't even know what I was saying. I didn't even know what I was thinking.

Except, Toppy's face. . . the tears in his eyes . . .

My heart tore and fell into a million pieces, and I started to cry, too.

When my grandfather scooped me up and pulled me into his lap like I was five, I beat on his shoulders for a few seconds. He didn't let me go, and he let me cry and say ugly things to him, and cry some more.

When I finally wore myself down to quiet sniffles, he kissed the top of my head and said, "This hacker business is out of hand, Max."

I didn't talk to him. I couldn't.

"My old Sienna will never make it cross-country. New wheelchair van will be here Tuesday morning, and I'll transfer the title to your mother so you two can take it to California."

"Stop," I whispered. "Don't. Just, don't, okay?"

Toppy rocked me, and I wanted to tell him to knock it off, but I couldn't do that, either.

"It won't be forever," he said.

"You're lying!"

"I never lie to you, Max. You know that."

After a time, he got up from the cold workshop floor, and he carried me to bed, telling the guard to shut off the heater and drive the chair inside.

When he put me in the bed and covered me up, I turned over and stared at the wall. I didn't want to look at him, and I didn't want to talk anymore. I didn't even want to keep my eyes open.

It didn't take long for me to cry myself to sleep.

I dreamed about a parliament of owls descending on Blue Creek, tearing everything apart with their bramble-covered talons.

19

DECEMBER 11

SCHOOL CANCELLED . . ."
  "ACCOUNTS ROBBED . . ."
  "CARS AND BUILDINGS VANDALIZED . . ."
"BEDLAM IN BLUE CREEK . . ."
"COUNCIL TO EVALUATE OPTIONS . . ."

I had about a dozen Facebook and iMessages from Jace and Cindy and other kids at school that I just didn't feel like answering. I checked the newsfeeds on my iPad every so often, wincing at the brutal headlines, and messaged back and forth with Lavender from the workshop.

Lavender: Is Toppy home?

Me: He left before I got up.

Lavender: The new corkboard looks cool.

Me: Cool but useless. I'm checking connections between the sites hit last night and also working on my chair. High school, nursing home, abandoned building, car lot. What do these places have in common?

Lavender: They're all in Blue Creek?

Me: Very funny. My new phone is almost charged. I'll call.

Lavender: I don't want to talk about you going to California.

Me: Me neither.

Mom finally came out to check on me around noon. She handed the trooper guarding the door a steaming mug of something-or-other, then brought over a sandwich and chips for me.

The second she put it down, I started getting hot inside, but when she set the plate down beside me, I made myself say, "Thanks."

I put my mock control box aside, but kept hold of my screwdriver, squeezing it way too hard.

Mom scrubbed her hands against her jeans, then rubbed her arms through her dark green sweater. I waited for her to sit, but she kept standing, obviously worried about something.

Finally, she came out with, "Are you angry with me?"

"Yes!" Too loud.

Too bad.

"I'm mad at you. I'm mad at Toppy, too!" My voice just kept getting louder. "And that disgusting hacker. And the mean, hateful City Council. Maybe I'm just mad at everybody."

My face burned. My head started to pound, right at the temples where it made my vision blur. "And I really don't want to talk about it. Why did you come out here?"

"I thought you might be hungry," Mom said quietly.

I had to quit breathing so hard just to hear her. I was out of my chair so I couldn't read whatever *Breathes* or *Fights* hadn't gotten wiped off yet—and I didn't feel like listing superheroes right now. No matter what I did to my chair or my heart or my mind, I couldn't haul this load.

Just don't hurt people, that therapist told me about when I got really REALLY mad and couldn't hold back. *Just don't hurt yourself.*

I threw the screwdriver as hard as I could in the other direction, away from Mom. It clattered against the shop's aluminum walls, and that felt good.

Mom didn't even blink.

I threw a second screwdriver.

Then I threw a wrench. It made a really, really loud noise.

"Cool," Mom said. "Like breaking plates, only without all the glass."

The throb in my head was easing, but every muscle in my body felt wrapped too tight. I stared at Mom, but at least I didn't want to hurl anything at her head.

"We'll make it like a winter vacation to the beach, okay?" she said. "We'll take your paints and markers, and your engraving tools, and I'm sure I can find you a garage that'll let you work on your chair."

Breathe. Come on, Max. In and out. Just keep breath-ing. I made myself look Mom in the eye. "Can I get a tattoo?"

Still too loud, but better.

Mom's mouth came open. Then closed. Then opened again. "That's cheating, Max."

"It was worth a shot."

We went several minutes without talking, and I did a lot of breathing, and made it all the way to Spider-Man in the Marvel S's. The heat slowly, slowly faded, and then I got a little cold.

"What have you been doing out here all morning?" Mom asked.

"I built a new model of my controls so I could exper-iment with what might shut them off without destroying my actual controls."

"I wouldn't have thought to do that," Mom admitted.

That made me laugh. "Yeah, well, I'm no genius. I blew up my actual control box last year, and since then I work on models first."

"Toppy never tells me when you blow stuff up," Mom said. "Which is probably for the best. Have you figured anything out?"

"Power surges will do it." I reached over and patted the chair. "If enough current goes through the control-ler, it overloads the wireless parts, and *zap*. Then, after a few seconds, it'll power up again."

"So . . . you were getting power surges at Thornwood?" Mom looked completely confused.

"I don't think so." I poked at my sandwich with one fingertip. Roast beef and provolone. I actually liked that, as long as she used spicy mustard.

"All the wiring in that place is probably decades old," Mom said. "Wouldn't that be enough to shoot a few sparks and cause the problem?"

"No, you don't understand." I picked up the sandwich and tried a bite. The tang of the mustard made my eyes water. Perfect. After I swallowed, I tried to explain. "If something was electrified, or that much power was traveling through stuff at Thornwood, we should have gotten shocked—or at least the people touching metal things or not on rubber wheels—and how would it travel through my wheels, anyway? I'm grounded the same way a car is if lightning hits it, you know?"

"No, I really *don't* know. Sorry. I know exactly nothing about wires and currents." Mom rubbed her hands together. "Would Ms. Springfield be able to tell you if there's anything electrical at Thornwood that's acting up? Or maybe Junior would know?"

"Couldn't hurt to ask, I guess." I reached over and scooped up my iPad and messaged the question to Lavender. Then I asked Mom about the blurry photo. "Have you had any luck getting us a clear image?"

"It's better, but you can't read anything yet," she said. "I've got some software downloading on my Mac. I'll keep working on it."

"Good luck with downloading on our Internet," I told her. "Toppy's connection isn't much better than dial-up. I mostly use the iPad's wireless signal for any data and surfing."

"Yeah, I figured that out." Mom's smile didn't quite reach her eyes. "I've been using my phone as a hotspot. Speaking of which, last night, Dad called me to ask which phone to get you. He wanted one that worked well with your iPad. Just wanted you to know he gave it a lot of thought."

"I really don't—I mean, he didn't have to do that."

Mom bit her bottom lip. "Have you tried the phone yet?"

"I'll check the charge in a few minutes and call Lavender," I said, really not wanting to talk about the phone, or going to California, or any of it.

"Sounds good." And then, "I really am sorry, Max. About . . . everything."

She sounded like she meant it.

"We're going to the City Hall for the Council meeting tonight," I said. Not a question. More like a bargaining chip. Give this to me, and I won't throw a fit about having to suffer in California for a while.

Mom gave me a stare just shy of one Toppy might muster when he was shocked by something I said or did. I waited for her to argue with me, but she stuffed her hands in her jeans pockets. "Okay," she said. "I'll work that out."

20

How did you get these made so fast?" I asked Lavender, gaping at the purple hoodie she handed me in front of City Hall, which stood across from the police station, on the opposite side of Town Square from Bot's Electronics.

Stenciled gold letters on the front read, *Support Toppy.* On the back, the letters said, *Punish Hackers, Not Victims.*

"Mom did them with the heat press at Something Wicked," Lavender said as she handed Mom her own hoodie. Lavender was already wearing hers, and when she jerked her thumb toward her mom, who was holding the front doors open, I saw that Ms. Springfield matched. To my surprise, Junior Thornwood was with her, and he was wearing a *Support Toppy* hoodie, too. He scanned the crowd beginning to surge into Town Square, and when I followed his gaze, I saw lots of State

Troopers, a local news crew, and a couple of news vans from Nashville, too.

Poor Toppy.

He hated attention like this.

I went straight to the restroom and put my sweat-shirt on, and touched the letters of his name. The message went well with the black-outlined yellow *STOP THE MADNESS* I had painted across the back of my chair. On my right leather armrest, I had written *Focus* in bright silver. On the left armrest, I had printed *Believe* in gold. On both arms, I had carefully inscribed *Strong*, using a blue paint pen.

Mom came into the bathroom behind me, holding her purple hoodie. She glanced around. "Wow, that stall is tiny."

"Yeah," I told her. "I wouldn't fit even on the side that's supposed to accommodate wheelchairs. Lots of bathrooms are like that. There's another in the back of the building, just a single toilet—I can go there if I need to."

Mom frowned. Then she pulled on her hoodie, cover-ing the nicer blouse she had picked for the meeting. Her hair got static-y from touching the fabric, and it poofed up, curling around her face in bright red rings.

She examined herself in the mirror. "I don't know about this," she said.

"Toppy says being quiet in the face of injustice never helped anything," I told her.

Mom didn't agree or disagree. She just looked nervous as she held the door for me to roll out. Without commenting, she followed me down the hall, watching as I dodged at least four people who didn't see the chair and almost stepped on me.

When a fifth person stumbled over my legs, Mom said, "I think I'll get you a boat horn."

"That would be awesome," I said. "I've always wanted to make people's ears bleed when they won't get out of my way."

She held the door to the City Council chamber, and I rolled inside.

Blue Creek was a small town, but the chamber was nice enough, with paneled walls, track lighting, and a very blue carpet. There were two large screens hanging on the far wall, behind seven chairs built into a wooden semicircle underneath the town crest. An American flag and a Tennessee flag bracketed the crest.

Each seat had a nameplate and microphone in front of it. The chairs faced a center table that had a bench built to face the Council seats. Behind all that was a gallery with theater-like chairs, only they weren't cushy and comfortable, just old, with rundown blue leather covers. A lot of people had crammed into those chairs, and more were standing in the handicapped section. When Mom asked them to move, they tried to throw her some attitude, and got Lavender, Ms. Springfield,

Mom, and Mayor Chandler in their faces.

As the interlopers hung their heads and shuffled out of the wheelchair section, Mayor Chandler motioned me forward. "Sorry about that," she said.

"Happens a lot," I told her. "You're lots better at getting people to move than the movie theater ushers."

Mayor Chandler, looking elegant in her black slacks and blue sweater, shot the rude people one last epic frown. Then she gestured for Mom and Ms. Springfield and Lavender to have a seat nearby.

"Is Toppy ready?" I asked the mayor.

"If by ready you mean dressed in his best uniform and pinkie-sworn not to holler at anybody for being ignorant, then yes." She smoothed imaginary wrinkles out of her sweater. "A little nervous about you being here, though."

"I know some people may say ridiculous stuff," I told her. "I won't believe any of it."

"I think he's more worried you'll tell them off." Mayor Chandler smiled at me. "I reminded him you were smart, and that you knew a lot better than that."

From somewhere nearby, Lavender broke into a full-fledged laughing fit. Her mother chastised her, but she kept right on giggling and snorting.

"I'll be fine," I told Mayor Chandler. "Except, when I murder my best friend, you'll help me hide the body, right?"

She saluted, face grave. "I've got your back, Max."

Then she gave me a pat on the shoulder and headed to the middle seat on the Council dais, the one underneath the city crest and between the flags. State Troopers filed in and took up positions here and there along the walls, eyes wide and alert.

"So many people," Mom said from my right, sounding anxious. Ms. Springfield and Lavender had the two seats in front of her, and Junior Thornwood was standing behind us, very close to one of the doors.

For a long time, people worked their way toward Council seats, while others went to the middle table. Most folks tried to find places in the gallery, and to sit where the television cameras would miss them. It wasn't until Toppy came in, his uniform all pressed and his buttons and pins shining in the bright chamber lights, that the whole thing started to feel scarily like a trial to me.

I gripped my armrests and stared down at my arms.

Strong.

Strong.

"Strong," I whispered like one of Mom's yoga mantras. "Strong, strong, be strong." Nobody was sending Toppy to jail. Nobody would hurt him. The worst they could do was suspend him, or maybe fire him, and sentence me to California forever.

Toppy sat down at his table, facing Mayor Chandler on the dais. For a split-second, I saw her face go soft and worried before it iced over into something more detached and professional.

Next to me, Mom pulled out her Mac and started tapping and chewing on her lip. Lavender fussed with her phone, and Ms. Springfield tried to get Junior to come sit next to her. He wouldn't do it. I wasn't sure, but I thought the crowd might be bothering him like it seemed to be bothering Mom.

My eyes went back to Toppy. He sat very straight in his seat. I straightened up in mine. Then, for no reason at all, I thought about making his tea and his oatmeal tomorrow morning, and how I wouldn't get to again for a long time—*maybe ever,* some terrible part of my brain whispered—and tears tried to punch their way to my eyes. I took deep breaths and watched the city's six aldermen get seated instead. There were three women and three men, mostly business people from Blue Creek. I knew one was a real estate agent, because I saw his face on signs all over the place.

All six of them looked grim.

Burning knots formed in my stomach. I reached into my arm pouch and pulled out the phone Toppy had bought for me. I had synced it with my iPad, so except for the smaller screen and thumb-typing, I could do a lot of the same work. I went into the message I had sent Lavender, pulled my list from the corkboard into Notes, and read it over.

Tired of Being Invisible.

Might Have Been Overshadowed By a Bad Person.

Might Love a Bad Person Even Though They Know the Person Is Bad.

Probably Knew About Detention.

Probably Local.

Probably Knows Us Pretty Well.

Has Good Computer Skills or Money to Hire Hacker.

My gaze shifted toward Junior, who seemed to be getting redder in the face as more and more people stuffed into the Council chamber. I so knew how he felt.

Thump, thump, thump. The noises made me jump. My attention snapped back to the Council dais, and I saw Mayor Chandler tapping her finger on her microphone. The screens on the wall flickered to life, showing the mayor and the other chairs from the front.

Mayor Chandler started speaking into the microphone. "Everyone find seats, please. Let's get settled in so we can call this meeting to order."

At first, nobody listened to her, so she said it louder. Then, when people finally did quit moving around and chattering, she said, "This meeting of the Blue Creek City Council will come to order. The clerk will call the roll."

The room got really quiet then, and I could hear the thud of my own heartbeat as an older man stood at the foot of the dais and called out seven names. Each of the aldermen and the mayor answered with, "Here."

"We have a quorum present," the clerk told the mayor.

I looked up "quorum" and found out that he meant enough Council members were present to make the proceedings legal and binding.

"The Pledge of Allegiance will be led by Alderman Smith," Mayor Chandler said. "Please rise."

Everyone in the room besides me stood. I kinda hated everybody-stand things, but I tried to sit even straighter and taller, and I put my hand over my heart as one of the aldermen, a lady with long white hair pulled up in a ponytail, led us in reciting the pledge.

After that came a prayer from the Methodist minister, and a text from Lavender telling me, **Oh geez, this is going to take all night.**

By the time Mayor Chandler called for a vote approving the minutes of the last meeting, I texted back my agreement.

But then one of the aldermen, John Eastland, according to his nameplate, stood. "Mayor Chandler, I move to go out of the regular business since this is a called meeting, and get to the issue at hand—the management of our local police force and the attacks on our town."

The mayor paused for a moment, then said, "Hearing no objections, you may proceed, Alderman Eastland."

The alderman, who seemed to be around Mom's age, straightened his suit jacket and tie. He faced the gallery—or the television cameras, more like it—and said, "Our city's general funds have been drained in a hack attack, as have the bank accounts of innocent citizens of Blue Creek. Many local business owners are here to discuss the impact of the recent cyberattacks and vandalism. I call the first of these, Danique Mitchell, owner of Danique's Foods on 317 Bypass Road."

There was some rustling behind me, and then Danique, a tall woman fond of wearing a bright green smock dress, came to the table where Toppy was sitting. She took an open microphone and explained first her hurt feelings over the nasty stuff getting published about her grocery store, and then the damage to her profits from the reduction in Internet sales of her "boutique foods," from the bad publicity, and from the denial of service attacks that kept crashing her web page.

"This hacker seems focused on you, Chief Brennan," she said. "And you haven't been able to find out who it is. I'm sorry, but I'm not sure you can stop this—and it has to be stopped."

She yielded to Evan Dourling, who owned the hardware store. When he changed places with her, I saw how many people had formed a line to go talk, and I wondered if having a screaming fit would speed things up or slow them down.

"Chief Brennan," Mr. Dourling said, "I realize that one of this hacker's goals might be to get you fired. I don't want to give in to what amounts to blackmail, but this mess is really hurting my bottom line. It's putting my business at risk."

I winced, then went back to my list.

Tired of Being Invisible.

Might Have Been Overshadowed By a Bad Person.

Might Love a Bad Person Even Though They Know the Person Is Bad.

Probably Knew About Detention.

Probably Local.

Probably Knows Us Pretty Well.

Has Good Computer Skills or Money to Hire Hacker.

I couldn't do much to search about the first three things, and *Probably Local* included every resident in Blue Creek. Clearly—and a lot of people were really mad now, some at the hacker, but apparently at Toppy, too, because he couldn't find the person making all the trouble.

Probably Knows Us Pretty Well, now that was better. *Good Computer Skills or Money*—harder. People didn't wear stamps on their heads discussing their computer proficiency, right?

In Notes, I thumb-typed **Local + knows us + good computer skills or money + knew about detention.** Then I typed the names of my teachers and the principals I could think of, and spent a few minutes doing Internet searches on their names.

I found Facebook and Twitter profiles. Ms. Kendrick's cousin had died last year, and I found his obituary. One of our principals had a dad who kept getting DUIs.

Hmm.

I copied my notes to Lavender.

A few seconds later, she wrote back, **But Principal Legon was on vacation when the school fire happened. Hawaii, I think.**

I scratched him off the list.

She sent me some thoughts and search links on officers Toppy worked with, but I shot each one of those down. **Out of town, too nice, very loyal to Toppy, Toppy helped pay his student loans . . .**

I sighed and listened to the owner of the Blue Creek Country Store and Hoedown Emporium explain how he'd cancelled tonight's square dancing competition out of fear of more fires being set. "I use a lot of straw, Mayor Chandler. It'd go up so fast no fire hose could help. Plus, my business and my personal accounts have been hit. Right now, I'm flat busted. I can't even buy milk for my granddaughter."

My grandfather's back stayed very straight, but his shoulders had started to round a little. "Strong," I muttered, and wished I could message the word to him, or go write it on his arm.

When I went back to my Notes program, I stared at Local + knows us + good computer skills or money + knew about detention. I added, Some connection to Blue Creek High School, nursing home, car lot, empty building? and sent that to Lavender.

Another alderman got to her feet. Her nameplate read *Alicia Tulley.*

"Chief Brennan," she said to my grandfather. "Could you respond to these business people and explain the steps your department is taking to stop both the cyber-attacks and arson in Blue Creek?"

Toppy stood and cleared his throat. In the bright chamber lighting, I could tell he wasn't flushed or angry. By his posture and tone, he was frustrated and worried—but I thought maybe he was more concerned about the town and the people in it, and probably me and Mom, than his own job.

"As soon as I realized this was going beyond just personal jabs at me," Toppy said, "I asked for the assistance of TBI and the State Police. Now that public and private bank accounts have been robbed, we'll be able to get federal assistance as well."

He went on to explain how he had changed patrol schedules, approved overtime, altered routes to give more coverage to the business district, and assigned officers to be at the disposal of arson investigators from the state. One of the aldermen asked where those investigations of the fires stood, and if anyone had figured out the connections between the sites that got hit last night.

My eyes went back to Notes and what I had written. **Some connection to Blue Creek High School, nursing home, car dealership, empty building?**

The high school thing and the computer skills fit with my sense that maybe this was somebody younger, and definitely local. But then the nursing home, car dealership, empty building—that made it seem like somebody older.

I looked up all six aldermen as Toppy answered question after question about his actions, his competence, and his department's competence. Alderman Eastland, who owned a shipping and receiving business near the abandoned building that got damaged by one of the small fires, seemed to be getting louder and harsher each time he spoke.

"What I can't understand is this, Chief Brennan," Alderman Eastland said. "I hear you saying you care about the businesses and you care about the town. I hear you saying you care about your officers and your family—but as we all have acknowledged, the hacker clearly wants you out of your job. Why has it not occurred to you to step down, or at least take a leave to see if the attacks on the town would stop?"

He sounded like Ellis and Bot, talking about how

Toppy should just give the hacker a win, and—

And I went very, very still.

The Council chamber got a little blurry.

In my mind, I heard—no, remembered the words, *I could come keep you company. Blue Creek High's not much on detention . . .*

Riley's voice.

OMG, I typed to Lavender. OMG, OMG, OMG!!

What? she asked right away.

Riley and Ellis and Bot knew about us being in detention. WE TOLD THEM.

I couldn't even hear what was happening around me right now. A message came in from my mother. I didn't open it. I just watched the little moving dots that told me Lavender was typing.

You can't seriously think one of those guys would hurt Toppy, she typed. Or you. Or anybody.

I shot back with, Local + knows us + good computer skills or money + knew about detention.

Okay, Sherlock, then how are they connected to Blue Creek High School, the nursing home, the car dealership, or that empty building?

We need to find out, I typed. Let's go ask them.

Lavender banged her head on the back of her chair and sent, You gotta be kidding.

Frustrated, I looked away from the iPad and caught Mom's eye. She seemed to be waiting for something.

Oh, right. The message she sent.

I opened it.

It was a photo. No, wait. It was the picture of Toppy's crime board, mostly unblurred. I expanded it. A list of eight names hung on the left. Four were marked out. Three I didn't recognize. One name I knew very well.

I stared at the mug shot and arrest record sheet for a young-looking man charged with criminal mischief and fraud. The arresting officer? Thomas Brennan. And the young-looking man, I might not have recognized him at all, except for the name listed in bold letters right below the photo—the same name I recognized from the list on the left:

David Botman

21

I almost ran over Junior Thornwood as I rolled out of the wheelchair box and out of the Council chamber. My mother and Lavender followed me, and Ms. Springfield followed Lavender, and Junior Thornwood followed Ms. Springfield. We all ran straight into Captain Coker, who had taken point at the main City Hall entrance.

"Hold on there." She put up her hands. "Where's this little train headed?"

"Across Town Square." Lavender pointed toward the blob of blinking Christmas lights that marked the front door of the electronics shop.

Captain Coker frowned at all of us. "I can't let you go out without an escort, and we're tied up tight here, folks."

"But it's Bot." I stared at Captain Coker, heart racing. "He's local. He knows us, he has good computer skills, he knew Lavender and I were in detention that Friday—and Toppy arrested him. It was a long time ago, but it fits. We just need to understand the connections to all the places he burned."

The stern lines of her face shifted to slack confusion. She glanced at the small crowd behind me. "Is she babbling?"

"Don't ask me," Ms. Springfield said.

"Dunno," Junior offered.

"It's Bot," Lavender said. "Probably."

I grabbed Captain Coker's hand. "Bot needs money because he just lost a big contract. And don't you understand? If we don't stop the hacking and stealing and vandalism and these butt-faces fire Toppy, I'll have to go to California, maybe forever!"

Her answer was a shocked expression and an intense silence.

My brain rushed over details about Bot and the hacks and the fires—but a small corner of my mind remembered that Mom was here. As in right with me, behind me. I turned in my chair. "I'm sorry. But I don't want to leave Toppy. I don't want to live somewhere I don't fit."

Mom's expression went flat. "The truth is what it is, Max."

I winced and turned back around because I knew she was trying to sound like it was no big deal, that I

SUSAN VAUGHT

hadn't hurt her feelings. That's exactly what I would have done, and I hated it when Mom and I did stuff exactly alike, because it got really obvious that we were related, and I couldn't not like her or even be mad at her when that happened.

"Let me get this straight," Captain Coker said, mostly to me. "For some reason, you've decided Bot Botman, the man who owns the electronics store here on Town Square—that he's your hacker-slash-vandal-slash-thief-slash-Thornwood's-Revenge scary bad guy?"

"Yes," I said.

"Why?" Junior Thornwood asked.

"Be quiet, Biker Boy," Lavender snapped. "Just be glad we don't think it's you anymore."

"Lavender Dusty Springfield!" Ms. Springfield crossed her arms and leveled a glare at my best friend that might have withered a soul who hadn't spent half her life shooting imaginary death rays out of her wrists.

"It's okay, Joy," Junior said with a grin. Then to Lavender, "So I'm in the clear now?"

"You're lucky," Mom said. "I'm surprised I'm not still on their corkboard."

Captain Coker ignored all of them and kept her gaze on me. "I'm struggling with the fact that your answer to deciding that Mr. Botman is a dangerous criminal is to charge straight over to his store and confront him."

"Um," I said. "Yes! Maybe. I guess?" When she put it that way, it did sound ridiculous. I jerked a thumb toward Mom and Junior and Ms. Springfield. "I was taking adults, see?"

"I don't think the girls are totally sure," Ms. Springfield said. "More like, they have a theory, and we're going to help them explore it."

"I see," Captain Coker said in a totally I'm-not-letting-you-do-this tone.

"Max needs to stay busy," Mom added. "She needs to do something to help her grandfather instead of listening to all that negative mess in the Council chamber."

Wow. Points to Mom.

"This could really hurt Bot's feelings," Ms. Springfield said to Lavender.

"Look at our case information here, on my phone," Lavender said to her mom. Then a bit more grudging, "And show Junior, too."

About a minute later, Ms. Springfield, wide-eyed, held the phone up for Junior, then passed it to Captain Coker. I watched Captain Coker's brows draw closer and closer together as she scrolled through the case facts and theories Lavender and I had assembled, right up to the unblurred mug shot of Bot.

"Well." Captain Coker lowered the phone, looking more like the stone-hard trooper who had first walked into Something Wicked nine days earlier. "Hate to admit it, but you two may be on to something."

She motioned to one of the two other green-uniformed officers on post at the chamber doors. He came straight over. "Trooper Allen," she said, "do me a favor and stand here while I escort these ladies and gentleman elsewhere. We need to talk to somebody."

"Yes, ma'am." Trooper Allen gave her a curt nod and immediately settled in by the main doors of City Hall.

Before we got halfway across Town Square, snow started to fall. I had to get in my arm pouch and dig out a baggie to cover my controller, because my chair's electronics despised any type of moisture.

As powdery flakes drifted onto our shoulders, Captain Coker and I led the way into Bot's Electronics, with Lavender, Mom, Ms. Springfield, and Junior jingling the bell right behind us. I had expected Riley to be waiting in his elf suit with his candy bowl, but for a few seconds, I thought the shop was empty.

"Hello?" Captain Coker called over the too-loud Christmas music piping through what had to be twenty different types of speakers.

No answer.

"Huh," Ms. Springfield said. "Weird. They're so right-in-the-customer's-faces, usually. Especially near Christmas!"

"Anybody here?" Captain Coker moved toward the door to the back of the shop. Her hand lifted slowly, coming to rest on her holster and sending my already fast heartbeat into a galloping frenzy.

I rolled forward—and my chair turned off, along with a bunch of the shop speakers.

Mom banged into my handlebars with an "Oooof."

I stared first at my chair, then at the speakers that had shut off. I recognized some of the brands and colors, since I had coveted a few of them and had them on my Amazon wish list.

"What's with your chair, Max?" Lavender asked. "I thought that only happened at Thornwood."

Captain Coker eased through the back shop door, but I couldn't focus on her, only on the speakers. "The wireless ones," I muttered. "All the wireless speakers just turned off."

"Is this one of those power surges that isn't a power surge?" Mom asked as she walked around the front of my chair.

I turned my controller back on and it lit up.

"It's EMI," I said, suddenly understanding.

Lavender hit my shoulder. "Electricity-ese! Stop it!"

"What?" Mom and Ms. Springfield and Junior said all at once.

"Electromagnetic interference." I glanced from one of their faces to the next. They all looked clueless.

I pointed to the speakers. "The wireless speakers all turned off when my chair did. I have components in my controls that function like Bluetooth, so the same EMI must have just blasted my circuits. My controller did the safe thing and turned itself off."

They still looked clueless, so I tried again. "It's kinda like putting an AM radio next to a vacuum cleaner."

Junior brightened. "I've done that before! You can hear the vacuum over the radio because the vacuum's motor overpowers the weak AM signal. Doesn't work on FM stations because—oh. I get it! Some strong wireless signal just swamped the weaker Bluetooth signals, right?"

I looked past all of them, my eyes roving over the store, trying to find what might have caused it. A spark on some inductor? Something with a signal so strong it could literally take over a weaker one—

Captain Coker came out of the back of the store with Riley, who looked both sad and confused.

"Hey, Max," he said when saw me. "Hey, Lavender, and Lavender's people." He paused at Mom. "And Max's people, too. Sorry I wasn't out here. Ellis's Internet setup is screwing up half the shop. Some sort of raw signal keeps shutting everything down. I was restarting the server to see if that would help."

Server . . .

Raw signal . . .

What's with your chair, Max? I thought that only happened at Thornwood. . . .

"Where's Bot?" Lavender asked, but I barely heard her. I unlocked my new phone and dove into the synced photo stream, swiping back to the pictures I took on my iPad during our first foray into Thornwood Manor.

There.

Right there it was.

I had been staring at it for days.

The picture of the fancy brass grate in the floor in the entryway, the one with wires peeking out of the corners. Wires, like somebody would use to pirate electricity from house lines, or boost a WiFi signal. Wow. I should have known what those wires were the second I saw them. I should have realized the hacker might be broadcasting right out of Thornwood Manor itself.

And . . . my brain kept throwing pieces into place—easy access to photograph and post the antiques on eBay. And the footprints in the dust . . . getting the best vantage point on our house, probably setting up a GoPro or some other small camera to keep an eye on Toppy and me, to make the cyberharassment that much easier. The hacker could record and even monitor from a distance, and always know when somebody was home.

"I really don't know where Bot is," Riley said to Lavender. "He and Ellis—they sort of had words over the Internet dysfunction in the shop, and over Ellis's attitude lately. Bot said he thought Ellis was headed down the wrong path. Ellis blew out of here pissed, and Bot went after him."

Captain Coker pulled a small notepad and pen from her pocket. "Do you know where Ellis lives? His address?"

"Sure—" Riley started, but I cut him off.

"They aren't at Ellis's house," I said. "They're at Thornwood Manor."

22

When I showed Riley the pictures of the wires, all the color left his face.

"Yeah," he confirmed. "The split on the left, that's Ellis's favorite way of amping a WiFi signal when we've got line-of-sight issues or poor coverage zones. He learned it from Bot, but he got lazy in the set-up, and he's been using unshielded wires. I think that's what's causing the shop's EMI problem, and so does Bot."

Everyone had huddled around my phone, with Captain Coker and Riley closest. The trooper gazed steadily at both of us. She pointed to the little wires coming out of the grate at Thornwood. "But why are they coming out of the grate?"

"No idea," Riley said.

"Thornwood's power and heat are on to protect the pipes—I think he's pirating electricity from the house wiring," I said. "Maybe running it somewhere else in the house, somewhere that didn't start off having power. When we went to Thornwood the first time, we could smell lemon-scented cleanser, but the place was still dusty except for a few places. I think the hacker cleaned up a hidden space for himself and his server."

Mom and Ms. Springfield and Captain Coker and Riley looked at me.

"You know how to pirate electricity?" Mom asked.

I held up both hands. "Hey, I learned my lesson with the fuse box mess. But maybe the hacker's running wires through the ducts, and also boosting signal off any nearby network."

"Who is the hacker?" Mom asked. "Is it Bot or Ellis?"

"Not sure," Lavender said. "We thought Bot."

Ellis. Wow. I had not seen that possibility coming. But, no. Ellis had been working to help us catch the hacker.

"No way," Riley said. "Just, no. Bot would never do any of the stuff the hacker's been pulling off."

"Does Bot have any personal interests in the buildings that got vandalized?" Captain Coker asked.

Riley opened his mouth to speak, but hesitated. I didn't think it was possible, but he got even more pale.

"What are you thinking, young man?" Captain Coker asked him in that voice I figured got just about anybody to confess.

"He—ah." Riley dug his fingers through his long

hair, his eyes drawing down to a squint. "The abandoned warehouse. Bot bought it last month for us to use as a second storage location. We didn't have anything in it yet, though."

Relief edged through me. *See? Bot. Not Ellis.*

Why was that better?

I rubbed my temples.

Maybe it wasn't either of them. That would be the absolute best.

"Was that building insured?" Junior asked, and when everyone looked at him, he held up both hands defensively, just like I had done. "Hey, I'm auctioning my lot up North, not setting it on fire for a payout."

"Bot would never do *anything* like that," Riley said. "He got in trouble once a long time ago for computer hacking and fraud. He told me about it, said he was angry and confused when he was younger, and he never wanted to live like that again."

"Didn't he just lose a contract with the schools?" I studied Riley. "He said so the other day. He seemed pretty irritated with both the middle school and high school, and they both had fires started for damage at different times."

Lavender pointed at the candy-strewn counters. "And all those packages that came in, the ones Bot had to send back because he got outbid by a big box store in Nashville, he lost a bunch of money on restocking fees.

Those drained bank accounts—that's good timing for somebody who needs cash quick."

"Bot didn't steal any money or set fires in trash cans," Riley insisted. "He was sad about that contract, sure. But he got over it and made the big Christmas sale even bigger to recoup some of the losses."

"What about the nursing home?" Captain Coker asked. "Did he have any issues with that facility? Any family go through there?"

Riley threw his head back. "Uhhggg, I don't know!" He sucked in a breath, then let it out slowly. "Look, Bot might have had family members there in the past, but most everybody in Blue Creek has had people in that place. The nearest other nursing home is what, fifty miles from here? And before you ask, the car lot—zero connection to it. Bot buys his cars in Nashville, and he's never tried to sell the car lot people anything. So you can stop stretching the facts to make them fit Bot, okay? He's a great guy."

I shut up then because I heard the hurt in Riley's voice, and I understood it. Bot was all Riley had. Bot was Riley's Toppy.

"Okay," I said, but I felt sort of sick.

"Tell you what." Captain Coker walked toward the shop door. "I want you to close up shop here, Riley, and come with us back to City Hall. I'm going to leave the bunch of you with the officers there and head over to

Thornwood to check on Mr. Botman and Ellis. I'll take Ellis's address, too, and Mr. Botman's, in case Max is wrong about where they are."

I wasn't wrong. I knew I wasn't.

Lavender seemed to know, too, but she got to fit-throwing faster than me. "We want to go with you, Captain Coker," she said.

The chorus of "NO" from every adult in the room almost popped my eardrums.

In under half an hour, Riley had locked up the electronics store, Captain Coker had dropped us off at City Hall and taken her leave, and we were back at the door of the chamber gallery, rubbing our hands to warm up our fingers.

Unbelievably, Toppy's meeting or trial or hearing or whatever it really was—it was still going on, with aldermen and business people and Mayor Chandler talking loudly to one another about what the town did or didn't need.

And my butt was slowly going numb. Great.

"It's getting late," Mom said, watching me shift my weight over and over. "About time for you to get out of that chair and lie down for a while, isn't it?"

"I don't want to leave Toppy here alone," I said.

Mom gave a quiet laugh. "Does it look like he needs us?"

Honestly, it didn't. Toppy didn't seem slumped or upset anymore. He radiated cranky and in-charge. "Guess not," I said. "You know, I almost feel sorry for the City Council."

"This could go on for hours yet," Ms. Springfield said. "And they may not make any decisions at all. Junior and I can stay. We'll hang out here with Riley and wait for Captain Coker. Callinda, you take the girls on to your house and I'll bring Toppy home and pick up Lavender when everything's finished."

I started to protest again, but Lavender said, "Sounds good to me."

Her tone seemed entirely too sweet and light. When I raised my eyebrows at her, she raised hers right back at me. Then she stage-yawned and stretched.

Oh. Right.

Going home was as close as we'd get to Thornwood Manor.

I yawned, too. "Okay. But text if they actually do vote on something to do with Toppy."

Riley gave me the thumbs-up. He didn't meet my eyes, though, and I wondered if he was still mad at me over making Bot a big suspect. Probably. I'd be mad at me, if I were him.

It took Mom a few minutes to let the troopers know we were leaving and to bring the van around, and the whole time, I thought about Riley and his faith in Bot. And I thought about how I believed in Toppy.

Was I being thick-headed like Riley? Was it really time for Toppy to retire because he couldn't keep up with a cybercriminal? As I left City Hall behind and rolled up the van ramp, as I fastened my chair to the tie-downs, as we pulled away from Town Square in the billowing snow with a state trooper car behind us, I refused to believe that, just like Riley refused to believe Bot would do anything illegal.

Mom and Lavender chatted in the front seat, and I tried to listen, but my thoughts looped to Toppy, then to Bot and Riley, and finally to Ellis.

Ellis, with the awesome computer skills who knew Toppy and me very well.

I clicked my chair off and on, off and on. Off, then on.

Ellis, who had been helping us catch the hacker, but hadn't really actually found anything but dead ends. I flicked my joystick and my chair spurted against the tie-downs with a *clank-click.*

Ellis, who went to the Middle School and High School. *Flick-clank-click.*

Ellis, who had tried to get a job all over town when his aunt died—maybe he had tried that car lot and held a grudge?

Flick-clank-click.

Ellis, whose aunt died at Blue Creek Nursing Home.

I squeezed the joystick hard.

The power on Town Square—maybe his lazy wiring had shorted things out, or maybe he'd done that on purpose to keep Bot and Riley busy, or give himself an excuse to disappear and vandalize a bunch of places.

But why would Ellis target Bot's storage building? And even more than that, what did Ellis have against Toppy? Against *me*?

Mom turned the van onto our road.

Instantly, Lavender and I both strained to look out the windows at Thornwood Manor. The blowing snow wasn't sticking to the presalted roads yet, but it made everything so hard to see.

"I think those are police lights," Lavender said, and sure enough, I could make out blinking blue on the hill above my house.

"Drive by, Mom," I urged. "See if Captain Coker's okay?"

"No," Mom said. "She's got a radio and a weapon and years of training. She can take care of herself." Then, more gently, "It really is a police matter, Max."

When Lavender and I didn't answer, Mom said, "Well, I see I'll need to lock you two in Max's bedroom tonight. You know, for safety. And to make sure you don't get any ideas about heading up to Thornwood."

Lavender stiffened in the front seat, but I said, "My door doesn't have a lock on the outside."

"Then I'll drop a sleeping bag on the floor in front of it," Mom said lightly. "Good place to have my evening chai and do some poses."

Oh, wonderful.

I ground my teeth.

Mom pulled into the driveway. As she was parking the van, my phone buzzed with the text tone, and I pulled it out to see a message from Riley.

Council just voted to fire Toppy. Mayor overruled. They're challenging whether she can do that or not.

My fingers and toes and heart and brain went totally numb.

I stared at the words once, then twice, then stuffed the phone in my arm pouch and shivered. The heat and the headache hit me like a wild spring storm.

They did it. Those buttheads seriously just voted to fire my grandfather. To put him out to pasture like some old goat.

Red danced at the edges of my vision.

I wanted to hit stuff. Break stuff. I wanted to scream.

From somewhere in the far regions of my brain, I noticed Mom lowering the van ramp into the garage like nothing was any big deal at all.

Tomorrow, I'd have to go to California with her even though she didn't really want me and I didn't really want her, and Toppy wouldn't have a job, and the hacker would still be after him.

My jaws ached, and I heard the grind as I nearly chewed through my own teeth.

The trooper who had followed us home parked his car on the curb, got out, and got the key from Mom to go in the house ahead of us, to check everything out before we went inside.

"You don't have to block us in," Lavender said to Mom. "Really. We'll be fine."

"Uh-huh," Mom said. "You coming out, Max?"

The Council. Toppy. Hacker. California. Blocked in. Helpless.

I gripped my joystick as I rolled down the van ramp and started to turn away from the open garage door.

My eyes flicked to my arms.

Strong.

Strong.

No.

I was helpless.

Red turned to crimson at the edges of my vision. My skin blazed so hot I barely felt winter on my cheeks. Why *couldn't* I have superpowers? Why? I hated not being really strong and able to do something—anything, *anything!* to fix this horrible mess.

Mom hit the button on the wall to lower the garage door.

Helpless, my numb, aching butt.

"Love me for who I am, Mom," I muttered.

Then I slammed my joystick forward, flipped my turbo switch, and shot out underneath the descending garage door, careening into night and the white, blowing snow.

23

The garage door slammed behind me.

Way behind me.

I was moving so fast.

Wind and snow made my eyes water and froze my nose and my fingers seemed to turn to ice on the joystick. Gloves would have been smart but I hated gloves. I hated the City Council. I hated the hacker. The heat inside me raged and raged, fighting the chill.

The turn to the Thornwood hill loomed in the dull streetlight ahead, and I flicked off the turbo switch. My battery bars blinked. There were six total, and I was at three from using the chair all day. Oops. Two. And I'd need a battery-sucking gear to get up the hill.

I pressed my gear button, setting it low for the pull, and pushed the joystick as fast as the chair would go without turbo. By now, Mom would be opening the garage door, maybe yelling for the trooper. Lavender would be plotting my death. When I got to Thornwood, I had Lavender's key, so if I could use it fast enough, I could get inside and lock them out.

And trap yourself in a haunted house with a hacker who might want you dead? Brilliant!

I wasn't seeing red anymore, but my breathing stayed fast and my jaw clenched so tight it made my head hurt right along with my crampy, numb hips. As I motored up the incline toward Thornwood, blue lights blinked, shining across my chest and face.

My phone rang.

I ignored it.

My text messages dinged.

I ignored those, too.

As soon as I had a straight shot through the Thornwood parking lot, I hit my turbo switch again and floored it across the marked spaces, skidding a little in the snow and swerving way too close to Captain Coker's patrol car. I panicked and let go of the controls, and the chair jerked to a sudden stop, then slid, coming to rest near the bottom of the ramp. I flopped forward against my safety belt, and it ripped. Not all the way—but it gave enough to make me swallow hard.

I glanced over at the patrol car. It sat running, lights flashing, doors closed, no one inside.

From down the hill, a siren yowled.

Oh, great. I'd be joining Bot with a felony record soon. I checked my controls. Nothing smoking or sparking. One battery bar.

Breathing like I'd run a marathon instead of driven my chair up a hill, I turned off turbo and eased the chair up the ramp into Thornwood Manor. At the turn, the wood popped enough to make me jump, but I kept going.

As I got onto the main porch, I could see I wouldn't need Lavender's key. The front door was open. A Thornwood Owl, bramble in talons, faced me. Low lighting from the entryway filtered across the Latin words.

Pecuniate obediunt omni.

Well, nothing tonight was obeying money, or anything that made any sense.

The hum of Captain Coker's engine blended with my chair motor, both nearly drowned out by the louder-louder siren coming up the hill. I eased my chair around the owls and brambles, and rolled into the entryway intending to look at the grate—

"Oh." I yanked my hand off the controls. The chair screech-stopped, my belt ripped a little more, and I had to grab my armrests to keep from falling forward over my knees.

There was no grate.

Instead, another giant hole had opened in the floor. It reached like a gaping mouth toward the open front doors, toothy boards dangling from all the edges.

"Captain Coker?" I called.

Oh, no. What if she came up here because of my theories about Bot and the floor collapsed and she got hurt, all because of me? I rolled forward and tried to see down in the hole, but I couldn't, so I inched around it, heading toward the main hall.

"Captain Coker?" I yelled again.

No answer.

I got to the main hall, turned my chair, and squinted down into the darkness of the hole. My cheeks stung from the snowy cold and the tears streaming out of my eyes. So dark. I couldn't—but wait.

I pulled out my phone and held it out, scrubbing at the screen with my finger. It lit up, and suddenly, I was looking into another stone basement, just like the one in the mansion's main room. So, Thornwood didn't have a priest hole. It was more like a priest mansion-under-the-mansion.

I had no idea why that one room had no doors or stairs, but this one did, off to one side—and a door on the other side. The stairs were stone, too, as if they had been carved out of solid limestone. I moved my phone farther and illuminated a too-modern desk, a lamp, a laptop, and a fat black box with dark lights that should have been blinking. A server with torn wires—wires that had likely been poking through the grate in my photo.

A car came rumbling into the parking lot as I kept

searching the little basement room, and my light fell on something I really, really didn't want to see.

A hand.

My chest squeezed tight, forcing out all my air as I followed the hand to a green-clad arm, to a shoulder, to Captain Coker's face. She lay on her side, eyes closed, boards and sawdust covering her legs.

"Help!" I yelled—then saw another leg, bigger, with a giant tennis shoe sticking out of the rubble.

"Captain Coker fell!" I sat up so I could yell louder and dropped my phone in my lap. "She's hurt and Bot fell, too!"

"Shut up," a voice hissed from behind me, and I screamed.

On reflex, I yanked my joystick backward and bashed straight into the big headshot daguerreotype of Hargrove Thornwood. Pinpricks of light danced on the opposite wall like lasers shooting straight out of his long-dead brain. I screamed again and held up my phone like it could fire back.

From out in the parking lot, Mom yelled, "Max? Max!"

Lavender yelled too, and a man's voice said, "We're coming!"

My head whipped to the Thornwood picture and I realized light really *was* coming out of its eyes. I tried to get a breath. Then I realized the steps I had seen along the far wall in the new cave-in room—they would lead into the closet under the main staircase. The closet must have a light inside, pirated if it wasn't built to have a light to start with. And the picture—it really was cleaner than all the rest of them, because somebody had dusted it off. Somebody had also scraped the eyes thin so they could see through them and catch whatever was happening in the mansion's main hallway. The closet light was shining through the picture's eyes.

I gulped a breath. Grabbed my phone and crammed it in my pocket. Tried to calm down.

Couldn't.

"Mom! Lavender! Help me!"

Hargrove Thornwood's portrait hissed, "Shut up!"

"No!" I rocketed away from that awful daguerreotype, blasting across the hall, into the study with the pink fireplace and the painting of Vivienne Thornwood, and absolute darkness. I let go of the joystick.

The chair screeched to a stop and rocked forward. My hands hit marble as I flung them out. My safety belt ripped the rest of the way, but I hung on to the chair arms and didn't fall. Safe.

For a split-second, Thornwood Manor got totally, completely quiet. I took a deep breath. Remembered how this room, too, had smelled like cleansers the first time we came, and how the inside of the fireplace had seemed cleaner than the rest of the mansion.

The door in the room under the grate . . .

And I knew how Vivienne Thornwood had smuggled out her daughter. Through more secret rooms and tunnels, which had to have hidden entrances, like maybe in the strangely clean fireplace.

I was probably sitting right on top of—

The boards underneath my chair gave a huge groan and pop.

The world shuddered.

My chair shook and pitched.

Wood turned to dust, and I fell through the floor, chair and all.

24

Slow motion.
　　But too fast.
　　Flying down.
My belly dropped fastest of all.
The chair tilted backward. Hit on its back wheels so hard every bone in my body rattled.
Bounced.
Who was screaming?
Me?
The chair tipped in the air and slammed onto its side.
Plastic and metal snapped under my right arm and leg.
My head hit limestone.
I don't know if it bounced.
The world swam and dimmed.

Came back.

I was staring at shoes. Right in front of my bleeding nose.

Black ones. Nike Airs.

"Size ten?" I mumbled.

Then I didn't see anything.

25

If I had a wheelchair made of unbreakable iron, I wouldn't need to be a superhero. If I had a wheelchair that could motor across water and jet through the air, I wouldn't need superpowers. I wished my chair could speed on highways and roll over bumpy fields and sand and gravel with no problem. If I could design a chair for myself, it would stand up for me and walk when I needed legs instead of wheels.

Why couldn't wheelchairs do all of those things?

If humans could make satellites that went to Jupiter and guns that killed fifty people in five seconds and cars that drove themselves and the Internet and toothbrushes for dogs, then why couldn't humans change the world so people on wheels could use it with no problem, or at least make wheelchairs that would really do all the things legs were supposed to do—and more?

From somewhere far, far, far away, I heard Mom and Lavender yelling my name.

And then, I didn't.

My head weighed six thousand pounds.

A few seconds later, I processed that somebody was carrying me.

Toppy?

I tried to open my eyes, but that made my skull throb, so I kept them closed. My legs didn't have much feeling, and they didn't work anyway, so I couldn't really tell if they were smashed to bits. I squeezed fingers and slowly moved my arms and head. I felt a little sore, especially on my right side, but I didn't think anything was broken.

Except my head, maybe.

That was probably bad.

The world went away again, but I thought maybe just for a little while.

Who was carrying me?

Not Toppy. The arms were too skinny. Wrong smell. Sweet spice, something commercial and newer. Toppy would call it "boy perfume."

Boy.

A few fragments at a time, the night came back to me. Thornwood. Captain Coker and Bot lying in the hidden room the hacker had used for his cyberattack center. My slow pulse picked up. I started breathing faster, and the spicy aftershave washed over my senses.

"Ellis?" I mumbled.

"Ssshh," he whispered.

For a few seconds I relaxed back into my fuzzy-headed brain-throb. Then my eyes fluttered open-ish again, and cool prickles of fear laced across my neck and shoulders. Why couldn't I hear Mom? Where was Lavender?

"It's okay," Ellis said. "I don't want to hurt you. I know I said some crummy stuff and made that abuse report, but all of that was just to make your mom come get you and take you away from this stinkhole town."

I kept my mouth tightly closed.

"That whole thing at Blue Creek Middle School— you were supposed to be gone. When I realized you weren't, I stomped out the fire in the trash can before the smoke choked you up."

I imagined a sooty footprint, matching the dusty footprint in Thornwood. "Thanks," I whispered, getting more terrified by the second but trying to keep my muscles loose so I wouldn't make Ellis mad. I caught a glimpse of his face, but mostly I could see the bottom of his jaw.

"All my fires have been small up to now, just to let people know they can't do wrong and get away clean.

Oh, and sorry I shined you on about helping you catch me." He laughed. "That was never going to happen."

But I trusted you, part of my brain insisted. The smarter part kept my mouth closed. Toppy had actually talked to me about situations like this, what to do if I got snatched by some freaky bad guy.

Stay calm. Pay attention to your surroundings. Consider your options. Remember your resources. Stay alive. Remember, Max, that's your only duty in a threat situation. Stay alive.

Did other parents do that kind of training, or was it just because he was a police chief? And if other parents did tell kids what to do if they got kidnapped, I bet they didn't always finish with a promise like, *And don't worry, they'll bring you back pretty fast, because you eat too much.*

Somehow, I didn't think Ellis was planning to feed me anything.

Stay alive. Yeah. That was about the shape of my current threat situation, and what I needed to do.

"Blue Creek is no place for somebody with special needs," he was saying. "It's no place for somebody special, period."

"Special needs." I so totally hated that phrase. I didn't have special needs. I just didn't have legs that worked, so I used wheels. Why was that special?

Don't get mad. Not here. Not now. He'll drop you, or do something worse.

"I was the best student in all my classes," Ellis said. "I had real talent—but did anybody care? No. I was nobody because I didn't have the right family or a big enough bank account."

Surroundings. Okay. I had to pay attention. On purpose, I slowed my breathing. Ellis wasn't walking fast or carefully, even though it was so dark I could barely see anything. The air smelled like cemeteries. Dirt. And wet rock. Now and then I saw twisty shadows above us, like tree roots. It was like we were inside, but outside, too.

"Well, who has the big bank account now?" he laughed. "And who has been staying in the most famous mansion in Tennessee for months? Thornwood Manor suits me. I'll miss it."

Why? Oh, no. WHY?

But before I could ask that, Ellis said, "I can go anywhere I want now. I can finally have what I deserve—and do you know why?"

I thought for a second, and I came up with, "Because all things obey money?"

"Smart girl." He sounded pleased. "Bot and that state trooper—they should have remembered that, and they wouldn't have gotten hurt."

"Are we somewhere near the manor?" I asked, trying to keep my tone curious and very light.

"We're underneath the grounds," Ellis said. "North

side. People thought Hargrove was a paranoid, sneaky guy—but he had nothing on his wife Vivienne. When he lost it, he built that first basement, sealed off from everything, and he started loading valuables into it through a trapdoor. That gave Vivienne ideas." Ellis laughed. "She got the workers who built Thornwood's basement to feel sorry for her, and she talked them into making a maze of tunnels connected to the rest of the mansion. It's all noted on the oldest drawings of Thornwood Manor that I lifted from the City Hall archives—and they have some notes about her supervising the construction, and gradually shifting most of what Thornwood salted away in his basement to her own hiding places. She sold his own stuff out from under his nose to fund her tunnels, and then she sent whatever money was left to her kids. No wonder the old guy kept accusing the townspeople of stealing from him."

We're underground in Vivienne Thornwood's tunnels, I thought dully. And Ellis seemed very familiar with them.

I thought for a second and asked, "We going anywhere special?"

"Nah, just near the end of this longest stretch." He sounded so happy it made me feel a little silly for being scared. "I've timed everything over and over— but I left myself a few minutes, just in case something unexpected happened. Like this." Another laugh. It sounded unhinged. "I can't let you stop me, Max, but I want to be sure the smoke doesn't get to you. I was going to escape this way, but I'll use my back-up exit in the front tunnels instead."

"Smoke," I managed to say calmly. "You're going to set something on fire?"

"A pissy little town like Blue Creek doesn't deserve Thornwood Manor," Ellis said. "And I need to be sure the City Council doesn't give your grandfather a second chance. Because of you, I'm not going to hurt him, though. Not unless he tries to come after me."

My heart ached. I wanted my grandfather. I wanted to see him and hug him and know he was okay, that I was going to be okay. I didn't care if he kept his job or not. I didn't care if we couldn't have cable or cereal or tea or Internet or anything. I didn't ever want to leave him.

Don't cry. Don't. I coughed instead, and thought about Bot and Captain Coker. Should I bring them up? Or did he want to hurt them, too? Would I make everything worse if I reminded him they were in the mansion?

"So, what did Toppy do to you?" I asked to keep him talking.

Ellis's grip on my shoulders and probably my legs,

too, tightened until it hurt, but I didn't make any noise. "It's not your fault. I know you weren't even born when Toppy and Mayor Chandler put my dad in prison."

"I thought . . . wait." I turned my head toward Ellis and stared at the bottom of his jaw. "You knew your dad?"

"My father's name was Frank Unger. I used Pritchard, my aunt's married name, so people wouldn't realize we were related. And no, I didn't know my father very well. Your grandfather stole him from me when I was seven."

Change a name, change your life. Who said that? Oh, yeah. Mom, when she was talking about Mayor Chandler.

"Dad had to do everything for me because Mom died when I was born," Ellis went on without me asking any more questions. "That's why he drank. But Mayor Chandler didn't care what he was going through. When he made a mistake and showed up to work smelling like beer, she fired him from Chandler Construction, even though he didn't miss a day. He couldn't pay our bills then, so he had to do something, you understand?"

No! I yelled in my head. "Yes," I said out loud.

"He only robbed that convenience store to make sure he could take care of me," Ellis said. "But Chief Brennan arrested him and sent him to prison. My aunt and I, we couldn't afford decent lawyers, so I never saw my dad again. I just got a letter when he died on the first of December, last year."

Oh. Oh, ouch. "I'm sorry," I said, surprised I actually meant that. Sadness flowed over me, through me, mixing with my fear, and I couldn't hold it back.

Ellis eased up on my shoulders a little. "It took me a year to plan this, to make sure Chief Brennan and the mayor and the whole stupid, judgmental town got what they deserved. Go to California with your mother, Max, and don't look back. Are you crying? Don't cry. I promise, you'll be safe."

"What are you going to do, Ellis?"

He slowed.

Walked a few more steps.

Stopped.

Then he bent down and gently set me on the dark tunnel floor. Cold immediately snaked through my clothes, slithering across my back and shoulders and neck and arms.

For a second Ellis stood there, staring at me. A tiny bit of light reached us from somewhere, and I could see his wide eyes, the bristles of his close-cropped hair, and I thought maybe I could make out some of his freckles.

He looked . . . the same.

He looked like Ellis. The boy I knew. The guy who sold me wires and circuits. Not some evil, heartless hacker, or thief, or vandal. Just Ellis.

More tears washed down my face.

"What's happening?" I asked the boy I had wished could be my older brother.

That boy stood up, and slowly, slowly, slowly faded out of my mind, leaving only a shadow hovering above me.

Then, in the tunnel's quiet darkness, that shadow answered me in a voice edged with ice and rage. "Thornwood's Revenge."

26

D on't leave me here!" I shouted after Ellis as he walked away.

"Once I'm clear, I'll tell them where you are," he called over his shoulder.

"Wait!" I cried so hard the word barely came out, but it didn't matter. Ellis just kept walking until he vanished into pitch darkness, back the way we had come.

Stay calm. Pay attention to your surroundings. . . .

Ellis had to be walking toward Thornwood, toward the rooms under the manor, but he told me the tunnels made a maze. Who knew how many twists and turns I didn't sense or remember? I wasn't even awake for all of it. Even if I could crawl as far as he walked, what if I ran into him? Or whatever awful thing he was doing?

He told me I'd be safe where I was.

And he was a wretched, lying creep.

Consider your options.

Without my chair, I had two choices: sit where I was, or crawl. I could yell, but my voice wouldn't last forever, and who would hear me down here, wherever *here* was?

I knew I was breathing too fast. And freezing. My teeth chattered. Still, my face got all hot as I got pissed off, because I *hated* that I didn't have wheels, that I couldn't move well with just my own body.

Remember your resources. Yeah. If pissed off and cold as heck were resources, I'd be set for life. Oh, wait! My new phone!

My heart gave a huge leap, and I dug my phone out of my pocket. Right away, I realized it had gotten bent and cracked when my chair fell through the floor and smashed into the granite floor beneath Thornwood. The broken screen stayed dark when I touched it. I bit my lip and pressed the power button, and . . .

It lit up!

"Come on, come on," I muttered, going back over everything Ellis said. He was about to burn Thornwood to the ground, with Captain Coker and Bot unconscious in that server room—and Mom and Lavender and that trooper had been trying to catch me when I ran away, and they might be in the house, too—

No!

The phone shifted to my home screen, and I managed to work the slider despite the fifty-billion crack lines. I pulled up the dial pad, pushed the numbers—

The call didn't send.

I brought the phone closer to my face and groaned when I saw the two little white words in the left-hand corner:

No Service

I banged my head once on the tunnel's stone wall. The phone illuminated dust and rocks everywhere. The floor here wasn't solid granite. It had been mixed with dirt. And—

"Notice my surroundings," I muttered, trying to pretend that wouldn't include counting spiders and beetles and ants and probably mice, and maybe even rats. My head twisted to my left. Yeah, there was definitely light coming from that direction. Not a lot, but some.

A bulb? A break in the tunnel? A way out?

Oh, no. What if Ellis's fire would only miss me *here*, right where I was?

Stay alive.

But didn't I have a duty to Captain Coker and Bot and Mom and Lavender and that trooper? What about to my grandfather? What if he was in Thornwood by now, looking for me?

My phone light bathed both of my arms, and I read the words I had drawn on them earlier, when my worst problem was the City Council going after Toppy, and maybe having to suffer through Mom and California for a little while.

Strong.

Strong.

Well . . . was I, or wasn't I?

"I had the case completely right in the end," I said to the bugs and rodents I imagined to be hiding in the shadows. "My profile. My assumptions. It wasn't somebody Toppy wronged—it was a family member of the bad guy, just like Vivienne Thornwood. I bet I could get a degree in criminology and do okay. If I don't get eaten by a cave snake."

Strong.

Strong.

Yep. I got the crime details mostly right. What I didn't get right was the life details. Like, being so mad over the City Council treating Toppy badly, and running away from Mom and Lavender, and driving my chair into creaky old Thornwood Manor even after everybody said the place was about to fall down. I tried to make myself haul a load I shouldn't have.

Toppy would have a lot to say about that when I saw him.

Because I *was* going to see him.

And when he told me off and grounded me forever, I wouldn't mind a bit. I'd write ten thousand sappy movie reports with zero complaining.

A few more tears squeezed out of my eyes. I let them fall, then slipped my phone into my pocket, pointed myself toward the faint gray light on my left, and started to crawl.

"No whining," I said to myself. "You played super-hero for years, right?"

Elbows down, plant, and pull. My body moved. Slowly. Good thing my *Support Toppy* hoodie was pretty thick, even though it was already torn in places.

My legs and feet dragged along behind me. I could hear them, feel the weight of them. I knew they had to be cold even through my winter jeans, but mostly they were just heavy. When I was little, crawling had been easy. Every year, though, it got harder.

"You read about superheroes," I said over and over, using it like a rhythm. Then I started naming them, DC first. "Adam Strange. Agent Liberty. Air Wave. Amazo."

DC had close to two hundred characters. I don't know how long I recited names, or how long I spent arguing with myself about whether characters like Green Arrow, where one died and a kid took over the role, should count as one or two when I was keeping track. Somewhere around Red Tornado, I had to stop, heart racing, and just lie there and breathe.

I did not feel like a superhero. And that gray light didn't look any closer.

I pulled out my phone and checked.

No Service

I put the phone back in my pocket and started again. Plant, pull. Plant, pull. After ten more pulls I had to stop, chest heaving. Okay, seriously, once I got out of this crappy mess, I was totally going to the gym, or making Toppy get me a weight machine. Screw superpowers. I needed a little muscle for times I got stranded without my wheels.

Elbows down, plant, then pull. Elbows down, plant, then pull. Forward. After a time, tears just slid down my face. I wasn't even sure I was crying. I swapped to listing Marvel superheroes, then decided I hated all of them.

Wasn't it heroic enough, just staying alive when life got this hard?

I stopped and flopped. Took a deep breath—and smelled something. Fresh sweat broke across my forehead and neck, making me clammy. Was I imagining—?

No.

I smelled smoke. It was coming from behind me, from the direction of Thornwood Manor. I dug my elbows into the sharp granite and crumbly dirt, and I pulled. I pulled and I pulled. No more DC. No more Marvel. No more mad or impulsive or anything.

Move. Stay alive. But I couldn't go far enough. I couldn't go fast enough. Captain Coker. Bot. Mom. Lavender. Toppy. All of them might be in that mansion—and because of me.

"Pull," I whispered, and moved. "Pull. Pull. Pull . . ."

Captain Coker, now there was a real-life superhero. Strong, kind—and she could sort of read minds. And what about Bot? He could practically touch people and turn them happy and make them sing Christmas carols.

"Pull," I said out loud. My elbows burned. They felt sticky and wet. Mom—well, Mom turned plain photos into scenes from other worlds and took people away. That was something, right?

Smoke billowed past me in little puffs.

Lavender and Ms. Springfield, both of them sparkled and brought color into everything and everywhere. Now *there* were some superpowers the world needed, right?

More smoke.

The sharp tang made my eyes water. I couldn't let myself think that any of the people in my life would get hurt in Thornwood Manor as it burned. My teeth hammered together, but I pulled. Weak, but not helpless. I could do this. Moving was super enough for me, for now, maybe forever. Plant, then pull. Plant, then pull. Watch the breathing. Rest for counts of three. Plant, then pull. Move. Move. Move!

I crawled past discarded brown bottles. Small. Old. I made sure not to break them. I didn't need glass slicing up my legs.

Plant, pull.

My grandfather was the super-est hero of Blue Creek. I couldn't even list all his great powers. If Marvel or DC drew him into comic panels, I'd name him Toppy the Wise and Exceedingly Grumpy. Plant, pull. Plant, pull. As I dragged myself through the endless tunnel, I suddenly imagined him with yellow tights, the same color as his Earl Grey teabags.

I giggled.

The sound scared me half to death.

Blood coated my arms. Everything hurt. Everything stung.

Plant, pull.

I heard something I didn't understand, a ping-like noise, and stopped. For a few seconds, the sound of my own ragged wheezing blocked out all sounds, but there was definitely more light here, and—

Snow.

Flakes drifted down in front of me, and I reached one shaking hand out and touched a few. Wet. Cold. Real.

I watched them hit the ground, but no. Wait. They didn't hit. They passed by my face and floated down, down into—

Darkness.

Oh, wow. I was on a ledge. I had crawled right through an opening in a dirt wall, and I had almost crawled straight off the ledge into a great big hole.

I pulled myself to the very edge of the overhang, careful not to go too far, rolled onto my back, and looked up into a dizzying collection of snowflakes, backlit by a single streetlamp. I could make out a circular opening way above my head.

Ping. Ping!

That sound again.

Wait. That was my phone's text tone!

I rolled to my belly and inched backward, off the ledge, until I was just inside the tunnel again. Then I fumbled with my phone and finally got it out of my pocket. My hands and fingers felt like floppy noodles.

I had a signal! But just one bar. I tried a call, but it wouldn't work. I knew texts would go through even when calls wouldn't, and I was getting those, so I opened them.

Before I read anything, I chose Lavender's name and sent a message:

Get everyone away from Thornwood. Ellis burning it down. Bot and Captain C in the front hall—fell through the floor. I think I'm under the grounds on the north side, in the well. Help.

For good measure, I sent the text to everyone on my contact list who wasn't Ellis, and watched each bar send until I knew the messages had gone through.

Then I started reading.

Riley: **Mayor C blocked the firing. Council pissed.**

Lavender: **You're a horrible friend, and I hate you.**

Ms. Springfield: **Lavender said you ran away. Don't do this, honey. It's cold out tonight and your grandfather will have a meltdown.**

Mom: We're coming up there and you are going to be SO sorry young lady.

Lavender: I AM GOING TO KILL YOU.

Riley: Dude, what did you do? Lav's freaking.

Lavender: Okay, Max, not funny. I'm scared.

The next text was from later, probably after the floor collapsed under my chair.

Lavender: Where are you WHERE ARE YOU WHEREAREYOU

And one more from a number I recognized but couldn't quite believe: C AI L

"Oh my God, the world is ending! Toppy the Wise and Exceedingly Grumpy sent a text." I started laughing. I didn't even think his flip phone *could* text. I laughed some more. Then I started crying really hard, and that's right about when I heard a rumbling-roar that sounded a whole lot like a huge Harley hog churning across grass and snow.

Less than a minute later, voices shouted above me. Flashlight beams cut across the circle above my head.

Somebody—Mom, I think—said, "Dad, don't. The well head's made out of stone, but we don't know if those dirt walls are stable!"

Then Junior Thornwood. "Here, sir. I got you. I'm plenty big enough to anchor, and I can pull you out on the bike."

"Ohmygodohmygod." That sounded like Lavender.

And then her mom. "It's okay, honey. The chief's here. He's got this."

A few seconds later, a shape blotted out the light, then dropped straight toward me and stopped right outside the hole.

I blinked at my grandfather, hanging there in his dress uniform, wearing a makeshift rope harness he had looped around both legs and his midsection until it looked like funny brown underwear.

"Are you hurt?" he asked.

I opened my mouth to tell him no, but said, "You need a cape."

He frowned. "You hit your head pretty hard."

I tried to gather my thoughts, but I just started crying again, gulping air between sobs.

"Max, look at me," Toppy demanded in his Chief-of-Police voice.

I obeyed. The sight of his sharp, focused eyes and familiar face calmed me enough to say, "Bumps and scratches. And yes, my head's kind of fuzzy."

"Crawl forward," he instructed. "Carefully."

But I was already moving. As I eased out of the hole, I reached for my grandfather and dropped my phone into the well. A count of two later, it hit way down below with a sick shattering sound.

Toppy gazed after it for a second, then made eye contact with me. "Good riddance," he said. Then he winked.

Another laugh-cry tore out of my chest, right about the time he swung over, snatched me up, and hugged me fiercely against his chest.

"Hoist!" he hollered to Junior.

A motor roared.

The rope started to move, slowly but steadily, towing us toward the moonlight and the snow.

I couldn't stop shaking.

Toppy kissed the top of my head as I asked, "Do you think the well gave us arsenic poisoning?"

"Nah," Toppy said. "But if you don't want to die a horrible death by poisoning, I wouldn't eat in Lavender's presence for a few months."

27

DECEMBER 18

A week after Thornwood Manor burned, Elvis Presley sang *Blue Christmas* from the living room as I put on water for two cups of tea, squirted a little honey in the bottom of two holiday mugs, and dropped bags of Earl Grey over the sides.

My fingers and arms still felt sore, but overall, I came out pretty good for somebody who plunged through a floor tied to a hundred-pound weight. Captain Coker, on the other hand, had a broken ankle from the hall cave-in. Bot, who had found Ellis's patched wires and figured out how to get down to the room where Ellis had his server, got a busted elbow and a concussion when the floor and Captain Coker fell on him.

Bot's heart took the biggest blow, though. He couldn't believe what Ellis had done, and Riley was working hard to heal his foster dad by selling out everything in the store to increase their holiday profits. Luckily, most of the money Ellis stole had been recovered by federal investigators and returned to accounts and city funds in time to keep the holidays from being a total bust for Blue Creek.

I hit the pewter Harley skull knob serving as the joystick on my chair, rested my elbow on the custom Harley heat-insulated wrapped exhaust pipe Junior had welded on as my armrest, and tried not to notice the roar of my repaired motor as I headed toward the kitchen table.

"I bet Elvis wouldn't have grounded his granddaughter over winter break if she almost died," I grumped, rolling up beside my grandfather.

Toppy, who was wearing brand new Superman pajamas I made him open from under the tree after he rescued me, gazed at me over his glasses. His pencil lifted from his crossword puzzle book, and his eyes shifted first to his steaming bowl of vomit-with-blueberries, then to my bowl, and finally to the notebook, pen, and brand new iPhone next to my bowl.

"Write your essays, Max," he said. "Or lose that phone."

I sighed and looked at my notebook, which had about twenty pages full of essay titles filled in by my grandfather, separated by three pages each. I had already written papers on Twenty Dangers of Interfering with Police Investigations, How to Assess Foundational Stability in Old Houses, The True Horror of Termite

Damage, and Thirty-Two Ways Real Life Differs from Detective Movies. The title of my next essay was Heroines Who Are Too Silly to Live.

I held back a groan. "What does this even mean?"

"Check the list of examples on the next page," Toppy said. "Think of how those ladies, and a certain other girl, got into trouble due to doing things about as smart as poking a rabid skunk with a stick."

When I didn't say anything, he added, "I want you to discuss how those film ladies might have made different choices, and, oh, I don't know, maybe ended up without a destroyed wheelchair, a concussion, stitched-up elbows, a bunch of bruises, road rash on both legs, and a best friend swearing to never speak to them again."

"Lavender's speaking to me," I said. "As of yesterday."

Toppy inclined his head. "Good to hear. And I finally managed to talk your Social Studies teacher into an incomplete over that paper you didn't turn in, instead of an F. He said he was willing to be patient, since Captain Coker and Bot probably would have died in that fire if you hadn't acted like you had no sense, and seeing as how you helped save the town and all."

"I got the paper finished last night," I said. "It's in my room."

The King of Rock and Roll switched to *Silent Night*. My alarm beeped, and I shifted my weight from one achy hip to the other. Then I turned my essay page, tore out Toppy's list of books and movies, and read through the titles.

"I'm not sure *Rocky Horror Picture Show* counts as an actual movie," I said. "And isn't this kind of sexist or something? I mean, heroes can make bad moves, too."

"That's your next essay topic," Toppy informed me.

My text message tone sounded, and I immediately checked my phone.

Lavender: Did you see the paper today?

The message had a link to the *Blue Creek Gazette.*

When I clicked it, I found myself staring at a picture of me in Toppy's arms, getting hauled out of the well. A second picture showed the little brown bottles I had crawled past without breaking.

"TRACES OF ARSENIC!" the headline blared, and I scrolled to the next photo—Vivienne Thornwood, gazing at me from underneath all those brown curls and that bright red bonnet.

"Wooooow, so Thornwood was murdered after all," I murmured. "Vivienne poisoned him and killed herself, too."

"Yep," Toppy said, still writing in his puzzle. "I figure she got her daughter out of those tunnels, maybe had her hauled up the well just like I took you out of there. And after that, she took care of business, because her husband's reign of terror over everyone in Blue Creek had to end."

I tried to take all that in, but had trouble wrapping my mind around it. "This is going to spawn a whole new bunch of legends, isn't it?"

"No doubt."

In the next few pictures, I saw Mom and Lavender and Ms. Springfield standing around the well, and the trooper who had been our guard for the night, and Junior with his big three-wheeled bike that had carried Toppy to me. Two aldermen from the meeting were in another picture running toward us with Mayor Chandler right behind them. In the background, Thornwood Manor burned spectacularly, tower and eaves shooting flames into the dark, snowy night.

Another headline called us "THE LAST VICTIMS OF THORNWOOD'S REVENGE."

"Oh, wow," I mumbled, realizing I had just become part of the Thornwood Manor lore forever.

I'm famous, I told Lavender. We're famous!

I know, right? she typed back.

The caption under the photo read, "Maxine Brennan."

"That's me," I whispered, reading the article below:

> Maxine Brennan, granddaughter of Blue Creek's long-serving police chief, Thomas "Toppy" Brennan, must have been exhausted after crawling for her life. Her family reports that she's

recovering nicely at home. Her mother, Callinda
Brennan, declined an interview before heading
back to California for work, but she stated, "I think
Max is stronger than ten superheroes."

Heading back for work. I almost laughed. Mom had
booked it out of Blue Creek just about as fast as she
could, before I even got out of the hospital, saying she
had to get ready for an art show. That was Mom.

Just a few months ago, I would have been so mad
at her that I'd have let it eat me up inside and turn me
mean, but really, what was the point? I was glad she
left, that I could have life back to sort-of-normal—if
you didn't count the Chitty-Chitty-Bang-Bang-looking
patched-up, welded, half-Harley-part-wheelchair that
clanked like an airplane engine whenever I drove it. I
didn't mind texting with her. We exchanged a few messages every day, which was more than we did before.
She told me she'd be moving to a new place so I'd feel
better visiting, but I filed that under, "Believe it when
I see it."

The article went on to talk about the fire, and what
happened to Blue Creek's most famous home:

The blaze, seen as a yellow glow in the winter
sky from as far away as the Nashville city limits, did
irreparable damage to Thornwood Manor. Blue

Creek's most famous home won't be reopened in the near future. Owner Junior Thornwood stated, "It's sad, but we'll be able to salvage a lot of the antiques—the eBay listings won't be back, though."

Thornwood noted that he plans to settle permanently in Blue Creek. His motorcycle dealership in Connecticut fetched a handsome sum at auction, and he reported that he and local business owner Joy Springfield are in the early stages of planning to use the proceeds to rebuild part of the mansion. "We're considering a museum and tours for the stone maze, under management of Something Wicked, LLC," Thornwood stated. "I might have the family problem with losing whatever money I make, but I'm counting on Joy Springfield's good energy to chase all that darkness away."

Springfield reported that interest in Thornwood Manor and its previously overlooked occupant, Vivienne Thornwood, has never been higher. "Inquiries are pouring in from all over the world," Springfield told reporters. "People keep asking about cursed antiques, and a Thornwood cousin mentioned that Vivienne kept a diary, which might be hidden somewhere in the warren she built to save her children from her husband's cruelty."

I looked up from the article. New legends? A hidden diary. Awesome.

Good thing I didn't say that out loud, or I'd be having to write Toppy an essay on better words to use than "awesome." He hated that one.

I scrolled down and at the bottom, almost like a footnote, I found one last small paragraph:

Ellis Pritchard, born Ellis Unger, son of felon Frank Unger who died in prison one year ago, was apprehended by Tennessee State Police on the ramp to Interstate 24, trying to flee the scene of his crimes.

He was arraigned on a list of charges so long I didn't even read them. It was too depressing. I doubted Ellis would ever get out of prison, at least not until he was older, like Junior Thornwood or Toppy. It kind of made me sad, the way his life got turned into a few lines of print, and his father was nobody to the world but a "felon" who "died in prison." Like Ellis and his dad had become evil things, not people. I frowned and put down the phone to find Toppy staring at me.

"I was reading a piece in the *Gazette* instead of working on my essays," I confessed. "Lavender sent it."

His eyes narrowed. "The newspaper had another

article? Have those ingrates on the City Council apologized to Maggie for threatening a recall vote when she blocked my termination?"

"Keep dreaming," I told him. "Have they apologized to you yet?"

That earned me a grunt just as someone knocked on the back door.

I grinned, because I knew who it was.

Toppy got up immediately and let Mayor Chandler into our kitchen for what had become our new morning routine. She shifted a stack of magazines she was carrying to the crook of one arm, reached up with her free hand, pulled Toppy toward her, hugged him, and gave him a quick kiss on the cheek. Then she surveyed his pajamas and said, "Nice. What was it Max said when you rescued her? Oh, yes. You need a cape."

Toppy actually smiled at her as the tops of his ears turned red.

I drove my rattling contraption of a chair to the electric kettle and punched the button to make Toppy's tea and hers, too.

When I brought them their steaming mugs, Toppy was actually eating his vomit-with-blueberries with no complaints.

Mayor Chandler gestured to the magazines she brought. "Look, Max. Mobility catalogues. Since Junior's settlement covers the damage to your chair, you can have whatever model you want. Heck, you can probably get two."

I leaned forward and gazed at the amazing wheelchair models, and my mouth came open as I spotted one that actually stretched up so I could reach cabinets and things on high shelves.

"Check this out," I told Toppy. "And look! Here's an all-terrain model for beaches and stuff."

"Wonderful," he said. "Those will make it so much easier for you to get into trouble."

"I saw your friend Lavender and her mom up at Thornwood just now," Mayor Chandler said. "Junior has a crew of archaeology students from Vanderbilt using ground-penetrating radar to map the chambers they haven't excavated yet. He says there are caves, too."

"Can I go up later and help?" I asked Toppy. "Please?"

He started to say no, but at a raised eyebrow from Mayor Chandler, he relented with, "Maybe. If today's essays get finished."

"Okay, okay," I said. But before I could start back to work on the silly heroine summary, I got another text. This one was from Captain Coker:

Hi, Max. I want you to look at this. If you're interested, I'll go as your aide so they'll take you a little before age-limit. It's accessible.

I clicked the link she sent, to Camp CSI: Birmingham.

"Oh, man," I muttered, reading about the forensic science summer camp at the University of Alabama, Birmingham. "Listen to this! 'Camp CSI: Birmingham is designed to show high school students the reality behind the forensic science depicted in such television dramas as *CSI* and *NCIS*, develop their interest in science and the scientific method, and provide information on forensic science education and career opportunities.'"

"That sounds like a huge bunch of fun for you." Mayor Chandler sipped her tea, then grinned at Toppy. "A way to channel all that investigative energy, maybe?"

He took my phone and read more off the website, and even used his finger to scroll. As Elvis shifted to *Peace in the Valley*, he said, "Maybe."

"If I'm not grounded," I said.

"Something like that," Toppy agreed.

"I'm already legendary," I said, going back to my too-silly-to-live essay. "Might as well become a crime-fighting superhero, right?"

"Wrong," said my grandfather, putting his pencil on one of the mobility catalogues and circling the wheelchair that stretched up to shelves and the all-terrain model, too.

I thought about describing the two or three modifications I had already thought about making to both of those chairs, but I didn't. There are times even legendary crime-fighting superheroes should keep their bright ideas completely, totally, and absolutely to themselves.

For now, it was super enough that sunlight had found our kitchen, and the Elvis CD wasn't hitching, and the air smelled like pine from Toppy and vanilla from Mayor Chandler and Earl Grey tea.

"I wonder if any of the Thornwood antiques got cursed or something," I said, glancing toward the hill above our house. "And what if Vivienne Thornwood really did hide a diary somewhere? And we should find out if the place is haunted or not. I mean, scientifically. One of those ghost-hunter shows—"

"Essay, Max," Toppy said.

"Right." I grinned at him as Mayor Chandler laughed, and I started writing.

EPILOGUE

FEBRUARY 14

S uper Max the Mighty Invincible can no longer see a haunted house from her bedroom window," I told Lavender as freezing wind whipped the blanket on my legs. "Kinda sad, right?"

When she pulled her purple scarf over her nose and mouth instead of answering, I rolled a little farther under the construction tent next to one of the dark front doors salvaged from Thornwood Manor and raised my iPad. "In years long past, sexism reigned," I read from the screen as the door's owl glared balefully in my general direction. "No one believed women had any brains. They all feared Hargrove and his threats dark and hairy, when Vivienne Thornwood was twice as scary."

Lavender's eyebrows lifted so high they disappeared under her hair. Behind her, propped against a tent pole and waiting to go to storage, Vivienne Thornwood's damaged portrait gave me an equally haughty stare from underneath her sooty red bonnet.

"That was truly heinous, Max." Lavender pulled her purple coat tight with both purple-gloved hands. "Poetry is not one of your superpowers."

"Well, somebody should do something to honor her," I said. "You got anything better?"

"I'm planning to write a novel," Lavender announced. "It'll be a best-seller, and I'll make it into a play and a ballet—and I'll do book signings at Something Wicked. Good enough?"

"Maybe," I grinned. "If Vivienne doesn't like it, I'm sure she'll haunt you."

Lavender groaned. "Look, it's *freezing* out here. I'm waiting for the ghost hunters in the van."

She bounced off without another word, leaving me alone with the pile of rescued artifacts from the burned mansion, and the remnants of Vivienne's long-ago life.

"Lavender doesn't believe in ghosts," I told Vivienne, but it was hard to look at her for very long. The edges of her frame had been scorched, and she had rips that crossed her throat and hoop skirt. The canvas flapped in the icy breeze, making dull, sad pops. Even two months later, the air still smelled like char and ruin.

I studied the painting in front of me. "It's not supposed to be this cold in Blue Creek on Valentine's Day. Are you doing this?"

Pop, pop.

"See, unlike my best friend, I do believe in ghosts."
I tucked the edges of my blanket around my jeans.
"I know you beat Hargrove in the end—but you lost
your youngest daughter, and that broke your heart,
didn't it?"

Pop.

The portrait's torn pieces rippled as wind caught
them, making it seem like Vivienne's hands fluttered
against her red-striped gown. Her painted eyes gazed
into the distance, as if they could see the big sedan rumbling up the hill toward the parking lot, towing a white
trailer with the ghost-hunter logo I recognized from
television. Right behind them came Toppy in his patrol
car, providing escort and scaring off any local autograph
hounds.

Would she hate her secret places being prodded
and measured and shown on national TV?

Probably.

I didn't know if the ghost-hunting team would find
"proof" of haunting, or whatever. I did know that interest in Vivienne Thornwood's life had picked up, and
people had been writing articles online, wondering
which of the Thornwoods would have most appreciated
Ellis Pritchard's attacks on our town.

With Vivienne dead for nearly two centuries, there
would be no fresh declaration of doom for Blue Creek,

Tennessee—but there could be no denying that a new legend had been born.

"You died sad, and probably furious, too." I reached out and used my mitten to clean a bit of soot off the canvas. "I'm betting that if Thornwood Manor really is haunted, you're the spirit to reckon with."

For a split second, the torn portrait blew back into place, making Vivienne Thornwood whole again. In that instant, her eyes seemed to drill through the approaching convoy, and that smile of hers turned colder than the frozen Valentine's Day.

I leaned back, heart thumping.

"Max!" Lavender yelled from a distance. "Come on. All the people are here!"

On the edges of the wind, I caught Toppy's music as he opened his door—Elvis, of course. "Take a walk down lonely street to Heartbreak Hotel. . . ."

I glanced at the parking lot, and Toppy lifted his hand to wave at me.

I waved back.

When I looked at Vivienne's painting again, the torn pieces had sagged, leaving her damaged and quiet and pitiful. I gave her a moment of silence, and a respectful nod.

Then, rolling away to the distant beat of the King, I left Vivienne Thornwood behind. Her portrait would be restored, and she would preside over the rebuilt section of the old house, and the new museum and tourist attraction at Thornwood Manor.

I had no doubt I would see her again soon enough, vibrant and refusing to fade or disappear.

She was a legend, after all.

AUTHOR'S NOTE

In 2013, my son, JB Redmond, wrote a piece for Disability in Kidlit, titled "What You See . . . And What You Don't See." In that article, he wrote, "I've never found too many disabled characters in the books I enjoy, unless they're villains or buffoons." Then he talked about what he typically found when stories include characters in wheelchairs, and how it hurt him. He talked about how he wanted to see real characters with realistic disabilities, living their lives and not being pitied or seeing themselves as weak or ineffectual.

Over the years, I have written many types of characters with many different issues, but I never gave my son the character he asked for—a person who uses a wheelchair, effective, strong, and realistic, having real-life adventures—until now. I think it was too emotional for me the first few times I tried. I couldn't get the voice right. I couldn't bear to delve deep enough to touch that character's pain and fears. And then came Max. She burst into my head as I was reworking a piece, she rolled over my brain and took over the story, and sometimes I swear she typed for me. And I'm very glad she did. I'm glad Max had the courage I was struggling to find.

Every day, I share Toppy's role with my wife, Gisele, and we will keep that role until the day we both leave this world. Without us, given the current social programs and structure, there's a very good chance JB would have no option but to leave his man cave and his extensive movie and book and *Star Wars* and *Star Trek* collections and all of his pets and move into a nursing home, and that's not okay. Programs and supports and options need to be better. Wheelchairs and technology need to be better. JB (and Max) deserve full access to the same world we live in—all the time, every day, every moment of their lives.

I hope everyone reading *Super Max* understands JB's life and his dreams a bit more. I think I do. Most importantly, *he* thinks I do, and he feels like I understand him more. Mostly, he feels like Max is Da Boss, and he wants to explore the tunnels under Thornwood Manor (after he goes to another planet, becomes a wizard, stops a nuclear crisis like Jack Ryan, tries out being a werewolf, becomes a Shadowhunter, and . . .).

—S. V.

Find the article: Redmond, JB. "What You See . . . And What You Don't See." N.p., 11 Oct., 2013. Web.